KEEP ME
IN
SIGHT

Publisher's Note: This is a work of fiction. Names, characters, places, and incidents are a product of the author's imagination. Locales and public names are sometimes used for atmospheric purposes. Any resemblance to actual people, living or dead, or to businesses, companies, events, institutions, or locales is completely coincidental.

Keep Me In Sight / Rachel Blackledge - 1st ed.

ISBN: 978-0-9907804-6-5

This book is dedicated to Les Brown.

"The most dangerous liars are the ones who think they are telling the truth."

- Jim Rose

CHAPTER 1

INMATE 6881

Initials mar the bench of the holding cell; a sea of letters scratched into the paint by the forgotten ones, marking their existence.

So and so was here. There's a lot of gang insignia, too. I see a skull done up quite nicely. That person had some talent. Wasted, clearly.

Keys clank against the metal gate. Wanda stands there, sliding a key into the slot and twisting. She's one of the nicer guards, which is why she works in the out-processing unit.

Wanda's uniform strains against her bulk. The heavy-duty

leather belt cinched up tight sections her belly into top and bottom folds. She's an older woman, approaching retirement, I hope. What an awful place to spend her golden years.

"Case dismissed." She pushes the gate open, looking me up and down. "Let me take a picture. It's not often I see a murderer walk free."

"Murderess," I say, rising to my feet and straightening my prison issue garb. I smooth back my hair and walk freely out of the holding cell.

"'Scuse me," she says, following me down the barren hallway. "They all come in here howling about how they're innocent little lambs. And the justice system has done them wrong and they deserve to be set free. Except none of those smart lawyers on the outside can never seem to find a single reason why."

I'm thinking about all the unfortunates who lack the ability to plan the perfect crime. Poor them.

Behind me, Wanda labors for breath, a wheezing sound that keeps time with her footsteps. Then we reach the last gate before freedom, the last time I'll be referred to as an inmate number.

"What's your secret?" she demands in a low voice, hand grasping the bars of the sally port door in front of us. "I saw your case file. You killed that guy deader than a doornail."

My gaze passes from the pockmarked metal bars to her fleshy hand, wrapped around the bar, knuckles rising up in soft mounds.

I recall Chris's hands wrapped around my neck, his nostrils flaring, his lips stretched across the tidy white line of his teeth.

Then I remember the gleam of my knife before I sank it in his belly.

"Foresight," I say with a wry smile. She smiles too, an involuntary reaction, but I can tell from her quick sideways glance that she's confused, trying to work out the meaning. While her wheels are turning, I nod toward the gate. "Shall we?"

I retrieve my articles, stored the night they processed me into general. No probation or bail for me. No way. A female killer? The authorities didn't want to take their chances, rare as we are. Women are supposed to be peaceable, not violent. What had driven me to kill?

Until they knew, nobody wanted the responsibility of authorizing my release. And who can blame them? Nobody wanted to face the possibility that it could happen again.

But it just might.

In fact, I wouldn't rule it out.

CHAPTER 2

BRYNN

One Year Later

Sunlight pours through our bedroom curtains, stupid gauzy things that I thought looked stylish when I bought them. But now, lying in bed with my arm slung over my eyes, I realize I should have splurged on blackout curtains instead.

Like sweeping radar, I'm remotely aware of grim aching in the balls of my feet (I swear on my life I'll never cram my feet into a pair of stilettos again), the plastered grungy feeling of make-up still caked on my face, a loud buzzing sensation in my ears (fried, still, it seems, from the deafening club music), and strength-zapping nausea.

Carefully, I peel open my right eye and glimpse Dan, lying next to me as still as a corpse, fully dressed in last night's crumpled outfit, his dark hair mussed, stubble emerging on along his square jawline, eyelids jumping as if he's reliving a terrible nightmare. Maybe he is reliving a terrible nightmare. We just survived an encounter with his ex-girlfriend.

It happened last night at Delmonicos, a popular bar in a trendy neighborhood close to downtown San Diego where we often meet up with friends, the starting point for Dan's departure party, his last hurrah before deployment. Dan and I had already pre-partied at the house with another couple, and by the time we all piled out of the taxi and rode the wave of euphoria through our group of waiting friends up to the edge of the bar, whispers started rifling through the ranks: *Erin is here. Dan's ex.*

I didn't know anything about her except that she had moved to Newport Beach after The Break. Her name had come up exactly once at a backyard barbecue, putting the festive mood on ice. Dan clammed up, of course. A whistle escaped his friend's lips, followed by another, who turned his back and pretended to be busy.

Dan's big blowout could have derailed right from the very beginning. But you know what? I liked her. We had a lot of fun. Okay, too much fun. As the night descended into hazy oblivion, somehow we became bosom buddies. Isn't that strange?

Lying flat on my back in bed, head pounding, I open my eyes experimentally and wait for my pupils to adjust to the bright light, but the blaze feels like stabs to the back of my head. So I roll over on my side and try to piece the night together.

There was singing. Mine. *Every party needs a pooper*, followed by Erin's rousing rendition that Dan didn't particularly enjoy. And there was drinking. Lots of drinking. I drank, at first, to quash my insecurities.

Dan had steadfastly refused to talk about his ex. But there I was, sitting across from the real life specimen, and I couldn't help but draw comparisons.

She's a platinum blonde with wavy layers that framed her face, parting around her prominent forehead. There was a hint of sadness in her wide set eyes. She wore minimal makeup, except for a lashing of red on her enhanced lips. And she has big breasts. Wasn't Dan more of a 'bum man'? That's what he'd told me.

That's exactly what I was thinking when she offered to buy me a drink, brown eyes glistening a little. She was so sweet about it. I could tell she was hurting. I felt sorry for her. I'd be hurting too if I happened upon Dan and his new girlfriend.

She returned with a bottle of wine in an ice bucket—*just for us*—and placed her hand on my forearm. We clinked glasses and a warm friendly feeling washed away my apprehension. She was so nice. Non-threatening. Funny, even. Why did they break up again?

Desperate thirst brings me back to present. I grope around for my water flask on the bedside table and knock it over. So I lie

6

there, listening to water drip onto the carpeted floor. Then I pull in a big breath and heave myself up to sitting.

The bedroom swirls around me; the biggest room in Dan's beach cottage with narrow-plank wood floors popular in the 1950s and a tiny overstuffed closet. When the four walls return to their original position, I swallow the last few drops in my water flask and half-heartedly wipe the puddle off the top of my nightstand, while my mind runs over the grooves from last night like a broken record player, trying to fix the glitch because something is missing.

We journeyed to the club, I remember. A group of us. Laughing. Confused. Led by the Pied Piper, a short guy who talked way too fast. I remember a VIP section. Red velvet ropes. Friendly strangers. Erin was there, of course. Then she wasn't. There's that black hole that Dan fell into, followed by his re-emergence and an after-party at someone's house.

The fragments dovetail, almost coming together, but then they disappear again into the foggy landscape of my mind. How did I get home? And when did I change into Dan's Navy t-shirt?

My body aches dully. My mind feels like fodder in a Jack LaLanne juicer. I can barely think straight, but I'm fighting a growing sense of dread. I think something happened last night. Something bad.

From the mist rises one specter. It's blurry and not well formed, this ghost, but I'm ninety-seven percent certain that I saw Erin leave.

And Dan follow her out.

CHAPTER 3

BRYNN

A few days have passed, but the mystery of Dan's whereabouts the night of his farewell party still haunts me. He says he's too busy to talk about it. And he is busy, getting ready to deploy. He's packing and preparing and sorting through his tactical and field medical equipment, carefully checking off items from his list. He's up early and home late with combat medic briefings and prep meetings. And he's definitely not interested in talking about that night.

But my mind is stuck on repeat, going back over the holes in my memory, trying to find something that makes sense because right now nothing is making any sense. Why would he leave and go somewhere with Erin?

I should let it go, I know. But this is like a splinter in my heel, inching toward infection. The only thing that will cure my condition is answers. So I'm back to analyzing the mystery.

There has to be an obvious and innocent reason why Dan went somewhere with Erin. Maybe the timing was awkward, and he never actually went anywhere with her. But his stonewalling only makes me more suspicious.

It's Monday evening, and I'm still a little groggy from our Saturday night blowout, but I manage to warm up dinner (leftover take-out) while Dan searches the cab of his truck for his compass. I'm washing the dishes and mulling things over in my mind, when I hear his phone vibrating against the countertop.

With both hands plunged into the sink full of soapy water, I lean over to see who's calling as significant others have done from time immortal, I suppose, and glimpse the name of the other woman. *Erin.*

My heart beats fast, fighting imminent implosion.

Why is she calling Dan? Maybe she butt-dialed him. Then something occurs to me. Why is her number programmed into his phone? Perhaps he forgot to delete her contact from the good ole days.

The phone keeps buzzing, shunting me in a surreal state of shock. Is this really happening? Is Erin back in Dan's life now, or is she elbowing her way back in?

The calls rings out. In the yawning silence, I find myself wondering about the nature of their relationship. Was it one of those love hate addictions? And the hate magically transformed to love the night of his going away party?

I know for a fact that he didn't drive up to Newport Beach and back. That alone would take four hours. Shagging would take some time, depending on the quality of the pillow talk. Besides, he's flat out, getting ready for deployment.

My heart sinks. Did she drive down here? Careening down the highway like a dog in heat, beckoning him over to her hotel room? That seems so seedy and gross. Something Dan definitely would not do.

Okay. Okay. Calm down. I need to think about the facts. So I think about Erin's enhanced bosom of all things. At least I can reach down and touch my toes.

See what venom lurks in my heart?

I hate that her missed call punted me back to my high school years, back when I was 'one of the guys.' I never was a show pony. I never sat in class, brushing my long sleek mane. I neither giggled nor jiggled.

But none of that matters now. I got the hot guy. Baywatch Babe can pound sand, as Dan would say. Trouble is, she doesn't want to pound sand. It appears she wants Dan.

The back door opens. Glancing over my shoulder, I see Dan walk in. He's wearing a ball cap with the bill pulled low on his brow, casting a shadow over his eyes and a hint of a sunburn on the bridge of his nose from his morning surf session.

"Can't find that compass," he says, going to his phone. "Maybe Riggs has it."

I turn back and look past the frilly half-curtains framing our kitchen window to the neighbor's stucco house beyond, focusing on his reflection in the windowpane, trying to look very calm and casual. I'm watching for his reaction as he checks his phone and sees that Erin called. But he slips his phone in the front pocket of his jeans and opens the fridge door. Business as usual.

"Do you want a beer?" he asks.

I don't reply. I can't. My heart is splintering around the edges. His calm reaction confirms my very worst fear. I knew something happened that night. Now I know what. They rekindled, and I sat there drunk, oblivious, while it all unfolded right under my nose.

What am I supposed to do now? Pretend I know nothing? Confront him as soon as possible? Remove the door handles on his truck? So many options.

The fridge door shuts. "Brynn? You okay?"

Anger props me up, but under the hot fiery current, runs a river of hurt. Well, now isn't the time to feel sorry for myself. Now is the time to get answers.

"No," I say, turning around and drying my hands on a dishtowel. "You have a missed phone call from Erin."

He scowls.

"Do you want to tell me something?" I ask, arms folded. "Because now is as good of a time as any."

"I don't know why she called me."

"Well, I have a few theories. Why don't we discuss the most obvious one first?"

His face freezes over. He knows the procedure. He's buckling up for a wild ride into Woman Territory, where he'll face any number of trials and tribulations, collectively known as *communication*.

"Did something happen that night we all went out?" I ask him. "I know you went somewhere with Erin. I saw you leave."

This is a shot in the dark because I *think* I saw them leave together. But his ribcage stills. And now I know it's true.

I suck in a quick breath. I can't stand the thought of Dan in anyone else's arms let alone Erin's. She's so different from me. It seems almost impossible that he could love her and me at the same time. The only explanation is that he never really loved her . . . or maybe he doesn't really love me. Maybe with me, he found someone easy, someone on whom he can wipe his feet.

"Did you get together or something? Is that why she's *following up?*"

Dan looks horrified. At least that's something. "Are you *serious?*" he cries, clenching his jaw and twisting the beer cap off with ferocity. He laughs caustically and stalks out of the kitchen to front room. I follow.

Bear, his Golden Retriever, sits on the couch, one fluffy ear cocked back as if he can't believe what he's hearing. Well, that makes two of us.

"I want to know if something happened that night, Dan. I want to know the truth," I say, bracing myself.

He snatches his cap off his head, tosses it on the coffee table, and rakes his hand through his dark hair. Then he sinks down on the gray couch next to Bear. I feel sick with anticipation. I'm not sure if I want to know the truth. Maybe I'm like Sheryl Crow. Maybe I want him to lie to me.

My heart twists thinking about Dan with Baywatch Babe, a fluffy Pomeranian poking its head out of her purse, her arm looped around Dan's waist in a proud and proprietary manner.

I sit down next to him. "Is this it? Is she back in your life now?"

Dan takes my hand. I sniff, trying to hold back my tears. I don't want him to see me weak and crying. I don't want him to know how bad he could hurt me. But the warmness of his touch is the salve that I desperately need.

"Nothing happened," he says, locking his hazel eyes with mine, and I find myself falling into his golden prisms, bright against a field of dark blue. He pulls his mouth into a wan smile, causing the faint dimple on his cheek to emerge, the dimple that I love to see. He leans over and nuzzles his nose against mine. "I could never do that to you."

I sit there for a few seconds, drinking in his words—nothing happened, he could never do that to me—as the pain in my chest slowly fades.

"Come here," he says, taking me by the hands and pulling me up to standing.

He hooks his fingers into my belt loops and pulls me close. I step forward reluctantly, closing the gap between us, my arms encircling his wide muscled shoulders.

"You insult my honor." One corner of his mouth lifts.

"You insult my intelligence," I say, trying not to smile. "What did she want?"

His body stiffens. I should have let this go, I know. I should have basked under the warm glow in his eyes, but I don't want any unanswered questions left to rot.

He rests his chin on the top of my head and sighs. "She wanted to talk," he says, his voice tired and bored. "I'm sure you can imagine how well that went over."

I can't help but laugh, picturing Erin trying to yammer at Dan. "Sounds painful."

"Pretty much," he says, glimpsing down at me. The light is back in his eyes. His mouth turns down, gauging my mood.

"So what in particular did she want to discuss?" I ask.

"Old times, I guess. I honestly can't remember."

Dan likes to talk with his actions, not his words. And so when I hear his soft tone of voice and feel his arms around me, supporting me, I let the terrible topic fade because I love Dan, and I believe him.

And I don't ever want to see Erin again.

Countdown to the day of Dan's departure turned out to be rough. We had another 'discussion' about *that night*. We tried to establish facts that had too many truths to count. And we made up again, his last day hanging over us like a storm cloud. We sought shelter in bed, soaking each other in, until finally, D-Day arrived.

It's a drizzly, overcast early March morning with out of season June Gloom, a blanket of low clouds that usually form in the summer months and burn off by mid-day. The weak sun breaks through the marine layer in bright patchy spots, but the air is still chilly and damp. Standing in the driveway, I wrap the flaps of Dan's cozy beach cardigan tight around me and try not to shiver.

Dan's pickup truck is loaded, almost ready to go. I watch as he puts his combat boots in the front seat and loads the last of his duffle bags in the bed of his truck, feeling like I'm attending a funeral. Then we hold each other one last time, my face buried in the nape of his neck, memorizing the feel of his body against mine.

"I'll be home before you know it," he says, but his voice cracks. I look up and catch him rubbing his reddened watery eyes.

"Oh, babe," I say, voice breaking. "You're not crying, are you?"

"Negative." But his eyes sheen, and he pulls me close. "Promise you'll be here when I get home?"

"Of course I will. Why would you even say that?"

He shrugs his broad shoulders. "I guess that Erin thing freaked me out."

I still have questions. *What do you mean, Dan? Why did it freak you out, specifically?*

But I'm tired of arguing. I don't want to squander our last few seconds together raking over pointless details. Dan said nothing happened. I believe him. And that night will soon fade away, destined for bad jokes.

He kisses me, pressing his full lips against mine. Then he whispers against my ear, "I love you, babe."

"I love you too."

As he gets in his truck, I admire how his jeans hug his narrow waist, how the thin t-shirt fabric clings to his muscled shoulders, how he cares about his honor, our relationship, and me. He drives away, waving, followed by one last thumbs up. I wave back, my heart full with love, but heavy with sorrow.

CHAPTER 4

BRYNN

Fitness Fun, a small local gym where I teach yoga fusion, is bright and jarring with pink carpet the color of Pepto-Bismol, clanking weights, and a bank of whirring elliptical machines.

But I push on. Dan has been gone for two weeks now, which feels like an eternity. Only five months and two weeks to go until he's home, I tell myself, feeling like riding one of those elliptical machines to the moon might take less time.

I wave to Michelle, sitting behind the front desk, and make my way over to the busy exercise room. People are putting away their weights from the 9 a.m. previous class. Others are rolling out their mats for mine.

I put my bag and mat down in the front of the studio, sync my phone to the speaker system, reminding myself to switch on airplane mode so that class won't be interrupted again by my Darth Vader ringtone in case my dad decides to call, and cue up today's playlist. The room feels like a meat locker so I walk over and crank up the thermostat. Then I roll out my mat, take off my shoes, say hello to a few of my regulars, and sit down to stretch, while the rest of the class fills in.

I'm bent at the waist, reaching over to touch my toes, when I catch a familiar figure in my peripheral vision. I look up.

Erin.

My stomach lurches. What in the hell is she doing here?

But she's here all right, purple yoga mat tucked tidily under her arm, a big Louis Vuitton bag hanging from her shoulder. She's *attending* my class, wearing a pair of super pricey yoga leggings with sheer panels cut along the thighs and a barre long sleeve top (clearly a size too small) plastered on her body. She gives me a little half-embarrassed wave, finds an open space over by the far wall, and unrolls her mat.

My mind races back to *that night*. Did I tell her where I worked? I must have because here she is.

The opening song plays. Class officially starts. After the third cycle of sun salutation, I move from student to student and make small adjustments—tuck your tailbone, square your hips, keep your ankle under your knee. Today, I'm careful to avoid the left side of the studio, where Erin set up camp.

She seems pretty limber, nailing the advanced version of Bakasana. Maybe she didn't hunt me down. Maybe she's just a

18

nice fellow yogi who happened to find a Saturday morning class that worked with her schedule, and that class happened to be mine.

Corpse pose concludes. The music stops. Class ends. While my students pack up and make their way out of the studio, I dilly-dally over by the stereo, fiddling with my phone, trying to busy myself while Erin leaves.

Janelle, one of my regulars, approaches me about modified yoga positions for her first trimester. She apologizes for taking up my time, but I'm grateful for the distraction. Erin will have plenty of time to clear out now because I plan on talking to Janelle for a while.

As we discuss Janelle's pregnancy, her life, and how she broke the news to the proud father-to-be, I watch Erin from the corner of my eye.

She seems to be taking her own sweet time, rolling up her mat and carefully inserting it into its carry case. She thoroughly dabs the perspiration from her face and neck, folds up the cloth, and packs it away. Then she checks her phone, which could take approximately forever.

Unfortunately my conversation with Janelle is coming to a close. "Thanks so much. I'll do that next time," she says.

"Okay, great," I reply. "I'm so happy for you. If you ever feel uncomfortable, stop what you're doing. And definitely don't roll onto your stomach."

"I won't be able to much longer," she says, patting her tiny bump. "See you next week!"

"See you then," I say to Janelle as she turns to leave.

"Hey you!" Erin calls out in a singsong voice that sets me on edge. She walks over, face flushed, carrying her bag and mat.

Uh-oh.

I pull my mouth into a smile, but I'm not feeling very friendly. She lives in Newport Beach, doesn't she? I think I remember her talking about managing some nail salon up there and employee dramas. *Nightmare!* she had shrieked that night, laughing, drink in hand. I definitely remember that. "You're far from home," I say, unplugging my phone from the stereo system and packing up my mat.

"I'm in the area today," she says, smiling and fidgeting with the edges of her rolled up mat. "I have some nail polish suppliers down here and I like to pick up the orders myself. That way I can count everything and make sure they're not ripping us off." She laughs and shrugs. "And your class just happened to fit in perfectly with my schedule."

"Oh, okay." We got along the night of Dan's big send off, but booze skews all reason. With her call to Dan in mind and now conveniently crashing my yoga class, I don't think she's very fun or cool. I think she's alarming.

"Anyway," she continues, shrugging in casual-cagey sort of way, "you said something about teaching yoga that night we all went out. And then you mentioned that your classes are only sixty minutes, which I *love*."

Did I say all that?

"And so I hope you don't think I'm a stalker or anything,"—she laughs and shrugs as if caught red-handed—"but I googled your name."

A shiver races over my skin. "I'm surprised you remembered."

"Brynn Masters? Hard to forget!"

Geez, she has a good memory.

"So . . . awesome class!" She looks around the exercise studio as if she's amazed with the white walls. Then another teacher walks in, followed by a few students.

"Well, thanks for coming, but I should get going now. The next class is about to start." I give her an officious nod, grab my mat and bag, and head toward the door. Maybe she'll take a hint.

"Yeah ninety minutes is so long, especially when you're sweating like a sieve," she says, following at my heels.

"It can be a bit much," I say, making a bee-line for my car, while Erin tails me. That seems okay, as long as she clears out when I get there.

We chat during the minute or so that it takes for me to arrive at my car. I thought about confronting her about The Call, but decided to drop it. That would mean engaging her in meaningful conversation. And I want to get out of here.

"Well, maybe I'll see you around sometime," I say, reaching in my bag for my keys.

Oouf. Why did I say that? Because I'm *nice*, that's why. I'm a people pleaser. Dan always brings that to my attention. He tells me to stop caring so much about what people think, but I can't help it.

It's the curse of the oldest child, trying to ride out a terrible divorce, trying not to upset anyone more than they already are, trying to keep the family together.

So I tried to be super good. If I was the best kid ever, then mom and dad wouldn't separate. Right?

Nope. Dad cheated. Mom cheated. And both descended into a haze of alcohol and work.

Except, old habits die hard. And I still strive to be nice, trying not to step on any manicured toes and all . . .

"Hey, Brynn?"

"Yeah?" I shift on my feet and hug my sweater close. Dark clouds threaten rain. I'm anxious to get going with my big plans for the rest of the day: homemade french toast for brunch followed by a movie binge-fest, curled up with a blanket next to Bear.

"I know this is a little awkward. But . . . I really need to talk to you."

First Dan, now me. This one really likes to talk. "What about?" I ask, wondering if there's a Stalkers Anonymous hotline. Maybe she can talk to them instead.

A chilly breeze picks up, funneling leaves around our feet. She shifts her weight, glances over at a beleaguered palm tree and back to me. Finally, she says, "It's about that night we partied. It's about Dan."

CHAPTER 5

BRYNN

Erin and I sit down at a small round table in a vegan restaurant, two doors down from the gym. I suggested this place because I'm friendly with the staff, and if things go pear-shaped, at least I'll have reliable witnesses.

Erin slides into the chair opposite me, stashes her yoga mat, and pulls her bag onto her lap, fidgeting with the long smooth handles.

Martin walks over, three-inch platform Creepers slapping on the faux wood floor.

"Hey, girl," he says. "What'll it be today?"

I want to make one of my usual cracks about his choice of footwear, but Erin is downcast and edgy, chewing on the inside of her cheek. What does she want to tell me? "I'll take my usual. Orange juice with ginger," I say.

"Super spicy . . ." Martin says, writing down my order with a smirk. It's literally a scribble. Then he looks up at Erin. "And you, hon?"

"I'll take a water, no ice. "

"Water, no ice." Martin makes a final scribble on his notepad and leaves with a flourish.

An awkward moment of silence stretches between us. Erin looks a little peaked. There are dark smudges under her right eye that I hadn't noticed before. Her lips are pale. I'm not sure if she sweated off her foundation or what, but she's not looking so hot.

"So, what did you want to tell me?" I ask.

She picks a ragged cuticle on her thumb, mutely studying the table. "Erin . . . I know you called Dan."

She looks genuinely shocked. Not exactly Oscar-worthy, but respectable. "It's not what you think," she says.

I look away and lean back. That old line? "Then why did you call him?" I tilt my head to the side, listening. This will be good.

But she doesn't reply.

"Look, Erin," I say, running my thumbnail along a groove in the wooden tabletop. "I know this is hard for you. Breakups are hard. I've had a couple bad ones myself. And I know we didn't make it any easier for you, but you really need to move on. Find someone else and . . . leave us alone."

That sounds harsh. I swallow, waiting for her to go Psycho Level Ten on me, and glance over at Martin, cutting oranges in half, oblivious to my combustible predicament.

But she doesn't take offense or try to defend herself. She presses her lips together, brow furrowed. She looks down at her clasped hands, deep in thought. Then she looks up at me.

"You're right. I shouldn't have reached out. It's just that something happened that night . . ." Like a shag? I wonder, but Dan said nothing happened. And I believe him. What else could it be? "And I wanted to talk to him before the police get involved."

The word 'police' hits me like a punch in the gut. Is she talking about rape?

She reaches into her bag, pulls out a photo from a side pocket, and slides it across the table toward me.

Carefully, I pick up the photo as fearsome as a snake.

It's a close-up of Erin's face with clusters of bruises around her temple and the corner of her eye and mouth. Her bottom lip is bloodied and bruised, her right eye swollen shut. Angry red scrapes like road rash mar the side of her forehead.

I drop the photo, afraid to touch it, and look at the shadows under Erin's right eye and a very faint yellowish patch—an old bruise?—over her temple that I hadn't noticed before.

She bites her lower lip and looks down. "It happened that night we all went out."

That night we all went out . . .

My mind races back to that big black hole of a night, jolted back to those foggy memories by this gruesome photo, whirring over as many scenes as I could recall, trying to solve this new mystery, looking at everything in a new investigative light. Who beat her up? And when?

We certainly were wasted. It was one of those rare times when the beginning of the night sparkled with fun and potential, and our thirst for drinks seemed bottomless.

The dead soldiers started multiplying. The empty glasses stacked up. More mysteriously arrived.

The wine went down like water. The music was bumping, my body moving. Everyone was deaf. *What? What did you say?* But it didn't matter. I wasn't there to blather. I was there to have a good time.

I was out with my lover, his hand on my knee, sending shivers of desire through my body. And then the booze took hold, filling the night with magic and laughter. Even the ex-girlfriend was so nice and fun.

There's the odyssey to the club. I remember that guy we called the Pied Piper, leading the whole gaggle straight to some VIP section, filled with strangers, laughing and drinking even more. I have no idea how we got in. But we were in all right. Where did the Pied Piper go? Did he do it? Did he beat up Erin?

There was boozing and laughing and dancing. Then the room started spinning, making me feel queasy. My voice came out all slurred and funny. I had to concentrate to say something other than utter gobbledygook.

By then, disorientation had set in. The room wobbled to the booming beat of the music. I remember wanting to go home and lie in Dan's safe arms until the world stopped spinning and my stomach stopped churning.

But he left, following Erin out of the club on unsteady legs. I got up to follow, I remember, but some horny wraith pulled me onto the dance floor. The wraith started bumping and grinding, pecking at my lips like a giant bird of prey. I pushed him away because—because I'm taken! I love someone. Someone who left to go somewhere with his ex . . .

I escaped the wraith and slumped down in the booth occupied by the friendly strangers. Did one of them beat up Erin? What about the wraith? Did he do it?

Who were the friendly strangers anyway? We all mind-melded at some point during the night's festivities, riding the same wave of drink and euphoria. Probably something else too, I would have realized if I wasn't so trashed.

But I *was* trashed.

Dan was missing, and I realized that all those fun people weren't fun anymore. They were on drugs, offering me some if I want to skip on over to the nearest toilet stall . . .

So I bailed, trudging down the sidewalk, shivering and hugging myself. My feet hurt. I needed help. I needed my boyfriend. Where in the hell did he go?

My night turned into a terrible nightmare at that point, not at all like the fun-filled night I had imagined. I tried to text Dan, but I couldn't see straight. Then I found him somehow, I guess, because the next thing I can recall is ending up at a house party with Dan, sans Erin.

There are black holes in my memory. Too many to count. How did we get to that house? How did I get home? Where did

Erin go? I have no idea, but I made it home all right, feeling grateful that the nightmare had finally ended.

Except now I realize that it didn't end.

It only just began . . .

"Who did this to you?" I whisper, afraid to ask, afraid of the answer.

Her eyes turn hard and brittle with hate. And she speaks the name that, deep down, I feared all along.

"Dan."

CHAPTER 6

DAN

Saying goodbye to Brynn was like a knife to the heart. The look in her eyes. The feel of her body against mine. I'm not exactly sure that I lied to her. I think about a polygraph test, strapped around my chest, monitoring my heart beat, and I think there's a good possibility that I would fail.

But lying when I have her best interests at heart doesn't exactly count, does it? I don't know. All I know is that I feel wretched inside for what happened that night. What was I thinking?

All during the long, endless hours of travel to Kandahar; first the long haul flight in the windowless military plane, then the dry jarring convoy along dusty unpaved desert roads, and finally the soulless processing onto base, I thought about that night.

What I wouldn't give to rewind that one single night and make it go away. What would I do if I had it to do all over again? I'd tell Erin to leave, of course. And if she sat there with that God-awful smirk on her face, making my blood boil, I'd take Brynn by the hand and walk straight out of there.

But I didn't do that. To my eternal regret, I didn't listen to my knee-jerk instinct that told me to run. I came back from the bar and found them sitting together, glass of wine in hand, talking. Intently. Then they started to laugh. Brynn, at first, followed by Erin, who brought her hand (I used to call it her claw) down on Brynn's forearm and squeezed. My hackles rose when I saw that. But then Brynn laughed again and sang that stupid party pooper song and smiled that beautiful smile of hers, and I thought to myself: *Relax, man. What could possibly happen?*

What did I drink that night? My legs turned to rubber at one point, I remember. I take pride in my ability to handle booze. But that night . . . what did they put in their gin bottles—jet fuel?

I haven't been able to eat much since then. Knowing what happened. I carry around that truth with me like a molten piece of lava in my belly. It smolders, day in and day out, burrowing into the folds of my gut, burning small holes into my flesh.

Why did Erin call me? She's such a nutcase. I wouldn't be surprised if she called to chat, imagining that we're best friends now despite everything that had happened between us.

I stood in the kitchen, looking down at my phone, knowing full well that Brynn was watching me. I could feel her gaze bore into me, even if she was staring at my reflection in the windowpane. When I saw Erin's name on my phone display, I felt my blood pressure drop as if someone had pulled a plug out of my heel. Brynn knew that Erin had called me. Of course she knew.

I find that I'm reminding myself to eat now, to get some gut luggage down there, or else I'll waste away and lose my strength. Then what will I do? How will I get though my missions? Don't think about it, man. It was a white lie. You told Brynn the part of the truth that she needed to know, the part she asked about. *Did you guys get together*? That absolutely never happened.

Good thing she didn't ask if something *else* happened, casting her net far and wide. Is that it then? I wonder. Is the truth on a need to know basis? I think so, yes. Yes, if I can swear it will never happen again. On that, I swear on my life.

But Brynn, she can't know what happened that night. She can never, ever know . . .

Briggs, our squadron leader, sticks his blonde sunburnt head into my bunk compartment. "Your beauty sleep ain't workin.' You're still ugly."

"I haven't heard your mom complaining."

He smirks. "Be ready to move out in twenty, pecker checker."

And it's my turn to smirk. "Yes, sir."

CHAPTER 7

GIA

It's noon on Saturday. Standing in the Newport Marina parking lot, I feel cold prickles sweep across my skin as the wind picks up. Early March isn't known for warm perfect weather, but for the first time in recent memory, the skies are leaden, threatening bad weather. I walk down the entrance ramp to the docks where all the boats are tied up, where my day sail with my best friend Nikki and the guy she's seeing, James, is set to occur.

They met at Nikki's twenty-fifth birthday party, while we were standing at the bar, ordering drinks. He bumped into her, wearing a wide grin and carefully mussed hair.

She fought her attraction to him because he's a Peter Pan Man, recently divorced, chasing his endless summer, not cut out for commitment or not any time soon anyway, at least that what his ex-wife would probably say.

Nikki gave me a slip number and the name of the boat, *Fair Thee Well*. I'll just walk up and down the floating walkway here until I find them. Easy.

Except it's not easy. There's about a hundred boats down here, a tangle of masts stretching up to the darkening sky. After I make my way up and down a row or two, I stop and unearth my cell phone from my bag. While I'm punching in my passcode, I hear Nikki call out, "Hey, Gia!"

I turn and find Nikki and James standing in the cockpit behind a faded red canvas cover, James with his arm resting on the frame, Nikki waving next to him. She's wearing her favorite pair of cropped chinos, matched with a nautical inspired polo shirt, and a striped sweater. Her chin-length blonde bob is tucked behind her ears, framing her high cheekbones.

"Glad you found us. I was beginning to worry," Nikki says as I walk toward them.

I glance up at the sky. "I already am worried. Do you think we should go out in this wind?"

"You can't sail without wind, can you?" James grins and moves to the side runnel, extending his hand toward me. "Welcome aboard."

"Thanks," I say, taking his hand, climbing up and swinging my leg over the wires that stretch around the boat. Then I catch the tip of my tennis shoe and stumble. It wasn't the most graceful of entrances. I hope I didn't look like an idiot.

I give Nikki a hug, and can tell by the glimmer in her eyes that she's thrilled to be dating a *captain,* a good-looking one too in charge of a real life sailboat.

Fair Thee Well is a lot smaller than many of the other boats docked at the marina, but it looks cute and capable. A sporty red stripe runs alongside two tiny topside windows. There's a confusing mess of ropes and lines and blocks and clamps, leading here, there and everywhere, and the sails are flapping half-heartedly in the breeze. Am I glad James knows what he's doing.

"I can't believe you own a boat. Wow," I say to him.

"Partly own. And sometimes I wish I didn't. You know what they say about boats?"

"That they're super fun to sail?" I ask.

"Ha! That they're holes in the water where you dump your money."

"Oh dear."

James chuckles and slips his arm around Nikki. "Good thing they're super fun to sail." Nikki looks up at him, smiling grandly, her half-moon shaped eyes disappearing into squints. "Go ahead and put your bag down below. I'll get the engine started."

Inside the boat, I find old ropes piled onto the faded canvas cushions of the couch. A bucket filled with tools sits off to the side, and a small wooden countertop topped with a single gas burner makes up the kitchen. The boat has a musty smell that makes me feel queasy or maybe it's the unsettling way the boat keeps bumping against the dock, knocking my sense of balance out of whack.

Quickly, I put my bag down and climb out into the fresh air again. The wind picks up, clattering ropes against masts all across the marina. Suddenly, I have a misgiving. I wouldn't call it ESP because I turned my back on my extra special power long ago.

But I do have an inkling. Call it nerves. I have a feeling that something is going to happen today, something big, possibly bad. Maybe it's just my imagination. What's that saying about fear? Is it something to be heeded or bravely pushed aside? I'm not sure.

I sit down next to Nikki, while James fires up the engine and checks a few dials. "Isn't this exciting?" She asks with a big smile, squeezing my hand with both of hers.

"Mmhm. Yeah."

"You okay?" she asks, her smile fading.

"I'm just a little nervous, I guess."

"About what?"

"I don't know. Maybe I'm just being a worrywart."

She smirks and wafts a hand. "Don't worry. James knows what he's doing." She looks over at him. "Right, babe?"

James chimes in. He's seen it all before, he's telling me. Big seas, bad weather, you name it. He sailed the boat to Catalina Island with six of his friends just a few weeks ago. Nothing broke. The boat didn't sink. Nobody died of privacy invasion. He's a real professional. People *pay* him to sail in inclement weather. In fact, he's off to a regatta on Martha's Vineyard in a few days to crew. "I'll get you home safe and sound," he's saying as he pats the yellowing deck of the boat. "She won't let us down."

"It'll be fun!" adds Nikki.

"Okay," I mumble. "Thanks guys . . ."

He's up at the front of the boat now—the bow—tossing ropes onto the dock. Then he hurries back and slips the engine into gear. So I sit back and try to relax as the boat pulls away from the dock, while James steers us into the great windy unknown.

CHAPTER 8

GIA

It's definitely windy. Gusty, James calls it, with blasts up to thirty knots. That's what his little wind-o-meter reports anyway, he calls it the Windex. I squeeze my hands between my knees and think about blue cleaning fluid. Thirty knots seems to be his threshold for concern. He's looking very busy now, and Nikki is looking very green.

"Keep your eyes on the horizon," James tells Nikki, who turns to the side and stares out into the distance.

"Can you winch in the sheet?" he asks me, voice raised against the wind, pointing at a thingy. Boats have a lot of thingies. Thingies with names that don't make any sense. I look around for said sheet, trying to find a big white fabric-like item that one might find in bed. Does he mean the sail? I know what a sail is. Sheets and sails are kind of similar. Both are big and billowy. Right?

"The rope!"

Nope. Okay, I see a lot of ropes. There's a thin blue one, a red one with black specks, and a dirty white one.

"The blue one. Put the winch handle on the winch and crank it up!"

Okay. Okay. I can do this. I grab a handle-looking device and try to fit it into the star shaped hole on top of the winch, but no matter how hard I push it won't go in.

"Push the button!" he yells into the wind.

I find the button on the top of the handle and engage it. Some edges retract, allowing for easy insertion. In it goes, and around I crank, praying the wind will die down, praying the sun will come out and rescue us from this worsening situation.

I look up at the leaden sky. Storm clouds are gathering thick and dark now. I'm definitely frightened. And if it wasn't for James' sailing skills, I would be crying right now. Instead, I'm teetering on the brink of 'terrified' and retreating back to 'shaken up.' Rinse and repeat.

"Twenty-five knots!" he cries, a wide grin plastered across his face, while my hair is plastered across mine.

Nikki and I hold on tight to the arched canvas covered frame that thankfully blocks wind and seawater spray. He calls it the dodger. I call it our lifeline.

"I think we should stay close to land," I suggest, staring longingly at the coastal cliffs. I contemplate jumping over board and swimming to terra firma, where I won't lose my lunch, where I don't have to pull on sheets and cling to dodgers, where I will never, ever, capsize and drown.

"No way!" James cries. "That's the worst thing you can do. You have to aim for the open ocean and ride it out, otherwise you risk running aground." He motions toward land, where heavy waves crash and crumble over a wide bed of jutting rocks that lead up to the cliff face.

"Seems like a wise thing to do," I mumble, grateful that James knows what he's doing, especially when, clearly, I have no idea.

Through the boat opening, I can see that my beach bag spilled its contents inside the boat. My suntan lotion rolls from one side of the boat to the other. A tampon makes a similar round-trip journey. I want to slip down the ladder and tidy up my belongings, but another gust of wind bum-rushes us.

"Hang on!" James cries.

I hang on, mostly to my big fat baby tears, and *ride it out*, thinking about my other problems. My queasy stomach, for one, feeling worse every time boaty smells waft up from down below. I stare at the horizon alongside Nikki and pull in deep breaths. Except it isn't helping. It's making me cold. Shivering, I look down at the rattling sleeves of my cute pink 'wind breaker' that breaks exactly zero force wind.

I hadn't bothered my head about performance when I bought it. It was cute, on sale, and had a sufficiently technical sounding name. The flimsy jacket was really built for a pleasant afternoon breeze, not Cyclone Mary here bearing down on us.

It'll be fun, Nikki had said. This is not fun. And I think Nikki would agree. She leans over the cockpit railing and dry heaves.

"Are you okay?" I ask, moving over to her. I put my arm around her, holding her hair away from her face, doing my level best to keep my stomach contents down where they belong.

"I'm fine," she mumbles.

"Nikki, take in deep breaths," James calls out. "That should help."

"Did you hear that, Nik?"

"Yeah," she says, "I think I need to lay down though . . ." And she settles her head onto my lap, while I huddle under the red half-dome of the dodger, looking out of the windows made of thick plastic sheeting to the wind-blown sea.

"Is it going to get worse?" I ask James, not sure if Nikki and I can take much more.

"It's just a squall," he replies, strong hands on the big wheel he calls the helm, steering us out to sea. He points toward a lighter area in the sky, past a dark shelf-like cloud that hovers overhead. "See that? It's called a squall line. Once we pass it, the wind should calm down."

Thank God for small mercies. Literally.

"When will we pass it?" I ask.

"Soon! Let's just hope I'm reading those clouds wrong,"—he motions toward a billowing cloud mass on the distant horizon, dark on the underside, puffy and white on top—"cuz that looks like lightning and thunder to me."

Well, James must be a weather genius because the next thing that arrives after the wind dies down some is thunder and lightning. This makes him nervous.

I nearly jump out of my seat when the first bolt thunders out of the sky. It's one thing to sit in the comfort of your own home, watching Mother Nature in her full glory. It's quite another to have a front row seat to her fury, while sitting on bobbing little cork in the vast churning ocean.

"Is that bad?" I ask.

He nods. Affirmative. "A direct hit can take out all the electrical equipment. The maps, the navigation instruments . . . everything."

"Everything?" I ask, looking around. I gaze out at the steely gray horizon, and for once in my life, I pray for bland weather.

We sail on for another half an hour or so, while I hang onto the dodger frame for dear life, watching the lightning spark on distant whitecaps. Then one strikes pretty darn close to home.

We've all heard stories of people getting struck by lightning. Those are the types of things that happen to the unfortunate segment of society called Other People. Not me. I'm not Other People. I'm me. Gia Eastland, the—

Crack!

The mast sparks, and a faint current of electricity races through the palm of my hand. Was that a direct hit? Lightning kills people, but here I am, pretty much alive. It must have been a trick of the eye, I reason. Nothing to worry about. Nothing—

"Shit," James says, tapping on a screen mounted on the helm station. He doesn't need to say any more. I already know. The lightning struck, frying all the electronics, ushering us into the terrible calamity that he just detailed.

Looks like we're about to spend much more time together than we originally planned.

"Can you go down below and flip the master circuit breaker?"

I stare at James, aghast. "What? Are you off your nut? I don't know anything about boats!"

"OK. You can either flip the circuit breaker or steer. But I can't do both." I think about it for a second. How hard can it be to steer a boat? It's not like we're going to hit anything.

"You ready?" James motions me over to helm. "Make sure you drive up on a wave or else we can capsize."

Never mind. "Where's the circuit breaker?"

"It's behind a panel underneath the nav station."

I blink.

"The nav station is where all the maps and crap are. The panel is below the table. It's white. You can't miss it."

"Maps and crap," I mumble. And to Nikki, "Hang on, Nik. I'll be right back."

I much prefer James to handle all the circuitry, but he's busy manhandling the helm, driving up waves, making sure we don't capsize. And Nikki is out of commission, so I make my way down the ladder and inside the boat.

Electricity makes me nervous. I'm not sure how much this little boat carries, but I'm pretty sure it's enough to make my hair stand on end. Plus, there's the problem of the thick malodor inside the boat, smelling of dried saliva, old fish, and diesel. The diesel part is especially hard to handle for some reason.

I descend the short ladder and I find the maps and crap on a little wooden table on the side of the cramped cabin. The boat pitches and bucks. I wobble over, landing a good handhold on the desk ledge. Made it.

I pause for a moment and hold my breath, trying to calm my stomach. Focus, I tell myself. Just open the panel, flip the switch, and get out of here pronto before something embarrassing happens.

I grab a flashlight rolling side to side on the nav station and turn it on. Thank God it works. Sorta. I point the dim beam of light at the panel and tug on the handle until the door pops open.

Inside I find our salvation: the master circuit breaker. It's a circular switch with a lever that twists to the position at three o'clock marked ON. Right now it's tripped to the twelve o'clock position marked OFF.

"Did you find it?" James yells from outside.

"Yeah," I call back, staring at the mechanism. I swallow and reach into the murky darkness as careful as a kid playing Operation.

You've done this before, I tell myself, thinking about the time my banker's lamp blew a bulb and plunged my apartment into darkness. I remember the jolt when I flipped the circuit breaker. But I survived, as I will now. I hope.

I grit my teeth and twist.

Nothing.

"It's stuck!" I call out.

"Try harder!"

Harder. Okay. I stick the end of the flashlight in my mouth, keeping the dimming beam of light on the switch so I can kind of see what I'm doing. With both hands now, I twist the lever as hard as I can, but still it won't budge.

"Anytime now . . ." I hear James exclaim.

My initial trepidation fades. Instead, I feel a surge of frustration tinged with my old friend Fear. If I can't get this stupid switch back into the Action Jackson position, we're going spend the entire night out here getting thrashed around. And how much more can this floating can of beans take? Right now, there isn't anything I want more than to get off this beater of a boat.

I try again, twisting so hard my fingers ache, pushing through the pain. Suddenly the switch jumps to the three o'clock position, and my hand slips off, striking a wire.

Zap!

A sizzling current surges up my arm, striking like a great snake. The power of the sting takes my breath away. The flashlight falls to the floor, killing the light.

I scramble backward, body buzzing, holding my aching hand up to my chest. A wave of nausea washes over me. Grey fuzzy stars dance before my eyes. I hear the distant sound of waves washing against the side of the boat, followed by, sometime later, the rustling sound of James' foul weather jacket as he rushes inside the boat.

"Good news, I got the autopilot working," he's saying. I can hear his distant voice, but he's far away, in a brutal reality that I don't want to go back to. "And the wind is dying down . . ."

I fall into a dark widening aperture, where the ocean is gentle and soothing, where everything feels warm and cozy, and languish there until my senses begin to return, until reality presses down on me like an anvil. I groan and roll onto my side.

"Gia? You okay?" James asks, grabbing my arm.

A shiver races over my skin. My vision shifts. The inside of the boat fades from view as if covered by a thin veneer.

It's happening. It's happening again. My long dormant psychic ability is overwhelming me and pushing through. I squeeze my eyes shut, trying to deny it, but it comes nonetheless.

Distantly, I hear voices. *Congratulations, Daddy.* I see hugs. I feel a rush of elation, making my throat feel tight with emotion. A sense of amazement and relief and happiness washes over me. James and his wife had been trying for some time to have a baby. The stork hadn't forgotten about them, after all.

Charlotte, it is. Charlotte Marie Taggart.

"Charlotte?" I wonder, trying to parse out some meaning from my swirling thoughts.

James lets go of my arm as if stung. "What did you say?"

And then I hear sobbing, a terrible rending sound that tears at my heart. I hear the rapid pulse of a fetal heartbeat, and then I hear the resounding silence of a little life lost forever.

My baby!

I squeeze my eyes shut. "Born still," I whisper.

The vision fades, leaving behind a dull impression of sorrow, pain, and terrible, grinding loss. The boat bucks and sways in the churning seas.

But the weather outside seems trivial compared to the storm raging inside James' heart. He's not a commitment phobe. He's not a Peter Pan Man. He is a man running though, running from terrible, crushing grief.

I look into his unblinking, glassy eyes. "I'm so sorry," I whisper.

He works his mouth, as if to say something. Then stops. The boat continues to buck and sway. A ceiling light flickers on and off, shifting the shadows that entomb us. Lightning flashes, holding his pained face in bright contrast, then dumps us back into darkness.

"It happened on week thirty," he says, at last. "They didn't know why."

I look away, tears filling my eyes.

"They said these things—that it happens. They said that because Jen was older—thirty-four—that maternal age could have had something to do with it." He puts air quotes around 'maternal age,' his voice thick with anger and condescension. "We ended up burying my baby girl in the tiniest coffin you'd ever seen. It was like burying a doll . . . a tiny lifeless doll."

He looks down at his open palms, laying face up on his lap. "Jen was beside herself. I said we could try again, but Jen, she— she couldn't think of trying again. The grief just consumed her . . ." He meets my gaze. "And in the end, it consumed us both."

CHAPTER 9

GIA

We finally limp into the marina at one in the morning. I go down below and collect my bag, careful not to wake Nikki, who fell asleep in the back cabin. As James walks me out to my car, I think about giving him some words of encouragement or sympathy, I'm not sure which, but he's probably had his fill of trite words.

"That was interesting," I say instead.

"Sorry about all that," he says, though it feels like I should be the one apologizing.

"It's okay. Thanks for getting us home safe. You sure know what you're doing out there."

"I try." His mouth lifts into a smile, but it doesn't carry up to his eyes. In them, I can see that he's haunted by what I saw. Well, me too.

"Tell Nikki bye for me. Tell her to call me when she wakes up."

James reaches up and scratches his brow. "Okay I will. I'll tell her when she wakes up."

"Okay, I'll talk to you soon, James. Thanks again."

I drive home in a daze, cruising through a yellow light, and arrive at my apartment. I park, turn off the engine, and somehow end up on the couch in my living room, cuddling my little rescue dog Jack, staring at the carpet.

It's back. The terrible and the wonderful. It's all come roaring back. I didn't want my psychic ability to come back. Not after I couldn't prevent the death of my best friend, Melissa, back when we were eighteen. But here I am, back behind the crystal ball, seeing people's pasts and the secrets that hide in their hearts.

I feel a little excited, but unsure about having my ability back, after what had happened so long ago. Maybe this is the past coming to find me, trying to make amends, the one that I had tried to escape from. I need to talk to the only person who will understand. I need to talk to Mom.

"Hallo?" comes her groggy voice over the phone.

"Mom? Hey, sorry to bother you."

"What time is it?" She has the phone pressed against her face, muffling her voice.

"Um. It's almost two."

"Ugh."

"Sorry. Do you want me to call you later?"

"No. No, I'm up . . ." She drops the phone. I can hear it clonk on the carpeted floor. Then she curses and fumbles around her bed, looking for it.

"Mom, I'm down here. On the floor."

Scrape. Scrape. "Hello?"

"Hi, yeah, I'm here."

She lets out a big sigh, and then falls silent. I think she's fallen asleep, but then she pulls in a deep breath. "Is everything okay? How did your sailing trip go?"

It's my turn to sigh. "Interesting."

"Interesting? Like fun interesting?"

"Not that interesting."

"Oh. But something happened. Otherwise you wouldn't be calling me at one in the morning. Remember what Nonna always said. 'Observe, observe and—'"

"'Take-ah the monney.'" I finish the sentence for her. We chuckle. It's a long-standing joke by now. Nonna, my Italian grandmother, was a tarot card reader and psychic. She worked tirelessly against quacks that brought her field into disrepute. She toured around the country giving parlor readings and talks about thought-transference and telepathy. And she wasn't shy about demanding her fees.

"She did have her pearls of wisdom, didn't she?" Mom's voice goes soft with nostalgia.

"Mom, I don't know how to say this, but . . . it's back. The superpower."

Silence.

"It's ... back? How is that even possible?"

"I don't know how it's possible. All I know is that I went out sailing with James and Nikki and this terrible squall blew in and lightning hit the boat, so James sent me down below to reset the circuit breaker. So I did, but then I got electrocuted and—and I saw that he lost a baby girl ..."

"That's horrible," she says with feeling after a long pause. "Maybe you had an inkling? You knew he was recently divorced, and so something had to have happened and—and electrocuted? Are you sure you're okay?"

"I think so."

"How do you feel?" she ventures. "I mean, after everything that happened with ..."

We don't even talk about it. The terrible tragedy. The aftermath of which gave me a nervous breakdown and a three-week stint at a *mental health facility*. After that, I turned away from my ability, refused to listen, denying it entirely, until finally, my ability fell silent.

But I'm better now. Stronger. Older. And I've healed. My psychic ability burned too hot for me back then. I was a cocky teenager, smarter than everyone else, and way too full of myself. I knew had clarity that evaded most adults. I knew had *the gift*. Except, I didn't know how to trust it. I didn't know how to use it properly. I didn't know how to save Melissa.

Like a lost love, I always carried a wavering, inextinguishable flame for my psychic ability, hoping someday we could reunite, when the time is right. Maybe the time is now.

"I feel a little buzzed and nervous, but I'm good. I feel good."

"Do me a favor then—will you go see a doctor at least? Just have him check you out. See if there's any lasting damage?"

"Like psychic abilities?" I ask.

She laughs. "Something like that." Then she sits up; I hear the bed squeak. "You know, maybe it's come back for a reason. Maybe it's finally time for you to heal."

"That's funny. I was just thinking the very same thing."

"I'm happy for you, honey. I think this is a good thing. It's time for you to embrace that part of yourself. To stop running . . ."

"I know," I say softly.

"Hey, I have an idea. Let's put on some training wheels on and start off easy. You can start with looking into me."

"But I know everything about you!"

"Maybe you don't." There are shadows in her voice that intrigue me. She actually had a life before I was born, a concept all kids find unfathomable. Maybe there was crazy boyfriend from high school, or a dead pet or something. I feel a twinge of apprehension. Would I see something else? Some dark hidden secret?

"Okay," I say, excited but apprehensive. I'm not sure how to get the ball rolling anymore. Back then it just came to me. Easy.

Superpower 1.0 was the ability to pick up information about people's pasts and their deeply held secrets. I could see into their hearts and minds. With my psychic laser goggles, I could see people's hidden dimensions and their past traumas.

Now that the era of Superpower 2.0 is upon me, I have no idea what to expect. Or how to get it working.

"Let me try . . ." I close my eyes and focus my attention on Mom. I visualize her spacious two-bedroom apartment backed onto a small nature reserve. In her bedroom with that ghastly floral wallpaper, I imagine Midas, her white terrier-mutt, snoring down by her feet. The scene set in my mind, I focus hard, trying to tune out all the ambient sounds around me—the refrigerator running, a car driving past my window, and a dog barking distantly—but I hear them all even louder, despite my best efforts.

Nothing. Am I supposed to rub my hands together and say a magic word? I didn't have to do that with James. But that happened after the electrical jolt. I hope I don't need a jump-start every time.

Still nothing. I sigh. "I don't understand why it's not working. I saw what happened to James. And—"

"Honey, I think you need some sleep, okay?" She yawns. "I need some sleep too. I have an early reading tomorrow morning."

Disappointment mixed with relief washes over me. I'm not sure I'm ready to embrace my ability, but I don't want it to go away either.

But maybe Mom is right. Maybe I need to see a doctor.

"Okay, Mumsie. Sorry I woke you up. Love you."

"Love you too, honey. Call me when you book your appointment, k? Night night."

CHAPTER 10

BRYNN

I need some fresh air. Clear my mind. Get my bearings. So I slip on Bear's harness and set out on a quick-paced jog down to the beach, eight blocks away. Bear's a good running companion. His energy levels are seemingly endless, and when my pace lags, which it will today, I can always count on him to carry me along.

If I can get my heart pumping, my blood moving, maybe I make some sense out of Erin's accusation and figure out what to do or who to believe. Because after tossing around in bed all night long, my mind going over every detail again and again, while I listened to the rain patter against the windowpane, I finally decided to get up and get moving.

It's golden hour, the first tender rays of a new breaking day. As Bear runs exuberantly in front of me, barking and leaping at birds in flight, I glance around at the soft light of post dawn. I'm never up early enough to enjoy daybreak, and despite the frazzled edgy feeling of looming insomnia, I find myself awed by the lilting birdsong, pink high contrast post-storm clouds, and sharp invigorating air.

After Erin had shown me the picture of her rearranged face, I drove away in a daze, absolutely blindsided, feeling scared and stunned, while conflicted thoughts ate me alive.

Somehow I ended up in the back streets of Clairemont Mesa, a hillside suburban enclave of modest houses landscaped with parched grass and gravel, searching for a place to pull over and park so I could think and not worry about getting rear-ended.

I stopped down at the end of a bleak cul-de-sac and turned off my car. The silence was deafening. And for the first time in my life, I was afraid to be with my own thoughts.

Who did this to you?

Dan.

Did he? Did he really?

I sat in my car, my heart twisting with pain and rage and fear. Then I had driven home, eyes glued on the menacing storm clouds forming on the horizon, apropos for how my relationship with Dan was unfolding, feeling numb and exhausted.

As I pick up the pace, I think about the facts that are working in Erin's favor. First and foremost, her evidence. Second, with a pit opening up in my stomach, I know that Dan had left with Erin the night of his party, and they had "talked." That's called a fact.

Sounds painful.

Pretty much.

Did he admit to beating her up?

On the other hand, I cannot actually believe that the man I'm in love with would do something this monstrous. I would have seen the signs, at least one of them. Wouldn't I? We've only been together for six months, but isn't that enough time to see *something* detrimental in his personality?

It's one of those weird, twisty things. You can't believe it, but you can't not believe it. Dan is smart and talented, hard working, and—okay, he has a black box of a past.

"Babe, I don't want to look back," he'd told me one evening at the beach about a month after we'd met, laying on a blanket and gazing up at the stars. "I want to move forward . . . with you."

I'd looked over at his handsome profile, okay, at his full lips, and when his captivating gaze met mine, I let the topic flit away. The past is the past. The future is for us. Does that make him guilty?

This is quickly becoming a war of fact versus feeling. I know Dan. And even though I saw Erin's swollen pulpy face in that picture, I know in my bones that Dan did not do that.

Except, suspicion snuck into my heart. Doubt began whispering little naked truths in my ear. *Remember the road rage incident? Remember how he punched that guy in the face?*

Oh right. That. I forgot about that. But that guy was a complete jerk. He deserved it.

Believe the actions, not the words.

And so, I find myself tallying up 'the actions.' The road rage incident. Dan's refusal to talk about certain topics in his past, his black box I called it. The questions surrounding what happened between him and Erin that night. He said nothing happened. Did he lie to me? But I stopped that line of reasoning because it scared me.

People don't like hearing the truth when it disrupts their own version of reality. I'm no different. I don't like thinking about Erin's evidence and the fact that Dan and Erin met privately that night (thus opening up the possibility that something *could* have happened) because it disrupts my original defense: Dan did not beat up Erin.

But if he can rough up a guy, he can rough up a girl too. Violence is violence, right? Had I batted away the red flags because they were getting in the way of my Dan the Man daydream? The man that I had journeyed to find?

When I had graduated from college, I packed up my car and drove west from Connecticut, feeling like Lewis or Clark, I wasn't sure which, forging on to the Great Frontier.

After a few months spent in Oregon and then Northern California, I'd headed south. I had some postcard images in mind after a brief stop in Monterrey. That place was both cold and expensive. The long stretches of Southern California beaches dappled with year-round sun beckoned to me.

I'd imagined myself traipsing around the golden hills of Hollywood with freethinkers and misfits. Cool people. I'd wanted to hang out with people on the cutting edge of independence. I'd wanted to find a place to lay down my restless soul.

Well, the freethinkers turned out to be celebrity-obsessed clones. "I know the pool man of the assistant to *Steven Segal*," one 'freethinker' advised me, clearly impressed with himself. They weren't freethinkers at all.

The misfits had turned out to be druggies. The golden hillsides turned out to be dry parched land, blighted with litter. And those open beaches drenched in sunshine? Cold.

So I kept driving until I reached San Diego, not sure what I'd find. My cash levels were still healthy. If San Diego proved to be disappointing, I had Australia in mind, home to the best beaches in the world apparently. I'd already looked into the visa situation. A few months picking fruit at an outback farm would get me a two-year work visa. Seemed like a nice exchange.

But I found something better than world-class beaches. I found Dan. Now, I'm losing him?

I think back to the day I found myself chatting with the desperately handsome Dan and falling in love with him. We had met by chance at a Fourth of July party down at Mission Bay, across the street from the iconic Mission Beach roller coaster rumbling along its wooden tracks. He's tall, a real plus for me because I'm five foot eight. His lopsided grin, dark wavy hair, and golden-blue eyes that glimmered in the warm evening light made me a little weak in the knees.

As we talked, I had the distinct feeling that he didn't hear a single thing I said, but somehow understood every word. After I had wedged my possessions in the trunk of my car and driven cross country, my journey seemed to purposeful, finally, because it seemed as though I found where I belonged.

I'll never forget how his gorgeous mouth curved into a wry smile as he asked for my phone number, while the fireworks boomed and crackled around us. I was nervous and giddy and wanted to make a sizzling impression. I felt like I'd landed a big sexy fish, but I figured he'd landed plenty of those himself.

He'd called a few days later and asked me out on a date. A proper one. He'd taken me out to fish taco dinner, followed by a stroll on the beach down by the water. When the sun slipped past the horizon and chilly ocean breezes washed over us, I huddled close to him and melted when stopped and kissed me.

During those tender days called 'getting to know you,' we'd fallen into bed pretty quickly. I remember lying in his arms, caressing his chest, laughing because we didn't know each other very well, after all. We'd soared high above the dating drudgery called twenty-one questions because we thought we were meant to be. All those other people, dutifully checking questions off their list? Desperate mugs. Ours was a real soul connection.

I didn't need to know the name of Dan's childhood pet to know he was meant for me, and I was meant for him. So if I was so sure about him, how could I not see this dark streak in his personality?

Maybe I had overlooked it. I'd fallen in love by then. I loved him, and I liked him too. I liked his simplicity. I liked his gainful employment. I liked his dedication; his work ethic, his cool job— search and rescue medic—and I liked that his friends called him 'Dan the Man.' There you go. Fantasy complete.

Except . . . this fantasy had just taken a hard left, veering into the realm of stark reality.

Bear and I jog up to the boardwalk and slow to a stop. Lines of big crumbly waves from the storm that blew in yesterday stretch around the promontory of Bird Rock, where surfers maneuver for waves. To my left, Pacific Beach pier marches toward the rosy horizon, waves smashing against the pylons. Down by the water, a lone couple walks together in the wet hand, hand in hand, jeans rolled up, bundled up in bulky coats against the cold.

I'm winded, but I have still have gas left in the tank, and Bear is straining at the leash, so we turn south toward Mission Beach, while my mind continues to grind.

Erin said she had a recording of what happened that night between her and Dan, and she offered to let me listen to it. I declined, stunned out of my underpants. A photo *and* a recording? Good God.

This allegation could completely destroy Dan. Even if Dan is somehow proven innocent, even if the picture is a fake, his life could be ruined with the accusation. His career that he'd bled and sweated for? Gone.

I can't dismiss the possibility that the picture is a Photoshop. I know it's possible. Did she show me a fake picture? And why would she do something like that? That requires a level of insanity that's hard to comprehend, and 'No Drama Dan' would never date a girl that's certifiable. Would he? He's a simple guy; allergic, he claims, to it. And finally, as if her photo and her voice recording weren't enough to give me permanent sleeplessness, she left words of warning that continue to haunt me.

Because if he did this to me, he'll do it to you . . .

And now, I regret letting the terrible topic of his whereabouts that night fade. I regret not asking twenty-one questions back when we were first getting to know each other. I regret skipping the interview process. And I regret not prying open his black box before moving in together.

I start off at a fast pace, my legs turning to jelly. Bear stretches to keep up, his mouth open in a wide grin, his tongue lolling out of his mouth. And I keep running and running, until finally, I can't run anymore.

CHAPTER 11

GIA

So I made the doctor's appointment. Maybe there's something wrong with me. Maybe a body scan will help. Maybe I have a hormonal problem.

I don't have any regular health problems to afford me a doctor acquaintance, so I flipped open my Blue Shield booklet and called the office closest to my house.

The following Tuesday, after talking to Mom, three days after my eventful sail with James and Nikki, I follow a nurse down the busy corridor into a bright exam room. I take a seat on the padded table, and the nurse takes my vitals.

She takes my blood pressure twice, as they always do when they discover my reading is ninety over sixty, followed by a little chat about salt.

Then she leaves. I pick up a gossip magazine and start leafing through it, hoping the doctor won't knock yet. There's a messy divorce I want to read about. Okay, done. I close the magazine and look around, hoping the doctor won't take much longer.

Then I text Mom. She's anxious for some comforting news. So am I. Over the course of the last few days, I tried to recover my long lost skill, concentrated so hard on making it happen that at one point I gave myself a headache.

When my friend Samantha invited me over on Sunday, I stood in her kitchen and tried some laying on of hands. Maybe it's touch activated, I reasoned. That didn't work either.

She was a good sport though, and poured me a glass of wine for my efforts. While I drank, I gazed at a light socket. Maybe a little jolt would get things going.

I wasn't stupid though. Before I stuck a butter knife in the wall and fried most of my brain cells, I ran my theory past Sam.

"You'll kill yourself," she said, taken aback. Then she launched into another story about how she heard of someone who knew someone who . . . .

So, reluctantly, I made peace with the loss of my superpower. It was a fluke, an acid flashback, a bionic arm that had stopped working. Lightning struck, literally, followed by a flash of insight. Now, I have nothing but a good dinner party story.

There's a quick rap on the door. A man walks though and introduces himself.

"Hi, I'm Dr. Keating." He shakes my hand, a firm grasp, and lets go. He's pretty fit for an older man in his late fifties, I guess. His salt and pepper hair is styled back, his waist nice and trim, and his buttoned up shirt fits well. He's wearing wears a stethoscope around his neck and stylish glasses. "How are you doing today?" he asks, shutting the door behind him and consulting his file. "Miss . . . Eastland is it?"

Suddenly there's a flutter in my stomach, and a word comes to mind as soft as a whisper. *Surgery.* My heartbeat picks up a little. Is my bionic arm back?

"Everything okay?" he asks.

"Yes, sorry." I look away. "I thought I,"—Stop. Stop right there. Don't you dare tell a board certified doctor that you think you heard a voice in your head. "I . . . had a little accident over the weekend. I wanted to come in and make sure there isn't any lasting damage."

He pulls a pen out from his pocket and starts taking notes in my file. "Can you tell me a little bit about it?"

"Yeah, sure," I say relieved that he's taking me seriously. Sam had pooh-pooh'd me. I'm ready to find out the truth of the matter, however depressing. "I went out sailing with some friends, and we got caught in a storm."

"The one that blew on Saturday?"

"Yes, that's the one."

He whistles. "That was pretty bad."

"Yes it was. Lightning hit the boat and the electrical equipment got fried. The captain asked me go down below and flip the main circuit breaker. So I did, but I guess my hand slipped or something because I got a pretty bad shock."

"Okay. Do you have any idea how much power was on board?"

"No, but I could feel my hair stand on end though. I actually thought my heart would stop beating. Electrical impulses and all that..."

"Well, luckily, the heart is a pretty solid piece of machinery." He puts his pen down and walks to the edge of the exam table. "I'll examine you first and see if I can find anything untoward. If you could lie back and relax..."

"Great. Yes. Examine away." I lie down, relax, and hope he finds something. Nothing deadly. Just something concrete.

He peers into my ears, my throat, and my eyes. He pokes around my belly, explaining that boats carry two types of power. Those made for the American market run on "one ten," meaning one hundred and ten volts. Or the boats destined for the international market, which sport a more robust package of "two-twenty," i.e. two hundred and twenty of those suckers. His boat runs on one ten, apparently.

"Both are survivable, in case you're wondering," he continues. "But there might have been some extra power stored up in the batteries that discharged when you flipped the master breaker."

Then he asks me to sit up, and tests my reflexes, fires off my funny bone, and says that he can't find anything untoward. He's writing notes in my file, recommending that I "take it easy over the next few days," when the words flash in my mind: *Surgery. Of the stomach.*

The inkling turns into an urge. This is definitely the tentative return of my bionic arm. I'm excited, but nervous. I don't want it to slip away again as elusive as a deer. I want to capture and keep it, but I don't want smother it.

I definitely don't want another James event. But I have a fleeting grasp on something powerful and mystic, something as delicate as a butterfly, something that I have missed.

Maybe I need to honor the inkling by speaking it aloud.

My mouth goes dry. I clench my teeth as the words come to me again.

Surgery. Of the stomach.

My heart pumps fast. I feel a little dizzy, but I speak anyway. "Doctor Keating, I'm sorry, I don't know how to say this, and—and please don't think I'm crazy, but I need to tell you something."

"Mmhm?" He keeps writing.

"Something about a—a surgery . . . of the stomach?"

He stops writing mid-sentence.

She needs surgery. Of the stomach.

I swallow. "I mean to say, she needs surgery . . . of the stomach."

He looks up at me, eyes wide with astonishment. "How did you know that?" he asks, voice small with disbelief.

I grimace and shrug. "I guess, I'm psychic?"

CHAPTER 12

GIA

Mom calls after my appointment with the doctor. I relate the most important detail: it's definitely back.

Then I tell her how I shared my strange inkling with Dr. Keating, who told me about his wife's ongoing mystery stomach complaint and the exploratory surgery that her specialist had recommended. Dr. Keating said his scientific mind wouldn't allow him to believe in psychic powers, but he cited placebo affects and other scientific mysteries that given him pause over the course of his career. He said he'd talk to his wife and consider moving forward with the surgery.

So I left, feeling good. Feeling helpful. Feeling like maybe my ability won't tear me apart again.

"So have you figured out how it works yet?" Mom asks. "I mean, do you have to say a magic word or something?"

I roll my eyes. "Mom, this isn't Lord of the Rings."

"Well, how do you know?"

It's a fair question.

I sigh. "I don't know."

"Well, don't you think we should try to figure it out? Maybe we should rule some things out."

"Like?"

"Well, like you said. You're not a wizard, so it's probably not word activated."

She's joking. I think. "Yeah?" I ask, laughing anyway.

"And you said concentrating doesn't seem help any."

"Mmhm."

"So try not to think too much about it because you can be really analytical, you know."

"Not that analytical."

Silence.

"Gia, remember that pie chart you drew up when you were trying to figure out if you should break up with that Marky guy? What was his name?"

"Mark Marshall." I forgot about that.

"Marky Marshall, poor guy. Awaiting the pie chart of doom."

"Mom, he turned out to be gay."

"He was?"

"Yeah, I told you. He took me on a date . . . to a gay bar."

Mom sighs. "Dating has gotten so complicated these days. I remember when I was your age, we didn't have all this internet dating and swipe right crap . . ."

"Another bad date?"

Mom doesn't reply. I had joined an online dating website and found Mom's profile. Shock. Horror. Mom is a beautiful woman, but like all women in their fifth decade, she's a little sensitive about her age.

Her profile picture featured a stunning ethereal headshot taken at the height of pixie hair 90's. It was one of those weird things, when you discover something about someone who you think you know like the back of your hand. Then the mask slips a little, and you question your knowledge of that human. Was Mom really into online dating? She'd had plenty to say about the *desperadoes* on dating sites. And why hadn't she put up a recent picture? It seemed a little dishonest.

But Mom had her reasons. She was eighteen when she got pregnant with me. Her father, Papa I called him, chucked the word *bastarda* around, wringing his hands with fear and anxiety and terrible, crushing disappointment. How could his good Catholic daughter get knocked up just out of high school? What would this mean for his only daughter, on whom he had pinned his hopes and dreams?

Nonna had a different view on the matter. She was a psychic much like her mother before her, making me a fourth generation psychic. She said my birth was written in the stars, albeit a little inconveniently, and that I'd become a powerful soul reader, one who would go on to help many people. So far, her prediction had proven to be questionable.

My grandparents, Nonna and Papa, had left behind their beloved Italy so that their daughter could have a life of options, of hope, of *monney*! And here, she'd gone and screwed it all up. "Santa Lucia!" Papa had cried, burying his hands in his thick hair. What now!

I can talk about this without fear of making Papa sound like an antiquated dickhead because he was there the day I was born, crying tears of joy when I came out yowling.

He was there, following the staff around with words of caution. "*Gentile, gentile*," he told any nurse who held me. Gentle, gentle.

"*La luce de meie occhi*," he said, when he finally got his turn to hold me tight. The light of my eyes. So Mom named me Gia, God's gracious gift, because my birth was the most glorious day of her life. I like to remind her of that day, particularly when I spoofed her online.

"Who wants to talk about bad dates?" Mom asks.

"Me." And we both laugh. "Well, anyway, about my *skill*. So far, I've been physically close to both James and Dr. Keating when my ability started working again," I say.

"So that's a common factor. And that makes sense because that's how it worked last time."

"That's true."

"But however it unfolds, always remember to listen to the quiet spirit within," Mom says, in conclusion of our discussion about my budding superpower. "Listen with your heart, not your head."

The next day proves to be a gleaming Southern California day, the same as any other, except when a storm blows in and gives me back my psychic power. I used to get excited when a cloud appeared in the blue sky, signaling drizzle mayhap.

Now, I'm happy for the grinning sun. I'm happy for predictable, uneventful weather because ever since my sailboat jaunt with James and Nikki my life has turned upside down.

Furry Baby, the boutique pet shop where I work, is a great place for me to build back up my confidence with intuiting. As I ring up customers, I gently open myself up to other people's energy.

Like putting on an old pair of house slippers, I'm finding that it's comforting to have my old friend back, even if I am still shuffling around the house.

This is a little bit like hopping aboard a spaceship, handling my newly awakened ability. I feel like I'm sitting in front of the warp drive nozzle, not sure how much pressure to apply, not sure which solar system to aim for. The answer will come to me, I hope.

It's closing o'clock. I need to rush home so I can take my dog Jack out for a wee; he's been home for over five hours, well into the danger zone of another potentially ruined area rug.

I'm zeroing out the till, when I hear the front door jingle. Hopefully it's the mailman, making his last zippy delivery for the day, and not an indecisive customer who wants to peruse the cat toy section. *Does this one have organic catnip?* I swallow the last dregs of my tea and look over at the door.

In walks a platinum blonde with slightly feathered (fried?) hair that falls around her shoulders in cascading waves, dark at the roots, almost silvery white at the ends. From her shoulder hangs a big, beige Louis Vuitton bag. Her eyebrows are shaped in a pretty arch over her eyes. The tip of her nose is bulbous. Her plump lips—inflated?—balance out the nose.

"Hi, I'm Erin," she says, walking toward me. She has a soft vulnerable voice, a stark contrast to her hard brown eyes. "I'm the manager of Nail Palace there across the street." We both look beyond the shop window, where she's pointing with her long manicured index finger. In the distance, above the blur of rushing traffic, I see a pink crown with some pink words on a storefront that I never noticed before. "We have some awesome nail art girls. Next time you need to get your nails done, you should come by."

"Oh okay, thanks for the invitation. I haven't been to a nail salon in forever though. A friend of mine got a terrible nail fungus, so I just decided—"

"Tell me about it." Erin plumps her bag down on the counter and sticks out her right sandaled foot, wiggling her long toes. "See that? There was a fungus among us. I lost my entire toenail!" Couched in her fleshy end of her big toe, sits a sliver of a toenail, shaped like a half moon, looking almost like an eye gouged out.

"Ouch."

"It's like having a deformity, losing your a toenail. So as you can imagine I'm super scrupulous about keeping things clean."

"I can imagine," I say, and then the words just come to me. *Hemorrhaging money.* "So how's business?" I ask her.

She blinks, a little taken aback. "Um. Okay, I guess. The colder months are tough because people tend to wear closed toe shoes. That's a fifty percent loss in revenue right there." She laughs. "Anyway, that's why I'm visiting all my neighbors." She reaches into her bag and pulls out a flyer with the words '10% discount' floating in a big pink bubble and hands it to me with a shy, embarrassed smile. "We're offering a discount to all first time customers, so come by anytime."

"Okay, I'll try," I say, not really meaning it because I don't see the point of paying someone to do something that I'm perfectly capable of handling. But as I grasp the paper, a strange distant sound comes to me.

Chugga-chugga-chugga.

It's a train, barreling down the tracks. Then I hear the sharp shrill blow of a whistle, and the ghost of a voice, too. With keen ears, I focus on the small wisp of a sound. What's it saying?

Nine one one. What's your emergency?

I step back, unnerved, setting the flyer down. After my sail with James, I've heard a lot of radio static: indecision at the kibble aisle, an attraction at the office gone wrong, and of course surgery of the stomach.

But this—this is something way beyond the usual. This is something tinged with shades of my friend Melissa, the one that I couldn't save.

"Sorry, I have to get going," I say, busying myself. "I need to get home and take my dog out for a walk."

"Oh I love dogs. What kind do you have?"

I perk up a little as I always do when the conversation turns to Jacky Baby. No need to be rude on account of my own hang-up. "He's a rescue that I named Jack-O-Lantern because he has a big orange head, but I call him Jack for short. He's some sort of Staffy-cross, Terrier, I think, but he's super cute."

"Staffies are way cute," she says. "I can recommend a great dog walker if you want. Her name is Sarah. She's a regular client of mine, and she's *super* affordable."

"Wow, thank you. I tried to line up a dog walker a while ago, but they're crazy expensive. So I just dash home as often as possible and hope for the best."

"Not Sarah. She'll take care of you." Erin smiles, and I smile too. Maybe she isn't spooky after all, but I can't shake an ominous feeling. "Here you go." Erin writes down the phone number of the dog walker. When she catches my gaze and smiles, I feel a chill race over my skin.

As Erin turns to leave, I open myself up a little more, waiting for more information to come through about the strange feeling I get from her, when the room suddenly tilts.

A cold wind blows. My heart races with fear. There's a blaring horn, bright, blinding light, and the train, thundering though my mind. Tightness like an invisible hand clasps around my neck, making me feel slightly panicky, and the faint shrieking voice is back, calling for nine one one. My mind races, trying to put the pieces together and figure out what it means.

By the time the shop door swings shut, the answer hits me like a brick through a cut glass window.

Erin is in trouble.

Big trouble.

"Closing early today, folks," I say to myself, locking the shop front door after Erin leaves. I think I'm losing it.

I lean on the checkout counter, loaded up with plenty of aromatherapy pet items, and pull in a deep breath, waiting for the lavender scent of RelaxDawg to travel up my nostrils and calm my grey matter. But my mind won't stop whirring.

What did I just see?

I saw that Erin's in trouble. But what kind, exactly?

I know that Nail Palace is struggling. But what does that have to do with a train, barreling down the tracks and the cold, biting wind? Is she on collision course with a terrible accident? My hand floats up to my neck as I recall the sensation of suffocation that I felt. Maybe someone is after her, someone dangerous . . .

I was tentatively optimistic about having my house slippers back. Safe. Sound. But I have a long ways to go before I'm confident again with warp speed. I need to learn how to walk first, before I run. Trouble is, I feel like I'm still shuffling.

I finish closing duties, put the day's earnings in a zippered pouch for a quick drop at the bank and double underline the final amount. Accounting all done, I close up the shop, thinking all the while about Erin's problem.

Specifically, what am I supposed to do about it? There are only two options. I can either a) forget about it, or b) try to help.

B seems like the dangerous thing to do. It also seems like the right thing to do. I think back to my conversation with Mom. *Maybe it came back for a reason.*

Maybe it has. Maybe I'm supposed to help Erin. So as I drive over to the bank, drop the money and make my way home, I think about that warp drive nozzle and turning up the dial. I think about what the doctors tell you to do when you're flat on your back and you need to get better: ambulate. Get moving. Baby steps though. No marathons. Just a little movement, something slightly more challenging than the ol' house shuffle. I should be able to handle that.

I can look into this thing called trouble. Just a peek. And I have a good idea how.

CHAPTER 13

BRYNN

I need a drink. That's not very zen of me. Paramahansa Yogananda, for example, wouldn't approve, but this problem has ballooned far beyond the power of meditation. And you know what? There's nothing wrong with a little wind-me-down glass of wine in the evening, particularly after a trying day.

Everyday, it seems, is very trying now. Well, at least I'm not popping pills. That's something to be proud of.

Wine, I reason, is a part of every civilized society. It's the water of the gods, I tell myself, going to the refrigerator and pulling out a bottle of Pinot Grigio. I like this stuff. It tastes like zesty water.

Okay, I like it too much, but if I give it up, I'll rob myself of liquid relaxation, and that's something I need in great quantities right now.

I keep my phone charged and on high volume at all times, should Dan find the opportunity to call, which he hasn't yet. I can't miss his call. I need to get this festering wound of doubt to go away. I need to find some closure. I need to know for sure that he didn't beat up Erin.

The image of Erin's damaged face is seared in the center of my mind. Everywhere I look, I see shadowy overlays of her bloodied lip. Her scratched temple. Her black eye . . .

The phone rings. I dive for it. Dan. Finally.

"Hello?" There's a long distance buzzing sound, as if the phone line is plugged into an electrical socket. I can hear echoes of Dan's voice.

"Brynn . . . can you hear me?"

"Yes. I can." I say, loud and clear. And I wait for the connection to clear up. After a long fuzzy pause, I ask, "Can you hear me now?"

I take another sip, waiting for him to reply. "Connection is shit," comes his distant voice.

"Yeah. I know." The pops and whistles fade away. "Dan? Are you there?"

"Yeah," he says, clearer now. "Yeah I am."

I sigh and sink down on the couch. "I'm so glad to hear your voice. How are you doing?"

He says he's doing good. It's going to be tough to talk to him while he's away, if his training trips are anything to go by. He's most likely in close proximity of thirty other smelly dudes, listening in on his conversation, hoping to overhear little nuggets of tenderness so they can humiliate him when he hangs up.

And if he's alone, there's always the threat of a sudden dropped call, so we can't settle into a deep conversation. We have to keep it light and sweet, waiting for the executioner to cut off the call, meanwhile savoring the essence of each other like fine Riesling. Except, I'm not feeling very light or sweet. I'm feeling angry, scared, and slightly buzzed.

"Dan, I need to talk to you about something."

"Okay, go." He's in military mode. He wants the bare bones facts, not dramatic embellishments.

I pull in a deep breath, overcome with emotion. I'm about to imply he's guilty of beating up another woman, just by asking him about it. How can I do that to him? Don't I trust him?

Trust or not, he needs to know what sort of nuclear bomb his ex is holding.

"Go," he repeats.

"Babe, Erin came to my yoga class the other day."

"Did you tell her to beat it?"

"No, I didn't actually. I went to a cafe with her."

"She your best friend now?" he asks after a beat.

Well that's a little insulting. Here I am trying to soften the blow, and he wants to make stupid comments. "No, she's not my best friend now."

"So what else is new?" he asks, clearly disinterested in the topic. If he beat her up, wouldn't he poke and prod a little bit, trying to determine if she ratted him out?

I don't know how to broach the subject of my boyfriend potentially pulverizing his ex-girlfriend's face.

So I find myself trying to reason through this again. In my effort to thoroughly leave no stone unturned, I consider another possibility: maybe Erin beat herself up. But the human body is biologically programmed to preserve itself, even if the owner has other ideas. And—is that even possible?

I recall a news report that I'd seen a while ago. It was grainy CCTV video footage of a psycho chick, who punched herself in an elevator and later blamed her boyfriend. I guess it is possible.

If Erin did this to herself, she's living on a whole new level of crazy, way beyond us mere mortals. And Dan needs to know about that, too.

"Dan," I begin. "I don't know how to say this, so I'm just going to say it the best way I can."

"OK."

"Remember that night we all went out? The night of your farewell party?"

"Yeah."

I pull in a quick breath. "Well, basically, Erin says you beat her up."

"What the . . ." And his voice fades into loud static.

"Dan? You there?"

Finally his voice breaks through. "I can't believe this. I can't—not on the hard line. This call might be monitored, Brynn."

"I know," I say in a calm, conciliatory voice. "I'm so sorry to bring it up here. I just don't know what to do. I can't get through to you on your cell phone and I just feel like you need to know what's going on. She says—"

"That's bullshit. She's lying. She's a bald-faced fucking liar! She—"

"She has a picture . . . and a recording."

"What?"

"Yeah. She showed them to me. The picture, I mean. I couldn't bring myself to listen to the audio accompaniment."

"She showed you a—a picture and says she has a recording?" His voice reaches high pitchy tones of total incredulity.

"Yes. But I mean, Dan, think about it. They could both be fakes." Or not. I slowly twist my wine glass left and right by the stem, trying to puzzle this out. "I don't know how you fake an audio recording exactly, but the photo would be relatively easy to pull off . . ."

"Of *course* they're fucking fakes!" he shouts. "For God's sakes, Brynn, do you think I'd do something like that?"

There's no way I could have fallen in love with a violent man. He's certainly never shown that side of himself to me. Is that because I haven't known him long enough. Gran's words of wisdom infiltrate my racing mind. *Make sure you know 'em for four seasons, eight if you can wait. Time reveals someone's true character better'n anything.* Except I don't have the clarifying benefit of time.

I've only known Dan for six months, that's only two seasons by Gran's accounting. And he *has* shown a violent streak by beating up that guy. Does that count? See, that's the problem. I drain my glass and set it down on the coffee table. I don't know, exactly. "Well, I—"

"Oh, great! You think I'm capable of beating up a *chick.* Just great. You know what? I should have left that night. I should have just bailed when she showed up and you two started singing that stupid party pooper song and drinking and laughing, but I just thought oh, what the hell. It's only one night. What could possibly happen?"

"It was such a crazy night. And we were all so hammered."

"And—and this. This fucking happened!"

I feel ashamed for asking and even worse for talking about it on a potentially open phone line, but I don't have a choice. None of my messages sent to his cell phone were acknowledged. I have no other way of talking to him. And the fact that Dan is continuing to talk about it tells me that maybe the phone line isn't so open after all.

"I believe you, Dan. I want you to know that. I would never take her side over yours. It's not like that. I just—it's just that I feel like I need to go over the details from that night and come up with something concrete, you know, in case she decides to take this to the police or something."

Cold, hard silence. If she goes to the police, there will be an official inquiry, and they'll go straight to Dan's commanding officer. I'm not sure about the exact protocol, but he could be pulled out of active duty with an investigation of assault and battery hanging over his head.

If she presses charges, moves forward with a criminal case, and wins, he'll be looking at a dishonorable discharge, a black mark that would carry over to the civilian world, rendering him unemployable. His life would be ruined. I don't even want to think about jail. The only problem is that I can't be his alibi because I lost that personage at the bottom of a bottle.

"Dan . . . I need to know happened that night."

"We talked, like I said. That's it. That's all I can remember."

"Can you try and remember something else? Because you said nothing happened, and then Erin showed up with a photo of her smashed face, saying you did it."

After a long pause, he finally speaks. "Brynn, I'm out here trying to concentrate so I don't get my ass filled with shrapnel, and you want me to remember some drunken night? I'm sorry for Erin. I really am. But I didn't do it."

"But how do you know? I mean, if you can't remember . . ."

Silence.

"Yeah, you know what? You're going to have to decide for yourself if you think I'm capable of doing something like that. Because I—"

"No, I—"

"Brynn, I'm putting my life on the line every single day. I need to focus, okay? I can't be bothered with Erin's flights of fancy. I did not do it. As for the rest, we'll have to discuss it when I get home seven months from now."

I sit up straight. "Seven months from now? But I thought it was only a six month deployment."

He hisses out a long breath. I listen to the static on the line, my heart aching.

"Maybe, I don't know. *If* I make it home. You never know," he says, sounding tired and worn out.

"Dan . . ."

And the call drops.

CHAPTER 14

GIA

I'm ambulating myself right on over to Nail Palace; I'm going straight to the source. Another encounter with Erin, this time prepared and charged up, will lend some insight into this trouble that I see brewing.

I pull up, park outside of the strip mall storefront, and go in, triggering a little chime announcing my arrival. Nail Palace is very girly, the type of 'girly' that makes my skin crawl. There's a pink Louis Vuitton wallpaper accent wall, two black matte chandeliers hanging from the mirrored ceiling, and a smattering of pink sequined throw pillows on each and every plush cream chair. Who in their right ming would blow so much money

sign at the top

decorating a nail establishment? Maybe that's why the business is taking on water.

"Hey," Erin says, walking toward me from the back of the salon, *squiling* at me. Mom likes to do that in photos—the squinty smile. She thinks it makes her look mysterious. I think it makes her look ridiculous. "I'm so glad you stopped by."

"I'm glad you're here." One of Sia's club songs plays in the background. It's good. Upbeat. Makes me want to tap my foot and get my nails done. Speaking of, "My nails need help."

"Well, you've come to the right place. What are you thinking?"

"How about a mani-pedi?" I'll have to splurge for a double nail procedure because I'm not sure how long it will take my superpower to boot up, if at all.

She shrugs. "Sure. Gel or polish?"

"Just some polish."

"What about the deluxe package? It's a little more expensive, but so worth it. I'll throw in a free foot massage."

"Sure," I say, focusing on the still small voice in my head that's going to tell me straight up what's the problem, but nothing comes to me.

"Go ahead and sit down." She motions to a white plush recliner with a sink at the bottom. "I'll warm up the water and get everything ready."

While she runs the water, I take off my shoes, sit down, and slip my feet into the warm sudsy water. Hey this isn't so bad. I can get used to a little pampering while on detective duties.

Erin grabs a plastic storage caddy full of implements from the next station over, wearing a smile that doesn't carry up to her eyes.

"Are you the only one working today?" I ask, glancing around at the empty nail salon. Where are the awesome nail art girls?

She takes a seat on a wooden stool, fetches my right foot from the warm soapy water and presses her thumbs into the arch of my foot. "Today was a slow day so I sent them home early and stepped in."

Does the owner step in too? Maybe Erin's worried about losing her job if the business goes under. Maybe that's the 'trouble.'

"So what got you into doing nails?" I ask.

"Oh, I've been doing them for years. My mom always said that your nails say the first thing about you, so you should get a manicure every two weeks. Three if you're lazy."

I must be catatonic.

"But that can really add up, you know? So I started experimenting on my own. Buying little nail art stickers and crystals and stuff. It was really therapeutic for me." She finishes up the foot massage, cleans up my cuticles, and puts my right foot back in the sink. "Besides, a penny saved is a penny earned."

Financial trouble for sure. Then she starts on my other foot, shooting me a bashful look. "That's what Daddy always said."

A jolt of alarm races down my arms. Daddy? Seems to me that any adult woman who still uses the word 'Daddy' needs help, and fast. But if they're so close, why isn't he helping her?

"Your dad sounds very wise about financial matters." There. That ought to get us going in the right direction.

"He was," Erin says, looking at me wistfully and blinking a few times.

My stomach drops. "Was?"

Oh dear.

"He passed away . . ."

"I'm so sorry," I mumble, feeling awful that I brought up the topic. But she doesn't reply. She's working intently now, probably trying not to cry. She seems so determined to help make this business a success. Whatever misgivings I had about opening up full throttle on my psychic ability is fading. Erin needs help, and I want to help her.

"It happened a long time ago," she says, picking up my hand. "What color are you thinking?" She's done with the prep work on my feet, which are both back in the tub, soaking.

Well, if she doesn't want to dwell on the topic, then neither do I. "Whatever you recommend, Erin. You're the expert."

"Red it is then. That's my favorite color."

While Erin cleans and tidies all my fingernails, filing them into a nice shape and laying down the base coat, I stay focused within. Fumes of acetone stab my nostrils. I welcome the sharp jolt. Maybe that will prod my psychic ability into action.

Erin starts applying the deep red polish on my fingernails. She works at a quick pace. I gently open myself up further, waiting for Superpower 2.0 to fire up, but it's silent on all counts. She finishes up both hands. Time is running out.

She moves down to the sink, pulls out my left foot from the water and starts drying my toes. In about ten minutes, my window of opportunity is going to close. Then what will I do?

Dr. Keating's voice comes to me. *Just relax.* So I settle into the plush chair, close my eyes, and pull in a deep breath, trying to relax. I'm breathing in and out, trying to clear my mind—

Chugga-Chugga-Chugga.

My power. It's back. I hold my breath, listening to the faint sounds of a rushing train overtaken with the deep driving bass of club music. It's a dark place, the place that I'm seeing. It's a club. Hands in the air. Flashing lights. Dry ice fog wafting over the crush of club-goers.

Then I get a sense of someone. My throat begins to tighten as I see a man, named . . . *Stop Dan, Stop*!

My heart thumps. I tighten my grip on the armrests, bracing myself and opening up a little more, trying to get a feel for him. I sense that he's tall, nice build, athletic and strong, with dark hair and eyes like iron. Then my sense of him tapers off. I wait a little while longer for more information about this new person to come to me, but nothing else comes except for a lasting impression of anger. Fury, even. Is he an angry person? A dangerous person?

"Hey, Erin?"

She looks up at me, eyebrows raised. "Yeah?"

I shift in my seat. This is called a defining moment. One that I'm not entirely really ready to face, but the chaos in my mind tells me that I don't have a choice.

"This is going to sound strange . . . but I'm a psychic, or at least I was before I wasn't—it's complicated." Do I need to tell her my whole life story? "But everything came back to me recently. The skill, I mean. I'm kind of getting back into it, and I feel like you're in trouble somehow. I got that feeling when you dropped off your flyer at my shop. And—and please don't worry. I want to help you. But I want to warn you, too. I'm not exactly sure what kind of trouble we're dealing with here, but do you know someone named Dan?" *Dan the Man.* "Um. Also called Dan the Man?"

Her head goes back a couple inches; her mouth turns down. "He's my ex-boyfriend," she says, at last. Then she looks down and continues painting my toes with nonchalance that seems strange. "I've always thought psychics were fakes," she says, finishing off my pinkie toe, appraising her handiwork. "But I have to admit that's pretty crazy that you mentioned Dan. Do you see something?" she asks, looking up at me. "Something about Dan?"

Screams now. I hear the pumping of the pistons. Faster, gaining momentum. The sound of a train drives into my ears, along with ghostly voices. I'm trying to focus and pick up on something concrete, but she's staring at me, anticipation glittering in her eyes, putting me on the spot. "You see something," she says, leaning closer. "What is it?"

Erin's eyes are glassy. Fixated.

Chugga-chugga-chugga.

The tragic squeal of the wheels sliding on the tracks fills my ears, along with urgent voices. I hear the wheels screeching again, and the deafening blow of the locomotive horn.

Erin looks at me, eyes fathomless. There are no tears in her eyes, only expectation. Is she being brave?

My fingers dig into the plush armrests. My windpipe aches. I'm trying to pull all the pieces together as they swirl around my mind in a vortex. 9-1-1. Frantic voices. I feel my throat closing down. And screams, I hear screams . . . .

I push the hideous sounds away. I'm not ready yet. Not yet! I'm closing myself down pronto—tamp it down!—but as the aperture stops down, the screeching metal and screams slip though the opening, filling me with fear.

"Something is going to happen," I say.

"What?" Erin asks. "What's going to happen?"

And then I'm cold, shivering, somehow feeling the sharp bite of howling wind. Then the train barrels down on me, bright light from the terrible monocle of its headlight, highlighting a cold, hard realization:

"Someone is going to die."

CHAPTER 15

BRYNN

After my call with Dan, I couldn't sleep. No surprise there. So I sat up all night, trying to piece this together. Through the long dark hours, I stared into the shadows, trying to figure out what happened that terrible night. Who is lying? And who is telling the truth?

But it's over now—that night—and I can't remember much, except a bunch of disjointed memories and cringey comments that I'd rather forget anyhow. By the time the sun breaks through my useless flimsy curtains, I find myself wondering exactly how much I know about Dan in the first place.

Turns out, not much at all. I know that I'm in love with him, and everybody says he's a "good guy." I know the basic facts about him, where he was born, where he went to college. He's an only child, but he's not socially impaired. I think Dan and I could probably win a few rounds in The Newlyweds Game, if it was still on the air. His mom is lovely, but distant. The topic of his dad also falls into 'Dan's black box.' All I know is that he left when Dan was young.

I drag myself out of bed, find my way over to the coffee machine, and make a pot, breathing in the invigorating aroma. Then I pour myself a cup, splash in some almond milk, and take a few sips, my mind beginning to awaken as caffeine moves through my circulatory system. Eventually, I'm able to form a coherent thought.

And then something occurs to me: I'm living in Dan's dang house, alongside all of his personal belongings. Why don't I just dig around and see what I can find?

Seems silly. What could I possibly uncover? An old high school yearbook? Perhaps. Some snaps of his exes? Maybe. Maybe I'll find nothing. Maybe I'll find the mother lode. But I have to do something to get to the bottom of this mystery.

Coffee down the hatch, I start in the master bedroom closet. I'm going to upend this house in my mission to get some answers. Dan keeps his stuff on the left side. My stuff lives on the right, and spillover goes in the spare bedroom.

I begin by searching every pocket of every item of his clothing. Truthfully, I hate doing it. I hate that this whole situation has driven me to snoop. No, I don't like knowing very little about his past. But I was okay with it. Now every time a pocket yields nothing, I feel both relieved and disappointed.

I cinch up my bathrobe, pound some more coffee, and keep going. I'm moving onto the top rung in the closet now where he keeps shoes and boxes and an old X-box game console.

In a sound and scientific manner, I yank everything off the shelf and start going through the pile, item by item. Bear wanders over and sits down next to the mess, swiping away the first layer with his blonde bushy tail. I shoo him away, so he jumps on the bed instead, watching me.

I keep looking at Bear, imagining that Dan can tap into his eyesight somehow. "Don't tell Dan, okay?" Bear tucks away his tongue and pricks his ears.

There's a cardboard box filled with knick-knacks, keys, an old spoon, pins, a broken watch, and fridge magnets from far-flung places that I never knew Dan had visited. I find a bottle opener with two big boobs for handles, the name of a "gentleman's club" emblazoned across the nipples. Is Dan into that? Visiting strip clubs? Thinking of women as objects? This is so far removed from the guy I know.

Then I find an old boarding pass to Oahu, dated over a year ago. I never knew he went to Hawaii. *Well, does he have to tell you every single little factoid about his life?* A snarky voice sounds off in my head. *No, just the important one, like whether or not he beats up women*, I reply.

The box goes back onto the top shelf, roughly where I found it, along with the rest of Dan's items. Then I move on. The closet is clear. No bombs in there. So I go to his home office, the second bedroom, where he keeps his paperwork. A large desk with two computer monitors sits under the small window. His file cabinet lives to the left of the desk, where incriminating evidence might be found. I zero in and find it locked, which only solidifies my resolve. Where's the key? I need to find it.

So I'm back in the closet, pulling down his box of knick-knacks and bringing it into the office. Each key gets my highest level of attention. Each goes in the hole, both sides facing up. Nothing. The final key (of course) attached to a red carabiner slides in smoothly in and unlocks the cabinet.

Slowly, I pull open the drawer. The top shelf has some reservoirs for pens and calculators. There's a compass tool similar to the one I used in high school to torment my brother. And there are some unopened letters from banks and investment firms.

I pull open the lower drawer and scan the tabbed subjects: Investments, Property, Crypto, Etc.

The first document in the hanging folder marked 'investments' is a financial statement, showing a balance of over two hundred grand. I did not see that coming. I always thought Dan was doing just fine on his military salary, not rich, but not poor.

I knew he played the stock market. In fact, those are the 'girlfriends' that he would talk about: Winchester, Moderna, and Soda. But this? I'm amazed. No, I'm not. I'm blown away.

And I keep going. There are more statements, stuff he's bought and sold. Funds. Blue chip and whatnot. He owns a second property in Arizona. A rental. And he plans on buying more. There are fact sheets, due diligence, and title reports. Geez, he's a busy guy.

I get to the et cetera file, my fingers flying through the documents. I'm thinking this is going to be unsorted mail, but there's a flimsy pink document wedged in the far back. It's one of those 'customer' copies, so I pull it out and unfold it.

It's a police incident report. My hands are shaking. I've never seen one of these before so I start at the very top.

San Diego Police Department. Date and time recorded. I do a little math and determine that this event occurred two months before we met. Incident Type/Offense: Disorderly Conduct.

Person(s) involved: Dan and Erin, followed by their particulars.

My heart twists.

There's the location that the incident occurred (an address in Ocean Beach that I don't recognize), the name of the reporting officer, followed by the narrative:

At approximately 23:19 hrs., I, Officer Cole, and Officer Lippman, arrived at the property and climbed the stairs to the front door, when a voice from across the street called to us. A woman approached with a wireless phone in her hand and told us that she called the police. The Caucasian female, later identified as Tammy Moore, said she lived two doors down and grew alarmed at the screams coming from within the house so she called dispatch.

I knocked on the front door. Nobody responded. Hearing loud yelling, I took it upon myself to open the door. Standing at the threshold I called into the premises. A white female, later identified as Erin Lazarus, entered the hallway, crying and shaking. I observed red marks on both arms. Her boyfriend, Daniel Evans, was very agitated. We then placed him in the back of a squad car.

Yes, and? I feel like I'm in a movie theater, on the edge of my seat, and the film cuts to black. I flip the paper over, looking for the rest of the story. I want to yell: *Then what happened*! But there's nothing else. A big fat zero.

Puzzled, I search the file cabinet looking for the rest of the story. But it's not in there. I then spend the next two hours painstakingly searching the house for the final conclusion, but it's nowhere to be found. Dan must have disappeared the conclusion of his incident report. Why? Is that because he's guilty of manhandling Erin?

It's late morning by now. I sit down on the couch, leg jiggling, thinking this over. The police were called in to help with 'disorderly conduct' otherwise known as domestic abuse. The parties involved were Dan and Erin.

There were red marks on Erin's arms. The cops, independent and impartial parties to the scene, saw it fit to place *Dan* in the back of a squad car.

Because if he did this to me, he'll do it to you . . .

And suddenly I feel very ill.

CHAPTER 16

GIA

In my hands, I hold a picture of my best friend Melissa taken on a hot summer day, two weeks before she took her own life. It's the only picture that I have of her; the only one that I could bring myself to keep. The photo is faded and peeling, but I remember that time of my life in Technicolor.

In the photo, she looks out into the distance, her caramel brown hair pulled around her shoulder. There's a hint of a smile on her face, her expression wistful.

She was the mysterious senior year 'new girl' recently transferred in from out of state, quiet, aloof, and not interested in typical high schooler concerns: who's dating who, crashing secret parties, or college prep. Normally, I kept my ability closed down so that I could get through the day, only opening up in certain circumstances, but Melissa had intrigued me.

We ended up in third period debate class together, and were put in the same small group for the day's activity, our chairs arranged in a small circle stating 'funny facts' about ourselves.

My funny fact was our family dog named Poopy Saint Clair. Melissa's was some goldfish story that I sensed she made up on the spot, so I opened myself up to her true story and saw that, a year previous, she'd endured a brutal gang rape. While she told the group about 'Goldie's adventures,' all the horrifying details of her ordeal emanated from her like a newsreel. With shaking hands, I gripped the plastic seat of my chair and listened.

An acquaintance of her older brother's had instigated the attack. Her brother blamed himself because he'd made the introduction in the first place, so he'd wrangled up as many witnesses as he could find and had strong-armed them into testifying, landing the perpetrator and his biker buddies ten years in jail.

And while justice had been served and the jury found the accused guilty, Melissa never got her happy ending. She'd unraveled shortly after the brutal witness hearing and made her first unsuccessful attempt at taking her life, before moving in with her aunt in California for a fresh start. And by the time she'd finished her funny fact story, I thought I was going to be sick.

When we first exchanged phone numbers, I heard a soft lilting singsong that I should have heeded all along:

Keep me in sight, or else I'll slip away

Hold me tight, and keep the wolves at bay . . .

But I didn't understand the meaning. I didn't catch the warning.

After the school year ended and we graduated, our futures lay before us like No Man's Land. Neither one of us had landed a spot at university, so we were community college bound, except that Melissa wanted to take a year off and get her life back together.

It was an unusually hot summer afternoon, the air as thick as soup. Melissa and I journeyed down to Huntington State Beach, the windows down, crisp ocean breezes softening the hard edges of heat. Once there, we parked and hunted between barbecue pits and lifeguard towers for the perfect spot, while music drifted down the boardwalk, the classic tunes of Cat Stevens, singing about wild worlds and moon shadow.

We laid out for a while and worked on our tans. I watched the water's edge, where kids played and shrieked, where rushing waves erased sandcastles and doodles in the wet sand.

Melissa never had very much to say. And that summer she seemed especially quiet. Her talk therapy was stalling. She wanted to quit and try to make it on her own. She had hopes of ditching her "zombie pills," while I'd tried to keep her focused on her future, her hopes, and her dreams.

We got up and went for a swim, walking down to the lazy break zone. I dove under rolling waves, the brisk temperature jolting me out of my groggy sunbaked haze, while Melissa stood at the edge of the water.

I spent a few extra seconds underwater, listening to the chirps and popping sounds of the ocean. Listening to the haunting sing-song—*keep me in sight, or else I'll slip away*—puzzling over the meaning and why had the song come back after so long a silence?

We swam and tanned and swam again until the sun sank low in the sky and chilly ocean breezes washed over us. Then we drove back to my house, pleasantly exhausted.

In my bedroom, soft pink light shone from my bedside lamp, enveloping my room like a warm amniotic cocoon. On my walls hung black and white photos framed with strings of glowing fairy lights. As we sat on my bed, I read Melissa's future with my tarot cards, and she read mine, even though she was never any good at it. We laughed and teased each other and climbed under my downy soft comforter and talked until we drifted off to sleep.

That night I dreamed of crashing waves and undertows, tugging on my legs and sweeping me away. I dreamed of hot rushing fear, of numbness and of pain, all the while listening to the haunting song.

Keep me in sight, or else I'll slip away . . .

When I woke the following morning, Melissa was gone. Mom and I called friends, family, acquaintances, and finally the police. The cops found Melissa's car, abandoned at the edge of a trailhead that led to a particularly treacherous part of the coast. It was a surf break called Smashers because of the way the shape of the land directed two currents against each other. It was a place where deadly rip currents were the norm; the place where Melissa took her life.

A woman found her limp body washed up in a tangle of seaweed several yards from the blonde strip of sand. The funeral took place on a dreary Sunday. Even the weather, it seemed, went into mourning. I stood at the edge of her open casket, breaking apart. She looked like a life-sized doll, bearing a surreal likeness of the real, live girl who was no more. Her lips were drawn on too thin with mortician's makeup, her hair brittle looking, her sunken eyes closed forever.

It was my fault that she slipped through my fingers. I should have known. I should have heeded the warning. I should have never let her go.

I put the photo back in a small keepsake box and close the metal lid. The still small voice is back now, and I don't like what it's saying. It's talking about death. An accident, possibly something more sinister.

But it's also talking about another chance to save someone's life, a chance to listen and heed the warning.

A chance that I am going to take.

CHAPTER 17

BRYNN

I'm not coping very well. This whole question of Dan's alleged assault on Erin is consuming me like flesh-eating bacteria. Morning, noon, and night, I can feel my body tingling with dread and uncertainty. Not made any better with the fact that I don't have anybody to talk to. I don't dare whisper a word to my family. My dad and I only talk about politics and gardening projects, definitely not personal problems.

My mom would worry herself into a dither and make everything worse. She's going to take the safe side, and nag me incessantly until I move back home.

I can't talk to Dan because he's at the mercy of his superiors to give him a window to call. Who knows when that will happen again? Contacting him on his cell phone is hopeless. And I can't talk to any friends, his or mine, because I don't want them to know about the allegation.

So I'm left struggling to carry the load of uncertainty all alone. The only person I can turn to is Dan's mom, Donna. Hopefully, she'll know something about the police incident. And she'll definitely tell me that Dan would never *ever* hit a girl. That alone will take four hundred pounds off my shoulders.

So the following Saturday, after I made my police report discovery, I drive up to meet with Donna. I called her under the guise of catching up while Dan is away because I didn't want to mention Erin's battered face over the phone.

She lives on the edge of Palos Verdes and Redondo Beach in a contemporary home overlooking the ocean with a vast glass panels and a slanted metal roofline. She sold her veterinarian practice and moved into the slower pace of retirement, but she keeps busy with morning jogs on the beach and writing a novel. She'd been "bitten by the bug," but she says it's really more like an untreatable infection.

I pull into her driveway, my nerves as frayed as old rope. I haven't been able to sleep very much since all this happened. Gastro stopped by for an unwelcome visit; my appetite cratered. I have a permanent knot in my stomach, and my stress levels are blowing up. I'm turning into an insomniac, which rhymes with maniac I realized last night at two in the morning while I was washing the kitchen windows.

Once I pull into Donna's double-wide driveway, I get out of my car and make my way up to her glass and wrought iron front door. My usual case of nerves takes hold. It's silly to be intimidated with wealth, but I can't help it. I grew up in a humble weather-beaten cabin stuffed into the dense forest of Connecticut furnished with lots of hand-me-downs.

I ring the doorbell and step back, checking my dress for last minute stains. Never know these days. Then I pull in a breath and try to shake off my feelings of inferiority.

My past does not define me, I think to myself.

But what about Dan's?

A blurry shadow falls on the opaque glass panels. The door opens.

"Hi Brynn," Donna says with her usual peppiness. "Thanks for driving up! Come on in."

She's an attractive woman in her late fifties with dark, curly shoulder length hair and eyes that remind me of a late summer storm.

She shows me inside, and I still can't get over my awe of her home. With the sleek granite countertops, smooth white stone flooring, and bright pops of color, I always feel like I'm wandering into a magazine spread when I visit.

A frosty glass of rosé arrives in my hand, and we settle on her outside veranda that overlooks the ocean. A cloud bank parts, flooding miles of sea with dappled light.

"Beautiful, isn't it?" Donna asks, looking out at the ocean with a peaceful expression.

"Makes you forget all your troubles, even just for a little while." I pull one corner of my mouth into something that I hope will pass as a smile.

We chat for a little while. I tell her I'm doing good—great! But I can tell from her crooked smile that she doesn't believe me. Her brow furrows with concern, but she can't blurt out how terrible I look because she's not my mom. She's Dan's mom, so she has to show some restraint.

I know I look terrible. The dark smudges are back, permanently camped under my eyes. I'm tired, and I'm scared.

"So what's going on?" she asks, crossing her legs, and leaning forward. "This is your first deployment with Dan. Are you holding up okay?"

"Not really," I say. This, she believes.

She rubs the top of my hand quickly. "You want to talk about it?"

I try to find the right angle of entry, a gentle slope that won't make her spill her glass of rosé. Then I sigh because I just need to say it. "We're kind of having a problem with one of Dan's exes."

"I know you asked before," Donna says, jumping on that old topic of conversation. I open my mouth to clarify, but she raises her hand. "I understand. I get it. You're just trying to do a little homework before you potentially spend the rest of your life with someone."

I'm not sure when I should steer the conversation over to domestic abuse, but Donna keeps talking.

"I remember you asked about Dan's past before. And I didn't tell you much because I feel like that's Dan's business to tell or not tell . . ."

She glances up at me, waiting for me to reply. I guess this is my window.

"Yes, you're right," I say. "I didn't want to pry and I still don't. It's just that one of them has kind of come back into the picture."

"Oh, really?" she asks, raising her eyebrows. She makes a face of surprise or distaste; I'm not sure which.

"Do you know someone named Erin?" I ask.

Her expression clouds over. Her brow deepens into a scowl, eyelids dropping into a glower. Donna knows her. "How did you two meet?"

"It was pretty random. Dan and I ran into her the night of his farewell party."

"Random?" Donna asks dryly.

And that makes me wonder. Was it an accident? The same sort of accident that brought her to my yoga class? She was alone at the bar. She said her friends had just left, and she was on her way home too, until we walked in . . .

"I guess 'random' is up for speculation. Dan wasn't very happy about it, that's for sure, but Erin seemed nice and you know how it goes. The drinks are flowing and everyone is out to have fun, not a big drama."

"Mmhm."

"Anyway, it was one of those nights where everyone kind of drinks too much and has too much fun and forgets what happened, exactly." I take in a big breath. "Except I remember. I mean, not very much. But Dan and Erin left to go somewhere together." I glance up at Donna, who looks completely horrified.

"And—and Dan said that nothing happened. And I believed him; at least I thought I did. Now, I really don't know . . ."

"Oh no. They didn't. Did they?"

I shake my head because what I'm about to say implies something even worse than cheating. It's unspeakable. Literally. My throat tightens up, making it hard to talk.

I blink, trying to clear an overlay of Erin's bloodied nose from my vision, trying to work up the courage to say it, to speak it aloud.

"Erin tracked me down," I say, finally. "And showed me a picture of something she said happened that night. It turns out that she—that someone beat her up."

Donna uncrosses her legs and moves to the edge of her seat. "What? That's awful. Just awful. What have things come to these days?"

My eyes sting with unspent tears. I'm scared that Erin will take the picture to the police and press charges. I'm scared that Dan might do something like that to me.

"She says Dan did it," I say as calmly as I can.

"Dan!" Donna leaps out of her chair and paces the patio, a breeze ruffling her kaftan. She stops and turns to me. "My Dan?"

I nod. "Your Dan,"—and in a low tone, I add, "My Dan, too."

"No way. She's lying. There's no way. There's—"

"There's a picture. And a recording . . . apparently."

The ocean crashes distantly on the beach. It reminds me of the many times Dan and I went to La Jolla Cove for breakfast and sat on a bench afterwards, looking out to sea, kissing, and talking.

It's such an incongruent memory. Dan the tender lover. Dan the abuser.

"Holy hell," mumbles Donna. Then she swallows a good portion of her rosé.

I want her to defend Dan's good honor, his gentle nature, his innocence. I want her to tell me that he doesn't have a mean bone in his body. But she's not saying that. She's not saying that at all.

Then she looks up at me, her lips drawn tight, her eyes wary. "Hate is such a strong word. And hating someone is like a constant surge of bile up your throat. I would know. I hated Erin. I hated every minute Dan stayed in that toxic relationship."

This I did not expect.

"Dan and I were always such good friends," she continues. "Sure we had our ups and downs. But we were always close. That is, until Erin came into the picture and tore us apart."

I feel a shift inside. Donna was always nice to me, but underneath she was unreachable. I felt like she treated me with professional courtesy instead of embracing me as Dan's girlfriend. I always thought it had to do with my humble upbringing, and she'd somehow deemed me to be unworthy. But now, I realize that it was because Erin had caused so much damage to her relationship with her son. So Donna is wary now. Once burned and all that. Well, I hope she has a fire suit.

"Donna, I found something in the house. A police incident report." My heart beats unsteadily. "Domestic abuse apparently. It states that Erin had red marks on her arms and Dan was placed in the back of a squad car . . ."

I pause, allowing her space to fill in the pertinent details. But her eyebrows draw up, and her eyes fly wide. "What?" she cries. "Dan was placed in a squad car?"

My heart sinks. I was so hoping Donna could tell me the end of the story. Something along the lines of: *Oh yeah. That. Well, that was a big mistake. Actually what happened . . .*

Instead she says, "Oh geez, Brynn. What a nightmare. I can't believe this is all coming out now that he's on deployment."

"Do you think Dan could do that?" I ask, cutting to the chase. "Beat up Erin?"

"No! I mean, I don't think so. Those things . . . violent tendencies . . . they don't just come out of the blue. And he has *never* hit another girl. But—but I have to be completely honest here." She focuses on the great expanse of the ocean with a faraway look, as if gazing into the past. "Their relationship was very volatile. I didn't recognize the person Dan had become when he was with her. He was quiet. Edgy. It was like he lost a part of himself . . . And if he did do something like that, call me a monster, but I'd be right there, sitting behind him in court." She looks over at me, one corner of her mouth drawing up into a sad smile. "All I'm saying is that it takes two to tango."

"Of course," I mumble.

"Brynn, I don't know what went on between them,"—she takes hold of my hand—"but I'm here for you. Whatever you need, just call."

"Thanks Donna," I say with a lop-sided smile.

And I left that day, wondering if I'll ever find a definitive piece to the puzzle.

CHAPTER 18

GIA

Erin is in trouble. This I know. And someone is going to die. This I also know. Well, it's something I deduced, technically, because I can't see the future, at least historically that was my limitation. This is more of a gut certainty, I would say, after what I saw at Nail Palace. It's also the official interpretation that I am going to stick with. Does this suggest that my ability growing and morphing? Giving me glimpses into the future?

I'm not sure. But I do know that die has been cast. The pieces have been set in motion. Erin is trouble. Dan seems pretty unhinged. I can't stop thinking about how my windpipe ached, the 9-1-1 call, the frantic voices, the screams, the train . . . I need to help her. But in order to do that, I need some specific information—Has she filed any restraining orders? Does she have a stalker?

First stop, Google. Except there's a bewildering number of people named Erin Lazarus. 'Lazarus' kind of seems like a fake last name, but on Facebook alone there are over thirty profiles. Are they all fake? Surely not. Plus, there's other social media accounts and other random offerings from what looks like bonafide people, none of whom look like my Erin though. I spend some time sifting through the profiles, the ones that aren't set to private anyway, until finally, I give up.

My best friend Nikki works at a private investigator's office that collaborates with attorneys handling white-collar crimes, the type of crimes that fall under the category of 'requiring a few brain cells to pull off.' These days, she helps with cases that have to do with doctoring flight logs, switching around private jet licenses, and creative money laundering schemes.

The following afternoon, after work, I take Jack outside for a walk around the neighborhood. While he zeros in on a bush, I call Nikki.

"Hey," she says when she picks up the call.

"Hey, Nikki. Do you have a sec?"

I hear some papers rustling in the background. "Kinda. Just finishing up this contract, but it's not super urgent, and my boss just left for the day."

"Oh, that's happy news."

Nikki snickers. "So what's up?"

"Can you look into someone for me?"

"Sure," Nikki says, her voice echoing in her water flask.

"Thanks, Nik. So, I'm trying to find out some information about someone named Erin Lazarus. I think that's her name anyway. That's what the Nail Palace website says. She's the manager. Do you think you could find out if she's filed any restraining orders or anything like that?"

"Hm. Okay let me log on to my handy dandy database here . . ." I can hear her keyboard clacking in the background. Nikki has any number of nefarious ways to dig up the dirt on people. An astonishing number to be precise. Why people even bother breaking the law in today's surveillance society is beyond me.

"So how's James?" I ask, while we wait for the results.

"I don't really know, to be honest. He's sailing in that regatta on the East Coast, apparently. I'm not sure when he'll be back . . . "

"Oh, I'm sorry to hear that. He seemed like such a nice guy."

"He's a great guy, but he's getting over a divorce as you know. And . . ." she sighs. "I don't know. He seemed really weird after we went sailing."

"Really?"

"Yeah, he just kind of shut down."

"Well, I may have an idea why."

"You do?"

"Something happened while you were busy turning green. I've been meaning to tell you. Actually, I just kind of thought he would tell you himself because it's not really my business to tell or not tell. I didn't want to spill his beans, you know?"

"Yeah but he hasn't spilled any beans at all. Like, not even one. He just backed away from me. Can you tell me what happened?"

I hesitate, remembering back to the few words we shared when he walked me out to my car that night. He didn't say anything like, *Don't tell Nikki*. So I'm not breaking any promises exactly, but it feels a little wrong to be sharing his personal tragedy. I can tell Nikki is hurting though, and she really cares about him. I also think she can help him heal, having survived her own personal tragedy: the loss of her younger brother to leukemia.

I pull in a big breath. "So when I went down below to flip the circuit breaker, I got electrocuted, which somehow jumpstarted my psychic ability and I saw that he lost . . . well, his ex-wife and him—they lost a baby."

"Oh my God," Nikki mutters. "That's heartbreaking. How did it happen? And—your psychic ability is back?"

"Yeah, it was so awful though. Terrible timing. I felt so bad for him. I saw that the baby was born still, but the doctor didn't know what had caused it."

Nikki falls silent.

"It's a lot to take in, I know, Nik. And that's probably why he's pulling back. He's probably trying to find his bearings. I think it was an old wound that I accidentally ripped open."

"Yeah, that makes a lot of sense," she says quietly. "Thanks for telling me."

"Sure. But let him tell you first, okay? I don't want to get caught blabbing about his secrets."

"Girl code. You can't keep secrets about the guy I'm dating!"

"That's true . . ."

"So your psychic ability came back? Wow. That must have a shocker, no pun intended."

"Har har. Actually, that's why I'm calling. It's like Grand Central Station in my head now, and I've got a bad feeling about something. Did you find anything about Erin?"

"Yep. Here it is. So Erin Lazarus is a blank sheet of paper. There's nothing close to what I normally find on people. No educational records. Work history shows only the nail salon. No credit history . . ."

"Um. That's weird," I say, head bent down in concentration, following Jack down the sidewalk.

Nikki leans back; I hear her chair squeak. "You know, secretaries get a bad rap for having boring jobs, but I think it's fun. You wouldn't believe how many fascinating facts I've managed to discover about people. Except this one."

"Mmhm," I say, kicking my neighbor's flowerbed edging with my toe, thinking about Erin and her lack of history. "Can you look into the person who owns that nail business? I think she's having financial problems. That might be a good place to start."

"Sure." More keyboard clicking, followed by a long pause. "Okay here's something. So it looks like someone named Denise Livingston is listed on the business license. And let me just run a quick background check on her. Denise Living-S-T-O-N. Search-o-ramma . . . doo dee doo . . . Okay, here it is. What the—holy *shit.* Whoa whoa whoa."

"What! What is it?"

"Denise's criminal record is what."

"What about it? What did you find?"

"Let me print this up and bring it over. You're gonna want to see this in person."

"Wow. Is it that bad?"

"Yep."

"Okay hurry up. I'll see you in a few."

CHAPTER 19

GIA

Nikki lets herself in the front door, calling out, "Yoo hoo! Anybody home?"

At the sound of her voice, I rush down the stairs to meet her; Jack hot on my heels. She's wearing a black pencil skirt, heels, and a pretty red blouse that flatters the color in her cheeks. Her sleek hair is tucked behind her nymph-like ears.

Jack runs to her, whimpering and wagging his whole body. "Heyyy Jacky Baby," she says, bending down to give him a quick cuddle. "You gorgeous little thing."

"Thanks for coming over so fast, Detective Nikki," I say, walking into the kitchen.

"You can thank me later," she says, plonking her handbag on the counter and pulling out a stack of papers.

We sit down at the kitchen bar, side by side, and pore over her discovery.

"So, check this out," she says, handing over the first document.

It's a court document cover page of some sort, a lawsuit, showing the parties involved:

DISTRICT COURT ARAPAHOE COUNTY
STATE OF COLORADO
PEOPLE OF THE STATE OF COLORADO
Plaintiff,
V.
DENISE M. LIVINGSTON
Defendant.

I can just make out the blurry case number and the name of the attorney on record. "Okay, so Denise has had some legal troubles. Bad business dealings, you think?" I ask, looking at Nikki.

"Not exactly." She slides over the next document, and I pull it in front of me. It's a document approving her removal from general prison population to the psych ward because of a suicide attempt.

"She tried to commit suicide? Oh dear . . ."

"Wait," Nikki says, thumbing through the papers. "It gets worse."

"Money-laundering type of worse?" I ask Nikki.

"Newp," Nikki says, passing over the next document, and it hits me like a stick in the spokes.

COUNT 1: MURDER IN THE FIRST DEGREE

My hands are shaking. This is big. This is terrible. "Denise *murdered* someone, Gia. But here's the strange part." She gives me the last document. "It's the verdict."

The jury instructions are going to say guilty, of course. But I read it anyway, curious how these legal matters play out, looking for the strange part. I see a filing date stamp on the upper right hand corner, followed by the signature of the Executive Officer. Then I read aloud the jury findings.

"We, the jury, find the defendant, Denise M. Livingston, *not guilty*, as charged in count one of the indictment." I look up at Nikki. "Not guilty? How is that even possible?"

"Well, there are some plausible explanations. It could have been a case of mistaken identity, where Denise was wrongfully charged and they dropped the case. Or maybe the prosecution couldn't get their body of evidence together and the charges didn't stick. I'm sure you've heard the phrase 'lack of evidence' before."

"I have . . ." I say, thinking this through. So Denise served time in prison, followed by a stint in a psych ward, after the suicide attempt. Did she have a nervous breakdown? I would have. She also owns the business where Erin works, the very same one that's suffering financial problems.

And to be found 'not guilty' of such a serious crime—is that what drove her to suicide? Or maybe she actually killed someone and walked free based on a technicality?

Despite the questions swirling around in my mind about the nature of Denise's jury verdict, I find myself afraid for Erin's safety. Forget Dan. Is *Denise* going to throw Erin in front a train?

"Is there any more information?" I ask, quickly sifting through the photocopies. "Who she killed or how she walked free? You googled it of course. What did you find?"

"That's the crazy part," Nikki replies. "There's nothing. Murder cases tend to generate a certain level of attention, especially cases that are unusual. And a female killer case is very unusual. Podcasters love to run their couch commentaries, news anchors, amateur Agatha Christies, and conspiracy theorists— they all love to speculate. But it's like the NSA got in there and wiped the internet clean."

"Is that even possible?"

"Well, yeah, sure. I guess. But it's not easy." She slides one of the documents over and points at a block of information. "This is the only identification information I could find. Her inmate number: 6881."

After a long silence, I tell Nikki that I have an idea.

"You can't call the psych ward!" she cries. "That's crazy. And—and are they even open?" She checks her big face wristwatch, pink bands encircling her small wrist. "It's already six fifty."

I roll my eyes. "It's a *hospital*, Nikki. It's not like everyone clocks off at five."

She rolls her eyes back. "What are you going to do? Call up and pretend to be Denise's lawyer? Looking for the rest of the case file?" She laughs.

"No, I wouldn't do that! I'm going to pretend to be Denise herself. Looking for my own case file."

Nikki laughs even louder and runs her hand through her hair, her shiny locks brushing along her jawline. "You're nuts. Go ahead and call. I'll count the seconds before they hang up on you."

While she stares at her watch face, I dial up the number listed on the psych ward document. A woman picks up on the third ring.

"Colorado State Psychiatric Hospital. Mandy speaking." She sounds a little out of breath, like she just made a heroic dive for the phone.

"Hi Mandy, I was wondering if you help me out with some documents?" My voice is high and approaching the sickly-sweet octaves of a politician pandering for votes.

"I'll do my best," she replies. "Can I ask who's calling?"

"This is, um, Denise Livingston."

"Denise?"

"Um, yes?"

"Hey Denise. It's me!"

Oh dear. Mandy and Denise, I mean *me*, know each other. She's going to take a little spin down Memory Lane and point out some road signs from our past, except that I won't recognize a single one.

"Hey Mandy . . ." I strap on my very best Denise impersonation, whoever she is, and look over at Nikki, my eyes wide. *Are you serious?* Nikki mouths. I shrug and look away, trying to concentrate. "Sorry I didn't recognize your voice," I say to Mandy.

"That's funny. I was going to say the same thing."

My stomach twists. Does Mandy know that I'm an impostor?

"Well, it has been a long time," I say.

"And I'm happy for that," she says. "I'm happy that you're not back in here, and that you're out in the big bad world, thriving. Hopefully. Are you? Are you doing okay?"

"Yes, I'm doing great. No, um, episodes to report." I think.

"Oh that's good. You remember that time the orderlies had to chase you down the hallway because you refused your medication?" She chuckles a little.

I chuckle too. "Oh ha ha. Yes that was . . . kind of my low point."

"And do you remember—"

"You know, I try to forget about those days. I try to focus on better things. Happy things. It's a part of my coping strategy for living out here in the big bad world."

I pull my shoulders up to my ears and grimace, while Nikki gives me the *keep going* hand signal.

Mandy seems like a cheerful sort with a soft, marshmallowy voice.

"Oh that's so great," she says. "I'm so proud of you. I always hoped you'd make a full recovery. I mean after everything that happened to you . . ."

What happened! I want to ask; instead, I say, "Thanks, Mandy. You were always so sweet and supportive of me." I hope so. She seems like a 'buttered up and sprinkled with sugar' type so I don't think I'm too far off the mark. "It was terrible—what happened to me," I say, even though I have no idea what I'm talking about. I hope she'll fill in the details.

"Mmhm." And that seems to be the end of her recollections. Of course it is. I just talked about staying as positive as Pollyanna.

"Actually, that's the reason for my call. I'm trying to get my paperwork in order, because I feel like I've forgotten so much of . . . what happened . . . and I feel like if I forget all the details, then I open up the risk of maybe it happening again." Does that make any sense?

"You feel like there's a risk that it might happen again?" She seems a little alarmed now, gently prodding the patient for some telling information.

"Well, no." I backtrack. "Not at all. It's just that I'm seeing a psychiatrist. And he's been so helpful. I feel like I'm healing from . . . my past . . . and all that. But we started to go over some raw wounds, you know, stuff that's still healing. And I feel like I'm ready to deal with everything. Including the case, the—details. Except I guess I forgot more than I expected. So I was wondering if you could send those to me? The case documents?"

Was that too much explaining? Guilty people try to convince. Innocent people convey. Well, I am a guilty person, trying to pass myself off as someone else. I just hope Mandy can't tell.

"Well, good on you," she says with a swell of pride. "I'm happy to help you out as much as I can. But you know patient files are confidential and I can't go mailing them off any which way."

"Of *course*," I say, trying not to sound too deflated. "Any information would be really helpful."

"Well let's see. Can I just verify some information? Gotta stick to the rules, you know how it goes."

"Sure," I say as calmly as possible, and give Nikki the thumbs up. All I have is the information in the photocopies. Let's hope she doesn't ask any trick questions. She asks for my case number, full name, inmate number, and a few other potentially trick questions that I answer with the help of the documents.

"Ok, good. Well, let me see what we have here," Mandy says, clicking away on her keyboard.

I wiggle my eyebrows at Nikki, who pulls one corner of her mouth into a smile and shakes her head incredulously.

"Thanks, Mandy."

There's a psychological element to using people's names. It's supposed to make people feel closer to you on a subconscious level. Salespeople are trained up in the matter of tricking people. Except it doesn't work with me. It annoys me. I hope it doesn't annoy Mandy.

"We've got your court records and the verdict. And here's the summary of your case file," she says.

I grab a pen and start taking notes, listening to Mandy mumbling and trying to catch nuggets of information. "Suicide attempt . . . Transferred to the psych ward . . . Subdued . . . Medication . . . Yadda yadda yadda. Seven stab wounds to the abdomen. Found not guilty by reason of self-defense." She huffs out a little breath. "You must have been terrified, you poor thing."

The world stands still. This Denise chick stabbed her victim seven different times.

"I'll never forget your case as long as I live," Mandy continues. "It's one of those things that you can't get out of your head, no matter what. And I'm so happy to hear that you're moving on from it, and you're getting help, and you're healing from it. If anyone deserves to be happy, it's you, Denise. Especially considering everything you've been through. What your *ex* put you through."

So Denise stabbed her ex seven different times. Was her ex a girl? Then it dawns on me. Maybe she's dating Erin, her employee, and a terrible crime of passion is about to play out. "Thank you," I murmur, wishing Mandy would fill in the details. Which she doesn't. "Yeah, it's been hard . . ." I add, fishing. "Learning to trust again."

"That ex-boyfriend of yours . . . what a monster. You must have the strength of an ox to recover from what he did to you."

Ex-boyfriend. Okay so her ex is a guy, not a girl. She could still be dating Erin though. But—but what did he *do* to Denise?

Mandy presses the receiver close to her mouth, her voice coming through loud and muffled. "You shouldn't blame yourself one bit for killing him. You were *protecting* yourself. It was you or him, and you know what? I would have done the exact same thing."

And the train is back, thundering down the tracks.

"Anyway," Mandy says, putting the phone back in normal position. "I'll just send these out to the address on file?"

"Oh, um. You know what?" I rattle some papers around and tap them noisily into order. "I think I found everything. Thanks, Mandy. You really helped me. Thanks again." And I hang up.

Fingers shaking, I set my phone down and look at Nikki. "Denise killed her abusive ex-boyfriend, seven stab wounds to his body."

"Wow," Nikki says, at last. "And how did she get off?"

"Found not guilty by reason of self-defense."

CHAPTER 20

GIA

It's Wednesday night, just past eight o'clock, one day after my call with Mandy. I should be relaxed, snuggled up with Jacky Baby, watching Whale Wars, but I'm strung as tight as a violin, googling Denise Livingston and the word 'murder' just to tighten up by search. But Nikki was right.

I find a lot of information about the murder part, and accidentally slip down a 'true crime' rabbit hole, knowing all the while that none of it applied to the real Denise (age is wrong, first name is wrong) but I read with gruesome interest anyway and finally close out the browser.

I feel a little shaky and nervous. Shaky because this whole thing involves a death. Nervous because of what I'm about to do.

I'm sitting on my couch, phone in hand, looking at Denise's address that Nikki had given me.

"So pretty much everything that relates to real estate is a matter of public record," Nikki had told me before she texted over the address. "You can even check this out yourself if you want. I think it's an invasion of privacy, but nobody asked me."

Denise's house is located about half way down Balboa Boulevard, on the bay side of the Peninsula. As I take a stroll with google maps, getting familiar with the area surrounding her house, I think back over Denise's crime, trying to find a link between her story and what I saw at Nail Palace, trying to figure out what it all means.

The train. The cutting wind. The tightness in my throat. How does this involve Erin? And then there's the missing link called Dan. How do these pieces all fit together?

I know that Erin is in trouble and she has a boss for a killer. So I find myself back to my last supposition. Is Erin dating her boss? Is this a love triangle gone wrong? Is that what this is all about? And what about Dan? Is he the accomplice? Or does this purely about the Benjamins?

The ghost of an answer is in there somewhere, lurking in the misty terrain of my mind. I can't find the common thread between all of these puzzles, so I decide to start with the only solid thing I have: Denise's address.

Eight o'clock seems like a good time to visit her house. Maybe I can find the truth lurking in the shadows. If she's home, the lights will be on. Then I will cruise on by and come back another time. If the lights are out, well then, I can dawdle outside and hope for psychic inspiration.

So I drive down Balboa Boulevard cautiously, near but just under the speed limit. It's a wide road with an island in the middle lined with parking bays, flanked on both sides by older modest bungalows, built back when homes were just places to live in—not vehicles to build wealth, alongside newer McMansions dotted here and there along the boulevard.

About half way down the Peninsula, the house numbers fall into proximity to Denise's address. I drive past a block of four newly built luxury townhouses and scope them out. The last one down, Denise's, is tidily painted with Cape Cod blue with white trim. A small American flag hangs from the porch column. Where does she get the money to live in such an expensive neighborhood? Maybe she's leveraged up to her eyebrows, hence the money pinch.

One block down, I pull over and park. I'm wearing my jogging clothes, so I can pretend to be out on an evening run if I see that someone's home. I lock up the car and slip my keys and my phone into the fanny pack that Mom had given me for Christmas.

Then I set off. Just ahead, geraniums spill over the decorative wall that separates Denise's courtyard from the sidewalk.

Once there, I check out Denise's windows. All the lights are off. So I bend and tie my shoelaces, trying to quickly boot up my psychic ability, furiously focused within. *Relax*, I tell myself. *Hurry up and relax.*

There's a dog yapping across the street. I glance over, feeling like a cagey criminal, while I finish tying off my shoes. There's a cluster of mailboxes, so I walk over like I'm checking my mail, waiting for some whiffs of intuition to come to me. Nothing.

My heart rate picks up, shunting adrenaline through my body. I am not relaxed. And if I can't achieve relaxation, it's less likely that my superpower will work.

Maybe I don't have to stand right in front of Denise's door to sense something. So I pull in some calming breaths, and walk away from the building, trying to slow my heart rate.

But as I pass the side of her townhouse, I notice a darkened walkway that leads to a back alleyway. And before I know what I'm doing, I'm rushing down the side of her house toward what looks like a side accessory door.

I place my hand on the doorknob and twist. The door—it's open. My heart rate picks up. I didn't exactly come here to break and enter. I came here for answers that I hoped would come to me just by being in proximity to her house.

But my thumping heart is overriding my ability to sense anything. I focus on my internal organs—*stop making so much noise!*—and pull in some long steadying breaths.

I can still leave. It's not too late. I can go home without an answer, but this might be the quickest way forward: snooping around inside her home. And the riskiest. But I need to know: *who* is going to die?

I pull the door open a fraction and peer into the shadows where a sleek red SUV is parked. Maybe I can go to the cops and convince them of my precog powers. Maybe I can slip inside and hunt around for some clues. Maybe—

"Hey."

Startled, I jump back from the door and look toward the voice. Erin stands there, her plumped-up lips pursed, her light-colored eyebrows drawn into a scowl. Where the heck did she come from? And what is she doing at Denise's house?

"Hey," I say, hand on my chest, feeling the thump-thump-thump of my pounding heart. "Geez, you scared me."

"You're scaring me . . ." She dips her chin and looks at me, the shelf of her brow casting a dark shadow over her eyes. "What are you doing?" she asks, but her flat tone of voice tells me that it's not a question; it's an accusation.

"I'm just—"

"*Spying*?"

"Me? God no. No, I was just—I was in the neighborhood, going for a jog. I love to run along the beach," I say, motioning toward the ocean, hoping I pointed in the right direction. "And I was walking past and thought I saw something strange in the shadows, so I just walked down here to check it out."

Erin also wears tight leggings, a tank top knotted in the back, and running shoes. She must have been out for a jog herself, and glimpsed me poking my head into a side garage door, so she slunk down the side of the house to intercept me. "Aren't you that psychic chick that came in for a mani-pedi the other day? The one that works at Fuzzy Bear or whatever?"

"Furry Baby, yeah. The one with the Staffy."

The deep lines of her scowl soften. "Right . . . yeah." And she nods as if some information is dawning on her. "You told me someone is going to die . . ."

My mind races back to the discovery about Denise and her dastardly deed, and Mandy, I'm thinking about her, too. What did she say? *Suicide attempt . . . Subdued . . . Transferred to the psych ward . . . Medication . . . Seven stab wounds. You must have been terrified, you poor thing.*

And then, in my mind, the truth begins to unfurl. The world seems a little off kilter. It's coming. Something is coming . . .

I hear a woman's voice, soft and seductive, so much like Erin's. *Why don't you come over, Chris?*

Followed by a man's voice, angry and accusatory.

Denise, you lied about everything. You set me up!

A jolt races down my arms. Denise set someone up. My mouth goes dry, my senses on high alert. The world stands still. The voices are coming in fast and thick now. Denise's. Chris's.

I hear a gurgling suffocating sound.

Stop, Chris. Stop!

And then I hear Denise's voice, strangled but triumphant. *Thanks for the evidence, asshole.*

No! It's a man's voice. Chris again. I can hear the panic in his voice, followed by muffled stabbing sounds of a blade meeting flesh. But he survives somehow—I hear him panting and struggling. My stomach sours. And I realize that he didn't hurt her at all. The floor falls out from under my feet.

She hurt him.

Nine one one. What's your emergency?

Help! I need help! He's going to kill me!

It's Denise's voice, I realize, as my heart rate climbs again. I hear blood pounding in my ears; I hear his screams. The train is back, thundering down the tracks.

I lift my gaze to meet Erin's. Her nostrils flare. Her eyes narrow. "Do you want to come inside?" she asks, motioning toward the accessory door. Her voice has changed into a deeper tone, the girlishness long gone, replaced by a cold, hard voice. A cold hard voice that belongs to Denise Livingston.

"Thanks, but I really have to get going." I back away and turn to leave, moving past Erin, and picking up my pace.

I rush down the dark side walkway toward my car, trying not to be too obviously freaked out, feeling Erin's gaze on my back all the while. Just before I turn the corner, before I move out of her line of sight, before I desperately dart to my car, I glance over my shoulder and catch a glimpse of the side accessory door opening and Erin, otherwise known as Denise Livingston, walking inside.

CHAPTER 21

BRYNN

Thank goodness I'm not an investigative journalist. I would have been fired long ago. I called the police department and tried to chase up the thrilling conclusion of Dan's police incident, but the unhelpful officer on the other end of the line advised me that privacy laws prevented her from handing out documents to "inquisitive girlfriends."

I believe I detected a hint of condescension, but I just thanked her for her time anyway and hung up. Questioning her tone of voice wouldn't improve her attitude or the outcome.

Donna never knew that Dan's police incident had taken place, and my online criminal history searches, which I paid dearly for, simply showed that Dan doesn't have a record. That only means that Dan's kerfuffle with Erin hadn't lead to a mug shot. It doesn't necessarily mean that he didn't put the marks on her arms.

So I find myself driving over to the Ocean Beach address on the police incident report and try to find that neighbor, Tammy Moore, who called the cops in the first place. Maybe she'll know something. I don't have much to go by, just a name and her location—"two doors down." Which way? I don't know. But I'll have to do some door knocking to find out.

My drive over to Ocean Beach is a quick one. Too quick. I loathe knocking on doors like a salesperson, but I'm not a salesperson, I keep reminding myself. I'm a woman searching for answers. Am I in love with a monster? Not a monster, I quickly concede. Just a guy who supposedly beat up his ex. Does that make him a monster?

The house where Dan and Erin's domestic event occurred sits on top of a hilly street that overlooks the placid Pacific Ocean, stretching as far as the eye can see. There's a scrum of smog on the ocean horizon, a faint yellowish brown line that obscures the blue. The house is a modern contemporary eyesore with glass walls, strange angles, and a color scheme that will need updating in five minutes. I park out front and start counting doors. Two doors up or down the street is my destination for the day. One of the two will hopefully yield the answers that I desperately need.

The house two doors down is a tidy small stucco home with a red tile roof. The front yard is fenced and landscaped nicely with a bright green patch of grass edged with flowering bushes. Seems like a cheerful place. I head over there first. There's an intercom box built into the stucco perimeter wall. I push the button, which springs back nicely, and wait. Nobody replies.

I push the button again, a couple of times, just to be sure, and wait. A breeze ruffles the fronds on a palm tree planted in the center of their lawn. Nobody seems to be home. It's early afternoon. I guess I should have waited until evening to catch someone at home. I guess I'll have to come back later.

Now I'm on to the other house, two doors up from the 'incident house.' I'm loath to knock on this door. The lawn is yellowing, the driveway cracked. There's a blue tarp draped over the side of the house, half covering all sorts of crap from disintegrating furniture to dirty discarded dog crates.

I knock on the front door and stand back, listening to a bunch of dogs yapping. A young guy opens the door with piercings in confounding places, wearing a dark sullen expression and black Emo clothes. His hair hangs in his face, which he clears away with one flick of his head.

"Yeah?"

"Hi, sorry to bother you. I'm wondering if I can speak to Tammy? Is she home?"

Four small dogs swirl around his feet, snarling and barking, but they don't dare to step over the door stoop. He looks over his shoulder and yells into the depths of the house. "Mom! It's for you!" And he leaves me standing there, dogs trailing behind him.

"Who is it?" Tammy calls from a back bedroom, her voice loud and rough.

"How am I supposed to know!" replies her son, and then he turns down a hallway lined with boxes, piles of clothes, and orphaned shoes.

One lone sentinel remains, a cream and black Chihuahua, manning the fort. He stands about four feet away from the front door now, barking himself into oblivion, while I wait at the threshold. I think we're both holding out hope that someone turns up sooner rather than later.

Tammy finally rouses herself from the back bedroom and waddles out toward me, blooms of flesh jiggling under her stained floral dress.

She makes her way over to the door, swiping at the Chihuahua with her leg, but missing. "Sheyuddup, Buster!" she yells at the little dog, who growls and nips at her slouching sock. Tammy is breathing heavily by the time she arrives at the door with beads of perspiration bursting out along her upper lip. "Yeah?" she asks, eyeing me warily.

Looks like cheerful greetings run in the family. I had envisioned a cozy chat with a conscientious neighbor. I envisioned a tidy home kept by a nice neighborly lady, who had some cookies and news to share. I had envisioned the house two doors down.

My heart sinks as Tammy stands before me, scowling, breathing hard in my face, gripping the doorjamb. How she managed to get herself out the house and down the street to meet the police officer is another enduring mystery, but I'm not here to delve into that unanswered question. I'm here to find out about Dan. She flicks her chin toward me. "Whaddaya want?"

"Hi Tammy, I'm so sorry to bother you." I start fumbling with the flimsy pink police report, unfolding it, readying it for easy reading if she needs her memory jogged.

"What's that," she says, peering down at the paper.

"Tammy, I don't know if you remember, but there was a—a domestic issue at the house two doors down a little while ago, involving a guy and girl. You called the cops? This is the police incident report."

I hold out the paper for her to view, and she does look at it very briefly, but then she looks up, beyond my shoulder, and scratches her sweating hairline. "Yeah I think I remember something like that."

"The guy that was involved in the incident is my boyfriend, and—"

"You're dating that guy?" she asks, eyebrows raised. I straighten. I hardly think *Tammy* is in the position to dole out dating advice, but she barrels on with her opinion. "Sweetie, you're as dumb as a nut if you think he won't do to you what he did to that girl."

I so want to be offended. And I do feel myself recoil, a little pucker, but my knee-jerk reaction is buffered by the hope of finally finding some answers.

"What did he do?" I ask. "What happened?"

She shifts on her feet, hanging onto the doorway. "Listen, I can't stand here forever and talk to you. I'm really busy right now, but I'll tell you what happened, if you really want to know."

I feel my knees give with relief. Finally, someone has some answers. "Yes, I'd like to know."

"There was a lot of yelling. And screaming. I believe that girl was screaming for her life. There was all sorts of racket, winding up my dogs and making me all nervous." She goes on about how events conspired to upset her and her peaceful abode and the heroic mission she undertook to call the police, all the while my heart is sinking. Will I ever get an answer out of this lady? But then she sighs, swipes her brow with the back of her hand, and says, "Hon, he hurt that girl as plain as day. That's what I believe."

"Believe or know..."

Tammy grows visibly flustered. "Nobody ever knows what goes on behind closed doors. Not you. Not me. Not anybody. So how about this. When someone shows you who they are, you better believe 'em." She flicks her chin in my direction. "You have a nice day."

And she retreats into the house, shutting the door behind her.

CHAPTER 22

GIA

The shock of discovering Erin's true identity reverberated through me long after I got home. The idea of using my ability to help someone had seemed right. Timely. Alluring even.

Now? I don't want anything to do with her. I thought *Erin* was in trouble, and warning her away from the 'trouble' would be manageable. Like telling someone to buckle up because I see a car crash coming. Well, I do see a car crash coming. And it's not a fender bender.

Someone is going to die.

Erin's fake last name isn't lost on me either. Lazarus of Bethany was the last resurrection Jesus performed before his own. Erin is rising up, resurrecting herself. Whatever she's up to, I don't want anything to do with it. Not with my superpower so young and untested. Not with Jack relying on me to come home every night. Not with the wound of my past still raw.

So the following morning, I call up Nikki and deliver the shocking conclusion of our investigation. The answer is likely to hit her like a roundhouse punch.

"Are you freaking kidding me?"

"No, not at all. I saw everything, like a straight-to-DVD movie playing right before my eyes. Erin *is* Denise. They're the same person. I saw how she killed her ex. I saw how she set him up, made him attack her first..."

After a short period of stunned silence, Nikki finally replies. "So *Erin* killed her ex-boyfriend and made it look like self-defense."

"Yep," I say, recalling the voice I heard when I went to Erin's nail salon.

Stop, Dan. Stop!

And in the same beat, I can hear the same words she cried out before Chris met his gruesome end.

Stop, Chris. Stop!

And now, I know she's doing it again, targeting someone else. She's setting up Dan the Man in the same way that lead to Chris's death. *Why* she's doing it or how, exactly, I don't know.

"Wow. I don't want to get involved in that," Nikki says.

I thought I was doing my best to stop a terrible accident from happening. I thought I was helping Erin. Now, I realize I'm hurtling myself into the dark mechanism of set-ups and secrets and possibly murder. Well, that's enough ambulating for me. I'm going to go back to shuffling around in my comfortable house slippers.

"Me neither," I agree.

So I get on with my life, trying to forget all about Erin. But every time the front door of the shop jangles, dread washes over me. Is that her? Is she back? After a few days, I neither see nor hear from her. And slowly, the whole jarring discovery begins to fade.

It's Thursday, and I'm feeling a little drained. Business is slow, so I decide to close up ten minutes early and skip my six-thirty Jazzercise class at the gym, so I can take Jack out for his evening walk myself. After I finish closing up, I send a text message to Sarah, the dog walker.

Hey there. I'll be home early today so I can take Jack out. Sorry for the trouble. Regular schedule tomorrow.

And I add a smiley face, hoping she's not too put out over the loss of income. I can see the three little dots, indicating that she's typing a reply. Great. I love quick responders.

Jack is with Erin. She said you wanted her to look after him for a while. You know more than me, I guess she'll drop him off soon?

I can hardly breathe. I call Sarah immediately. She picks up on the second ring, but I don't even wait for her to say hello.

"What do you mean he's with Erin?" I blurt, hands shaking. "Erin . . . took him? Erin has Jack? Jack—my dog??" Maybe she's talking about another Jack.

"Yeah, she said you were stuck at work." My mind is racing. "She said that she helps you out sometimes? She said she's known you forever, and I mean Jack didn't seem to mind. She had a treat for him and everything, so I—"

"Known me forever?! We just met!" I'm pacing the store, hand on the top of my head, trying to keep it place. Erin has no idea who Jack is! She's never even seen him before. How the heck did she get her claws on him? Erin recommended Sarah. Did they plan this? "Did you coordinate with her or something?"

"No! Of course not!" Sarah seems genuinely shocked. "I—I didn't know. She sent me a text and asked where I was when I was out for his regular walk at twelve. I wrote back and said I was at the dog park with Jack, and then she came over and picked him up. I thought you knew! She was so adamant about it. And—and I'm so sorry. I guess I should have called you first."

Yes you should have! I want to yell at her, but what good will it do? I need to get Jack back. Sarah is the only person who can help me. But then a horrible realization dawns. It's six o'clock now. Erin took Jack at noon.

My heart starts beating in strange irregular thumps. "Erin's had Jack for almost six hours? Oh my God. Do you have any idea where she went with him? Did she say?"

I want to be mad at Jack for waltzing off with a stranger. Doesn't he have better judgment than that? Maybe he didn't have a choice . . .

"No," Sarah says. "I have no idea where she went. But let me give you her phone number. Just a sec."

She gives me Erin's phone number, which I dial eight consecutive times. Each call goes to straight voicemail. I call again and decide to leave a voice mail.

"Hey Erin. It's me Gia. I'm not sure what's going on here, but you took my dog. I'm not even sure if that's even legal, taking someone's dog, but I'd like him back. Maybe it was an accident. I don't know. But please send me a message and tell me where I can pick him up. I want to come get him now. Thanks. Bye."

But then common sense swoops down and pecks at me. An accident? Who *accidentally* steals a dog? OK. Maybe it wasn't an accident. But Erin *killed* someone, even if she was found "not guilty." So I'd rather try and stay on her good side for the time being.

Besides, honey is supposed to catch more flies than a punch in the face, right? Except I've always found a punch in the face to be far more effective . . .

I'll punch her in the face later, if she refuses to give up Jack. In the meantime, I check my phone. No new messages. No missed calls.

Honey for now. Punches for later. Except later is now, and Erin isn't calling me back.

I send her another text message.

Erin, I want my dog back. Now. Please tell me where you are. I'll come get him.

Still using the honey—*please*—but I'm getting more agitated. My teeth are starting to sharpen into fangs. My hand is curling into a fist.

I don't know what else to do. She's not replying. So I close up the shop, get in my car, and start combing the streets for Jacky Baby. I fire off more text messages, but those go unanswered.

I scour the dog park, cruising past alleyways in the nearby neighborhood, eyes alive for signs of him. I find nothing. The sun sets. I flick on my headlights and keep driving.

After the rush of anger passes, a feeling of fear and loneliness sets in. Is she going to hurt him? Is she going to drop him off a million miles from home? Or on the other side of the San Diego-Tijuana border?

Fear spurs me into fighting mode. I pull over and call her up. She doesn't answer. Big surprise.

"Listen to me you—dog thief! I know you have Jack. I want him back. Right now. Do you hear me? What is wrong with you? Stealing someone's dog? If you have a problem with me, go ahead and tell me to my face. But don't involve an innocent animal! Give me my dog back, you—you *monster*!"

I push the red hang up button, but it doesn't quite have the same satisfaction of slamming the phone down. As I sit there, fighting back tears, I realize driving around is a fruitless endeavor. I check my phone in case Erin called with ransom instructions. Nothing. So, with my heart breaking and nothing else to do, I drive home.

Home is a desolate and strange place without Jack greeting me at the door. I want to sit down and cry, but I need to keep searching. I can't give up. I call all the local animal shelters, asking if anybody turned in an orange Staffy mutt.

"He's super sweet," I say, just in case, but nobody has any good news. The day is winding down. I don't know what else I can do. The long, dark and lonely night is settling in.

I flip open my laptop and google 'how to find a lost pet.' There's helpful tips and stories with happily ever afters. There's lost pet flyer templates that I can download for a small fee. And there's an email notification bubble in the corner of my monitor.

It's from Yelp, letting me know that the shop has a new review. I click on the bubble before it slides away. A nice review will help cheer me up.

From: E.

My mind races. E—as in Erin?

Oh dear.

The very first thing I see is a great big fat one star review, complete with a detailed description of how I verbally assaulted her. *Assault.* I'm having a hard time processing that word. Then this supposed customer states that she's considering pressing charges. The best part? She posted an audio clip as evidence.

But the audio clip . . . it's like a car crash, and I'm the rubbernecker. My cursor hovers over the big white play button. I can't stop myself from looking. Click! Suddenly my own voice roars back at me. "You—you *monster*!"

My mind races over criminal procedures. Can she press charges with a single sound bite as evidence? Of course the case will be dismissed, won't it? Isn't calling someone names covered under the First Amendment? What did I say exactly? I can't even think about what my boss is going to do. Not now.

My eyes scan the rest of the page, and I see a sea of shining one star reviews. My chin puckers. My eyes sting with tears. Jack is gone. And now the shop's reputation is in tatters. What about my job? What will Jeff, the overly pedantic owner, say?

My cell phone rings. I pick it up, my voice weak and desolate. "Hello?"

"Hi, is this Gia?" a woman asks.

I hear a volley of dog barks in the background. She's calling from a shelter. "Yes, yes it is." I jolt up to sitting up, ready to receive some news. Please let it be good news.

"Great. So this is Karen from Coastal Animal Shelter."

"Yes?"

"And we found Jack. Or at least we think it's Jack . . . he fits the description anyway. And we—"

"I'm on my way. I'll be there in fifteen minutes." And I hang up.

Technically, it's a half hour drive from here, but I was afraid she'd tell me to come over tomorrow if she has to wait for my arrival. I'll make it in fifteen, even if it costs me my driver's license. I can't stand the thought of Jack spending one night at the pound, surrounded once again by the terrifying sounds of desperation, abandonment, and loneliness.

She may not even have my baby Jack, but I take the chance anyway and blow through a few yellow lights, swerving around grandma behind the wheel, and it seems like grandma is behind every steering wheel.

I merge onto the freeway, glance over my shoulder, and cross three lanes at once. I swerve into the fast lane and put the pedal to the metal, leaning forward, senses on high alert.

Ninety miles an hour. One hundred. One ten . . . and here's my exit. I eat up three lanes and before I know it, I careen onto the shelter premises, double park with a screech, and go in.

"I'm here for Jack," I tell the elderly receptionist. "He's a staffy-cross. Orange. Big head. Karen just called me?"

"Oh," she says, looking at her computer monitor, clicking her mouse randomly. "We did? We don't usually call this time of night." She seems a little overwhelmed with modern technology.

"Do you mind if I check the kennels myself?"

She looks at her wristwatch. "Well, it's just that visiting hours are kind of over."

What is this a hospital? I can feel my fangs growing longer. I've had a rough day. If she doesn't help me out, and quick, I'm about to draw blood. "Look—"

A side door bangs opens. A woman walks through, holding the handle of a thin plastic slip leash. Karen, I presume. She has buzzed sidewalls, piercings that run along the edges of both ears, and lots of tattoos. She's wearing a black t-shirt that says: *I heart animals more than people.*

She rounds the reception desk, and at the end of the leash cowers Jack.

"Jack!" I cry, bundling him up in my arms. He's whimpering, crying, and licking my face. And I'm crying too, with joy.

"Well he sure likes you," she says. "Looks like I won't have to ask for proof of ownership."

"Thank you *so* much," I say to her.

"Well, thanks for picking up the phone. You wouldn't believe the trouble I have with reuniting pets with their owners. Sometimes I'm like, hello? Your frickin' pet is here. You wanna come get him?"

"I would never do that. I've been such a wreck since he went missing."

"That's because you're a good person," she says, reaching behind the counter for a form. "Some people should be banned from owning pets."

While Karen fills out the paperwork, I check Jack's collar because I'm damn sure he has an ID tag. It's an expensive crystal embellished one that says 'Jack's Mommy' followed by my phone number. But it's missing.

Instead, I find a little metal tube, clipped onto the D-ring. Surprised, I unclip it. I can see that it's a little screw-together barrel. Strange. I twist it open, and find a curled up piece of paper stuffed into one end.

With shaking fingers, I unroll the paper and read. *Stop snooping and Jack lives.*

CHAPTER 23

GIA

I'm completely horrified that Erin finagled the theft of Jack. Did she plan it from the very moment we met. If so, why? Did she read my mind? Or does she lay a foundation for entrapment with every person she meets? Seems like a lot of organizational work. Does she keep spreadsheets? Whatever her motivation (and her accounting system), I find her prep work to be chilling.

I drive straight up to my mom's house to drop off Jack. He needs to be safe and completely removed from Erin's grasp. I'm trying to get one step ahead of Erin. In order to do that, I need to think like a paranoid criminal.

Is Mom's house really the best place to take Jack? Will I be putting her at risk? The only way that I'd be putting my mom at risk is if Erin could track down her address somehow. So I threw away Jack's collar just in case she planted a tracking device. And if she goes to one of those 'mine for personal information' websites, she won't be able to find my mom through me because we have different last names.

I had legally changed mine in high school when "Ercolessi" somehow became Ergo Lezzie, followed by many guffaws about my sexual orientation. So, it's not ideal, taking Jack to Mom's house, but I think this will do for now.

As soon as I walk through the front door, Jack is gone, lucky me, darting around the front room with Mom's dog, Midas. Then he sideswipes a small decorative table and sends a lamp with a beaded shade tumbling to the floor. "Jack!" I cry, but he's not listening of course. So I pick up the lamp and offer the bog standard apology that every dog owner constantly mutters, "Sorry..."

"It's okay." Mom tries to corral Midas, but he slips away. I try to nab Jack, but he's zippy now, energized by looming entrapment. Then they both run, barking, into the back bedroom, dual flashes of orange and white. Well, at least Jack will be happy here.

"Do you think you could keep him for a little while?" I ask.

"Sure," Mom says, pulling his doggy dishes out from the pantry. "How long?"

"I'm really busy with work," I say, sitting down at the kitchen table. "My boss asked me to pick up a few more shifts." I'm trying to guesstimate how long it will take Erin to forget about abducting Jack again. "Maybe a few weeks?"

This is the first time I've ever lied to my mom. It feels strange and odious. I want to take a shower, but my overriding concern is for her and Jack's safety.

"Sure, honey," she says, "Did you have dinner?"

"No, not yet."

"OK, let me see what I can rustle up."

While Mom warms up some Bolognese, I read my text messages. There are several from Sarah, the world's worst dog walker—*Did you find Jack? Is he ok?*—and reply with news that I found him at the pound, followed by sharp words about job ethics. You never *ever* let someone take your client's dog. *Stupido!* Okay, I left the last part off.

Then I head to the living room and sit down on Mom's favorite reading chaise, thinking.

I decided that I didn't want anything to do with Erin's dastardly deeds. I decided to leave her dark secrets alone. But after Erin stole my dog and left those bogus reviews, threatening my livelihood and my dog's life, I'm furious. And I'm scared. If she's going to hold a gun to my temple, I'd better make sure I'm holding the bullets.

But there's something else churning inside. The last time I had dismissed clues dangling right in front of my face Melissa had lost her life, and I had fractured apart as a person. I'd turned away from my psychic ability, the one that had caused me so much confusion and heartache.

Nonna had said once that receiving psychic impressions is like an obligation. *Don't break-ah the contract.* After so many long years of healing and shoring myself back up again and, finally, hoping (albeit with trepidation) that my gift would return, I have been given a second contract.

But . . . should I try and stop her? Should I take the risk? I'll be stepping in Erin's way, a woman who has already taken a life. Would she have any qualms with taking another life? Possibly mine?

I don't know, but my sense of conviction returns, thinking about stopping her. Thinking about honoring *the gift*.

I think of Mom's words: *maybe it's come back for a reason*, and Nonna's prediction from long ago rises to the forefront of my mind. *Gia will go on to help many people . . .*

Maybe it's my destiny to stop Erin. Maybe that's why my ability came back. And when my decision solidifies—*yes, I'm going to try and stop her*—a sense of peace and determination washes over me.

Erin has a dastardly plan that involves Dan. I need to get to him. Fast.

But how? All the snooper websites require full names. All I know is his nickname: Dan the Man. I thought about calling Nikki and asking her to try and hunt up something, but she was very clear about her ongoing disinterest in Erin. *I don't want to get involved in that.*

Lucky for me, Google doesn't have a choice. I pull up the browser on my phone and type in "Dan the Man."

Jack trots into the living room, hops up onto my lap, and sits down, snuffling around my phone. He likes to surf the internet. He even has his own preferences. He likes to watch funny puppy compilations, the sentimental sap.

But not today. Today, I need to find Dan the Man. I start scrolling through the images. There are old men lying on the beach, wearing scanty pieces of clothing. There's a guy with big beard and a belly to match, followed by various images of half-naked and hair-free individuals.

I find pictures of seductive looking boy band groups, a hipster duo, and many Dapper Dans. Then I find a lot of other images that don't seem to fit the bill (no offense, Hot Man Killer.)

Facebook yielded way too many results to be helpful, so I close the browser and turn off my phone. What now?

My mind goes back to that day at Nail Palace, when I first intuited him. He seemed like a fit guy: nice build, strong, eyes like iron.

I got the impression that he's a physical guy, not a desk jockey. That gets me thinking about active jobs. Not dirty jobs. Though, I'm fairly certain that his job does get dirty at times. Is he a foreman? A personal trainer? A policeman? A detective?

That would be the ultimate irony. He investigates murderers for a living, only to find one hot on his tail. I grab a pen and scrap paper from the small spindly side stable where Mom stashes her books, and write down as many active, possibly dirty jobs I can think of.

I finish my list and look it over, waiting for one to stand out, waiting for my superpower to tell me clearly: the guy's full name is (fill in the blank); he's a (fill in the occupation); you may find him at (enter precise address). Except it doesn't work that way.

I sigh, feeling disappointed and a little panicky. I have no idea how to find this guy, or go about doing it, and this really is a matter of life or death. I run my hand along Jack's velvety fur and scratch behind his ear stumps. He's a clingy little guy. But of course, he would be, after what had happened to him.

I found him at the pound, while looking for a cat to adopt. Cats are independent and easy to care for, requiring only food, water, and plenty of neglect.

But there weren't any cats available that day, so I visited the kennel out of curiosity. I wanted to give reassuring pats and cuddles to the poor homeless fur babies, even if I didn't have the bandwidth to care for one.

A volunteer followed, pointing out some potentials. There were purebreds, I was surprised to find, including a Cocker Spaniel with dirty ears dragging on the floor. There were blind dogs, young dogs, some exuberant puppies rescued from off the street. I felt so bad for them all.

Sharp, anxious barking battered against my ears. I wanted to take them all home, but I couldn't. So I resolved to make a donation and continued down the aisle toward the exit. Out of curiosity, I stopped at the last kennel, silent within, and peered inside.

An orange dog with docked ears and tail lay curled up on the concrete floor, the ridge of his spine facing out. I could see his rib cage rising and falling, but just barely. He cuddled a dingy stuffed animal.

"His owner surrendered him a couple days ago," the volunteer said, fingers hooked into the chain-link fencing, looking into the cage. "Said she'd fallen on hard times and couldn't take care of him anymore. Since he was originally a rescue from a dogfighting ring, we have to be extra careful. Not a lot of people are interested in that box of chocolates."

I bent down and made little kissy sounds. "Hey little fella . . ." But he didn't move.

"If I've ever seen a dog die of a broken heart, this is it. We can't get him to respond to anyone or anything. He won't eat. He clutches his stuffed animal and just lays there, like he's waiting to die."

I looked over at his bowl of food, untouched.

"He needs a foster home, but we reached out to everyone on our list and they're all busy with other dogs." She sighed. "It's a toughie because people don't want to adopt a dog that won't interact with them, especially with breeds that are high risk. I don't know what to do. If we can't get him to come out of his shell, management is going to put him on the kill list."

I sit up straight. Kill List.

Mom has a deck of divination cards that she nicknamed Kill List.

I think about that mean-spirited deck. I like cards that are chatty and give me the whole balanced picture, both good and bad. Kill List just gives the simple brutal truth.

This divination deck, created and passed down by Nonna, offers no flowery upsides. It's based on a forty card playing deck with four suits—cups, coins, swords, and clubs—used for a popular card game in Italy called Scopa.

Nonna gave each card a meaning in latin based loosely on tarot. The cups signify thoughts, imagination and emotions. Messages in the coins suit have to do with the material plane.

Swords represent movement and time, and the clubs allude to power, transition, and outcomes.

Mom retired the deck after it predicted the sudden death of a client, which later turned out to be a car accident. Mom had to make up a nice story about a dream coming true, while insisting that her client take care, be careful, and buckle up.

"Mom? Do you still have Kill List?"

"What?" she asks, pouring some pasta in to a pan of boiling water.

"Kill List. Do you still have it?"

She looks over her shoulder at me. "Why do you want that deck? I put it away a long time ago."

"I know, I know. But I have a question that I want to ask Kill List."

She arches her finely shaped eyebrows, all the way up to the blunt line of her newly trimmed bangs. "Use the art deco deck if you have a question, honey. It's such a lovely deck. I'm really enjoying it."

"Okay, but I want to ask Kill List first."

She shakes her head as if she can't be bothered arguing and turns back to the stovetop. "I keep everything in my chest of drawers. Third drawer down. Come down for dinner when you're done."

I hurry up the stairs to the tall chest of drawers in her bedroom where she stashes her non-valuable valuables, while Jackie-boy trots along behind me. I should have named him Shadow, as in My Personal Shadow, but I'd already done up the paperwork.

I open up the third drawer and pat around the edges, scraping around the back of the deep drawer, kind of hoping I won't find it, but then I feel something hard and very deck-like.

Out comes Kill List. I remember the thrill of excitement and fear when I worked with this deck. It was like climbing on the back of a powerful, smart, and barely broke horse. Whatever message pours out of these cards will be clear, concise, and terribly accurate.

I sit down and slip the deck out of the sleeve, while Jack curls up between my folded legs and lays his oversized head on my thigh. It's been many years since I've read tarot cards. Hopefully, this is like riding a bicycle.

First things first. Reset the deck. I have to inject good energy into these long dormant cards and get them to behave.

I shuffle a few times and press Jack's paw against the deck. His energy is pure devotion and selflessness, mixed with bundles of gratitude. Then I clear my mind.

OK, done.

I continue to shuffle as I formulate my question. I don't need a long exposition, I remind the cards. I just need an answer.

I hope this tricky deck will spill the proverbial beans. Short and sweet. Done and dusted. I speak my question, loud and clear. "Where do I find Dan the Man?"

I keep shuffling, pushing down a growing sense of unease as I feel the cards awaken.

Jacky starts snoring. Well, if he's not alarmed, why should I be?

A card flops out, face up.

OCCIDO.

The hair on the back of my neck stands on end. I feel something akin to a dark cloud gathering around me. This is not like the Death card in tarot, which can mean the death of one thing in order for there to be the birth of another. Kill List doesn't put a happy spin on things. And this card isn't showing any ole death. Occido means 'slaughter or slay.' I feel a little queasy. Kill List wants to show me a death, and a very violent one at that.

"Where can I find Dan the Man?" I ask the cards, shuffling faster.

Out falls another card face down this time. I flip it over, hoping that it will answer my question, instead of more description of the future horrendous deed.

MOX. Soon, presently, shortly. My stomach drops. This guy doesn't have much time. Nonna built a time element in this deck. She was a very impatient person. So am I.

"Okay, okay," I say, cutting the deck. "I need to find this guy. I need to find Dan the Man. Dan the Man. Dan the Man." You have to repeat yourself. Sometimes the cards can be a little hard of hearing. "Where can I find Dan. The. Man."

One last card falls out. I hold my breath and flip it over.

BELLUM.

And now, I know where to look.

CHAPTER 24

GIA

The very next day, I arrange for my co-worker to cover my shift. Then I collect all the names of the bases and related outposts in San Diego, the epicenter of all things military. There's way more places than I expected. It seems like every time I zoom in to the map, more locations materialize. In addition to the Navy and Marines, there are the quasi-military branches of Homeland Security, Border Patrol, and the Coast Guard.

It looks like my new mission will take a long time. Time I don't have. So I decide to start at the northern-most base in San Diego—the Marine Corps base in Camp Pendleton—and make my way south.

I exit the freeway and follow the signs toward the San Onofre Gate of Camp Pendleton, a narrow road leading to a two-lane entrance flanked by cinder block security huts and a small metal-roofed admin office building sitting off to the side. One lane is blocked off, directing all traffic to the lane furthest to the right. I slow down and lower my window. I haven't planned out a script, but looking up at the scowling cadet, wearing his sharp uniform and sharper haircut, I realize that I may have screwed up.

"How can I help you today, ma'am?"

"Hi, I'm trying to find someone. Would it be possible to talk to someone in admin?" I smile, trying to soften my ridiculous request.

"Who are you looking for?"

"I'm looking for a guy named Dan . . ."

I cringe inwardly, while he presses his lips together, waiting for me to provide the rest of the information. Problem is, I don't have any.

"You're looking for a guy named Dan," he says. I notice this is not a question. It's a statement. "And does this Dan have a last name or rank?"

"Well, that's kind of the thing. I don't actually know his last name . . . or his rank." I smile again, hoping to get this guy on my side. He can cause me all sorts of problems up to and including detainment, if he deems my behavior suspicious.

He steps closer and peers into the backseat of my car. Then he meets my gaze. "Ma'am, are you aware that Dan is one of the most common names in America? My dog is named Dan. Are you sure you're not looking for someone's dog?"

I sigh and glance at my rear view mirror. Another vehicle is coming. My window of opportunity is closing. "Yes, I'm sorry, I know this sounds a little strange, but I need to find someone named Dan. He—he has a nickname." This'll be good. "It's . . . Dan the Man?" I wince.

He straightens. His nostrils flare. He probably thinks I'm playing a prank on him, ergo playing a prank on his beloved branch of the U.S. military. But I have to find this guy, offended parties or no. I have to save someone's life. I lean out of my car window and look up at the cadet. "He could also be known as Danny?"

Well, that ends my tour of Camp Pendleton.

He instructs me to turn around and leave the premises post haste, which I proceed to do. Before I reach the freeway on-ramp, I pull over and look at my long list of destinations for the day. Then I sigh and lay my head back on the headrest, overcome with the reality of my mission. I could go to every place on my list, but I'll face the same problem. Calvin Cadet will meet me at every entrance gate and point out the obvious state of affairs: there are millions of men in the U.S. Military, named Dan.

But what am I supposed to do? This is all I have. One life hangs in the balance, maybe more. So with no other option, I sit up, put my car into gear, and drive on to the next stop.

I experience what I can only summarize as 'same-same' with the following four stops. Calvin Cadet is proving to be rather unhelpful. Time for a change of tactic.

I'm driving over Coronado Bridge, death-gripping the wheel, keeping my eyes glued to the dotted white lines as I soar over the skyline and return safely to terra firma.

At the base of the bridge, I drive through the unmanned tollbooths and follow the GPS directions to the Naval base. This time, though, I have a plan. I decide to park in the nearby neighborhood, walk onto the base—okay sneak—and ask around.

It's risky, otherwise known as a big gamble, but I don't know what else to do. I can't get past the sentinels.

All the Calvin Cadets so far look like recent high school graduates polished up like chess pieces. These boys are also a little cagey looking and militant, working very hard to do the right thing, score some brownie points, and stay under the radar. Better do the best I can to stay under *their* radar.

It's a sunny Friday afternoon with a weak sun and light breezes. White puffs of clouds scuttle across the bright blue sky. I'm hoping Calvin Cadet will be in a little bit of an end-of-the-week haze, daydreaming about the upcoming weekend.

The streets on Coronado Island are charming and well maintained. The lawns are impossibly green and immaculate. I find myself wondering where the municipality gets their endless source of water. Cheerful blooming trees dot the neighborhoods, along with SoCal's renditions of Cape Cods, Colonials, and stucco plantation style homes.

I pull up next to a one-story home with a cactus garden for a front yard and hurry down the sidewalk toward a security hut on base about a hundred yards down the road, trying to look calm and casual.

As I approach, I watch another Calvin Cadet wave through a few vehicles and return to his hut. A group of three people in front of me, one military and two civilians, walk toward the entrance, past the hut, and make their way to what looks like an admin building. I decide to do the very same thing. But just as I walk past the traffic boom, I hear Calvin bark, "Ma'am?"

He's talking to me of course. I keep moving.

"Ma'am!"

As casually as possible, I tail civilians into the building. Right before I slip inside, I glance behind me and see Calvin dip his head toward the walkie-talkie attached to his epaulet, eyes glued on me. He's calling for backup.

I don't have much time. Backup is on the way. I push inside the admin building and rush up to the counter.

"Excuse me, sorry," I say to the woman sitting behind a computer monitor. She's in full uniform, hair pulled up slick and tight under her brown cap. There are some insignia sewn on her sleeves, and some medals pinned to her chest lapel. "Hi, I'm looking for someone named Dan. Do you think you might be able to look him up?"

"Dan? Do you have his last name?"

Ah, yes. That. "No, I don't. Sorry."

She shakes her head a little dubiously, but soldiers on, ready to query her database. "Okay, can you tell me his rank?"

"I don't know that either."

"Do you know his company?"

"Ah . . . no."

She takes her hands away from the keyboard. "Ma'am, you'll need to provide a little more information. Can I see your pass?"

She means my security pass of course, the one that I don't have. I make a show of trying to dig it out of my purse. "Oh, you know what? Actually, here it is." I hold up Nikki's new business card. "I forgot I wrote down his number on the back of this card. I'll give him a call. Thanks so much." Smiling, I leave, stealing a quick glance toward Calvin Cadet, noting with dismay that he's still talking on his walkie-talkie.

I rush to the nearest group of men in uniform. "Hi, sorry to bother you, but I'm looking for Dan," I say to the first one. "It's important. He has a nickname. Dan the Man." I glance back at Calvin. "Do you know him?"

"That's not much to go by," a man replies.

Another one chimes in. "Is this something serious?" He seems interested in helping.

"Yes, I mean, no. Not yet. But I need to get a message to him."

Both men shake their heads. I move on, stealing another backward glance, and see two young men walking toward me. They're here to escort me off the premises or arrest for me for trespassing.

I hurry to the next cluster of uniformed men. "Does anybody here know Dan? Dan the Man?" They look confused. So I move onto the next group and the next, not caring if I look like a crazy person. Well, okay, I care a little, but the image of Kill List's deadly prediction drives me on.

OCCIDO. Slay. MOX. Shortly.

I accost another group before the security detail catches up to me. Both men take a hold of me, one on each side, hands encircling my wrists like iron manacles.

"Please don't arrest me. I'm not here to cause any trouble. I just need to find someone named Dan. Dan the Man," I say to the gentleman on my left.

Dan the Dickhead? The words ring loud and clear in my mind.

Astonished, I look up at my captor. He's short, maybe five foot eight, stocky, so blonde his hair is almost transparent, and he has acne scars flaring along his jaw.

"You know him . . ." I say.

Blondie looks like he's been caught shagging a sheep. "Huh?" he asks, scowling. "I don't know him for shit."

Stop breathing so hard, Captain Cadet. You're stealing air from the rest of society!

Sir! Yes sir!

"You do know him."

He keeps his gaze locked on our destination.

How's training, son? You holding up okay?

My instructor is a Class A asshole . . .

"You—you think he's an asshole." And all the color drains from the young man's face. Blondie slows down. The other one keeps up the momentum. Soon we'll be at the security gate, where Calvin will mete out his punishment. "Please," I say to him under my breath. "I need to get a message to him. It's important."

We arrive at the gate and Calvin stands there, arms crossed, looking none too happy.

Time's up. Game's over. After all the risks I took to find Dan, I failed. I look again at Blondie, imploring him to help me. "Tell him he's in trouble, okay? Tell him to stay away from a girl named Erin."

And before he hands me off to Calvin, Blondie leans over and whispers fiercely in my ear. "His name is Dan Evans. And he *is* an asshole."

CHAPTER 25

ERIN

Gia is giving me the shits. She's a little too motivated for her own good. Why can't she just stick to her pet shop life? Ringing up customers, selling them overpriced "accessories" made with organic free-range sustainably sourced materials woven on a loom by seven virgins? I hate those sanctimonious animal-loving idiots with more money than sense.

It's a dog! I want yell every time I see a 'pawrent' presenting his or her smelly, slobbering canine with a doggy cake and posting pictures of their fat over-indulged 'furry baby' dressed up in some barf-inducing birthday bandana. Those people need help. Can't they think of anything else to spend their money on? Like starving children?

What a monumental mistake it was to go around and try to drum up some business for the nail salon. I didn't exactly plan on abducting Gia's dog when we met. That was pure luck on my part, giving her Sarah's phone number. Well, I better get my game face on because I can't afford to screw this up.

Christ. How did she find my house? That was a shocker. Seeing her standing there, poking her head in my garage.

Time to get going with my 'Befriend Brynn' plan. Pick up the pace. Lay my trap. Get her on side with me, and maybe even, talk to the police. Wouldn't that be a boon?

Brynn was another unexpected complication: finding out Dan has a girlfriend. I had to think quick on my feet that night. Thank God she's a gullible fish. Made my job a lot easier. What does Dan see in that breadstick?

Anyway, my plan has a time component so that I don't come across as creepy because when I showed up at her yoga class, Brynn looked like Penelope backing away from Pepé Le Pew.

So I decided to let a little time pass before moving into phase two, but Gia is messing with my plans.

What is she up to? Her finding my house was definitely a close shave, and I'm feeling a cold wind blowing on the back of my neck, where my long locks used to flow.

She's a psychic, apparently, and she did pick up on Dan when she came in for her manicure. So I can't underestimate her. Of course, she'll sleuth around for more information because she's trying to *help* me.

Well, I need to hurry up and help myself before she ruins everything. I hope I scared her into submission with my online review and the threat I left on her dumb dog's collar.

Someone is going to die, she predicted. Anyone with good sense would pipe down after that prediction. Get back to their regular life and leave me the fuck alone. Not Gia! Lucky me.

I need to keep my thumb on her. You don't get to where I am without understanding the nature of people, without heeding your own instincts about them. And my hunch tells me that she's going to try something else, a heroic Hail Mary to save this unknown person's life and solve her delicious little mystery.

Well, I'll have to cut that off at the knees. Unfortunately for her, she called looking for Jack. All part of my plan. Now I have her cell phone number. Tracking people through their cell phone is a little bit of an internet myth. There are a lot of apps that promise the Valhalla of trickery, but they don't really deliver. If I want to track an Android user, I have to physically load an app onto the target device. If I'm after an Apple user (like Brynn), I need to get them somehow cough up their iCloud password. Good luck with that.

There are other websites that promise to track the location of an individual by triangulating cell phone tower information for a small fee. But you can't be completely stupid, even if you are desperate. Why would someone put their credit card information into a tracker website that promises to deliver on a shady illegal deed?

The only reliable way to track people via their cell phones is to thoroughly break the law. And in order to do that, I need to find my clever Bangladeshi buddy on the dark web. It's scary what he can do with a shabby computer and an internet connection.

When we first met, we had chatted very briefly about the world of data mining. He calls himself a data broker and says he can get his hands on literally any piece of information that I'm willing to pay for, or erase it, which is how I made his acquaintance in the first place. I needed someone to clean up the search engines, wipe the stain of my misdeeds off of the digital pages. He did a good job, and I paid dearly for it, but it was money well spent, I think, though now I'm not so sure.

He also advised me to create a plethora of social media profiles to confuse anyone who tried to find me. Squid Ink he called it, blowing a big puff of black misinformation in someone's face every time they try to look me up. That took some time and some creativity to make up so many different people, but I managed it in the end.

But right now, I just need to track Gia's location. So I fire up my VPN, then my Tor browser and navigate to a forum where he usually hangs out. Then I leave him a message and close out my browser.

A few minutes later, I get a text message from a seriously random number, one of his burner phones probably, the identity scrambled across a VPN.

Yep?

Hey Raj. Need to track someone. Same deal as before.

.0089 BTC per

I tabulate the conversion: almost ninety dollars per request. Ouch. Prices have gone way up. That's not exactly happy news, but what price am I going to pay if I lose?

Ok, I reply, along with Gia's cell phone number. I get back on my computer, turn on my VPN again to mask my computer IP address, load up my browser, log in to my Bitcoin wallet, and send over the amount. *All paid*, I text. Then I wait.

A couple minutes later, a text message comes through with a screen grab of the I-5 freeway south, a blue dot plotted on Coronado Island. I sit up straight. Gia is in San Diego . . . hunting down Dan?

Shit!

I'm hustling now, balancing on one foot and then the other as I slip on my shoes. I'm dashing over to the kitchen counter and grabbing my purse, and then I'm out of the garage entryway door and fishing out keys from my purse, while I hop in the driver seat and jam the key fob into the ignition. Before the garage door rolls up completely, I ram the car into reverse, roaring out of the garage, and skimming the roof of my car on the bottom of the garage door. I cringe as the scraping metal rakes across the roof of my car, but I don't have time to stop and check the damage. I jam my finger onto the garage door clicker and drive away.

It's a bright sunny day. That means traffic is going to be a bitch. Rush hour has gotten earlier and earlier. Three in the afternoon used to be a nice time to cruise down the freeway, but little knots of red taillights are already flickering on about half a mile down the road, where cars are starting to bunch up. Great.

While I tap on the brakes, I think about Gia. What the fuck is she doing? Is she really headed to Dan's house? How could she have figured out where he lives? All she knows is his nickname! Did she intuit something from the spiritual world? Did some angel on high waft down from the heavens and plop Dan's address into her palm?

Maybe she's just headed down to San Diego for a day at the beach. I can feel my shoulders begin to relax a little and slowly ease away from my ears. Yes, that makes sense. She's in San Diego visiting friends maybe. There's no way she could have found Dan.

I haven't quite worked out my plan with Brynn yet. I need her on my side. I need her to testify against Dan. I had hoped to take my time and ease into her life, be that sympathetic listening ear now that Dan's on deployment. Earn her trust. Get her to turn on Dan. After I went to her yoga class, I promised myself: no more strange coincidences. Things need to unfold between us naturally, even though I'm going to engineer every interaction.

Maybe this is the opportunity I've been waiting for. I reach over and dig around in my bag, making sure my secret weapon is still in there. It's a gift for Brynn. Cost me a small fortune. Call it an investment.

I decide to guard the critically important spot, Dan's house. I'll park just down the street, out of view, and make sure Gia spends her day at the beach, working on her tan or whatever, and that she heads straight home after she's done.

Pray I get there in time . . .

CHAPTER 26

GIA

Dan Evans. I could have kissed that young cadet, but I didn't dare. Calvin Cadet and friends interrogated me for nearly an hour and dutifully recorded my particulars. They said they'd let me off this time, because somehow I convinced them that I wasn't working for a terrorist cell organization, but next time they'll take up the matter with the police.

Well, there won't be a next time because Dan's time is running out. As I drive back over the bridge, I wonder at what kind of crazy lives inside that perky package of a girl and the hell she plans on unleashing.

Once I reach the other side, I pull over at a gas station, get out my phone, and look for his home address. Nikki taught me that trick. *Pretty much everything that relates to real estate is a matter of public record.* Turns out public records are conveniently located online.

There are exactly five addresses in San Diego where 'D. Evans' resides. It's late afternoon by now, but I hope there's enough daylight left to visit each address. I hop back on the freeway because I have business to do, and very little time left to do it.

Pacific Beach. It seems like a happy, sunny place, where guys and gals jog around with surfboards tucked under their toned arms. It seems like a quaint pocket of yesteryear tinged with vibes from Endless Summer.

I follow the driving instructions and arrive at the first address. Nerves flicker inside my belly. I feel like a Jehovah's Witness, knocking on someone's door and helpfully advising him or her that heaven's almost full.

I park and walk up the cracked walkway to the front door of a beach bungalow with a narrow empty porch. I knock and wait. Nothing. Then I wait and knock. Nothing.

My stomach settles somewhat. 'Nobody home' seems to have a calming affect on my internal matters. Then I hear a frail voice yell from within, "Just a minute!"

This person is definitely not Dan. Maybe it's Dan senior, I reason, as I wait an age for the door to finally open. The elderly man stands there, wearing a terrycloth bathrobe tied around his gaunt body and hotel slippers on his feet. He squints at me through the screen door.

"Yes?" he barks.

"Hi," I say. "You don't know me, but—"

"Who is it?" cries someone from the back of the house. The voice sounds male. Not young. Not old. Maybe it's the right Dan, looking after his grandpa.

"What do you want?" The old man scowls and shuffles closer. "You want to tell me what my house is worth? Or what my neighbor's house is worth?"

"Um, no."

"Damn real estate agents," he mumbles.

A middle-aged man arrives at the door. "Sorry. My dad's hard of hearing."

The old man turns and shuffles away, yelling: "Well you know, Dan, they always come around here. Knocking on my door, telling me that so-and-so sold their house, and how much for, and why don't I keel over and die so that they can get the listing!"

Dan opens the screen door and props it open with his foot. "Sorry about that. Can I help you?"

"Are you Dan Evans?" I ask, heart sinking. This is definitely not the Military Man in question. It's clear, by his sloped shoulders and slight frame, that nobody ever bestowed 'The Man' on this fellow.

"You want to tell me what this is all about?" he asks.

"Sorry to bother you. I'm looking for someone named Dan Evans. You wouldn't happen to be in the military, would you?"

He shakes his head. "No."

"Okay, thank you. Wrong person. Sorry to bother you." And I leave.

The next two houses yield similar results. I find the exuberant fourth-grade son of Doug Evans, who wants a dog soooo bad!

I find Dawn Evans, the retired gardener, who takes me on a walking tour of her front yard. There's grumpy yuppie Don Evans in La Jolla, who's leaving for lunch at Del Mar. "Not him!" he says, shutting the door in my face.

And so off I go, back to my car, to cross another address off my list, my message of doom still undelivered. All in all, I'm having a pretty okay day, meeting some interesting people, and I find myself wondering why this wasn't a 'thing,' a sort of social treasure hunt.

The day comes to a close. Evening falls. I sit in my car and squeeze the bridge of my nose. Because it's not that much fun, actually.

I had hoped to get my mission over and done with during daylight hours. Only creeps go hunting around for strangers at night. I look down at my list again. Only one address left. I wish I could visit this last house some other day, but I don't have any time to waste.

So I make my way around the dark winding roads of La Jolla, inch down a steep road that runs straight downhill and deposits me onto La Jolla Shores, then skirts around La Jolla Village until I reach North Pacific Beach.

According to Jeeves, my GPS advisor, my destination is "three hundred metres to your left." That seems right and proper, so I slow down, search the darkened exteriors for numbers, find the right one, pull over, and park.

The house is a tidy weatherboard home, painted gray and white, with a small porch flanked by two narrow columns. An overgrown bush grows in front of a bay window next to the porch. Light spills onto the walkway from an illuminated fan light above the red front door.

I climb a couple of steps to the front door. Just as I raise my hand to knock, I hear an argument break out inside the house. A woman is yelling. I can't quite make out the words. Then I hear loud and clear:

"Fuck you, Dan! You asshole!"

And I know she's talking to Dan. The right Dan. The one I'm looking for! Finally, I can share my news and be done with this heavy, horrible burden. Except that now seems like a really bad time.

I knock softly, nervously, but nobody answers. Confused, I stand there, wondering if I should come back at a later time. But I made such an effort to get here. And what if I came back and find the house empty? Besides, I don't have any time to spare. I need to get this over with. Rip off the bandage, I tell myself, raising my hand to rap on the door again. Maybe she didn't hear me the first time.

Right before my knuckles strike the door, the lights flick off, plunging the house into darkness. I'm standing there in the shadows, wondering what on earth just happened. Is there a power outage? I glance across the street and see other well-lit houses. Did she blow a fuse? I hope it's not a tripped circuit breaker.

I walk down the porch steps and edge my way between the bush and the front bay window, pulling up my hoodie to keep the scraggly branches out of my hair. Where is she? I know she's here. Is everything okay?

The window is covered; the blinds shut tight. I'm trying to see around the edges, trying to figure out where this woman went. I peer through a gap and see nothing but darkness. There's no movement inside the house at all. So strange.

Where did that chick go? If I can't talk to her, I'll have to drive all the way back down here. And there isn't any time. Maybe I can write her a letter and put it in her mailbox. But what will I say?

"Hey stranger, someone you hopefully know, named Dan Evans, is about to get whacked." No, no, no. That's not very sensitive. How about, "I'm a psychic with a message from the beyond. Stay away from someone named Erin Lazarus."

That seems a little better, but she'll probably think I'm crazy. I'm edging my way over to the other end of the window, wrestling with the overbearing bush that's poking me in the back, when the slats slam up.

There stands the figure of a woman, framed in darkness. Stunned, I stumble backwards, buffeted by the bush for a second, then burst through anyway, falling onto my rear end, heart hammering in my chest. The branches close with a swift *woosh*, blocking her from view. And before good reason can prevail, I'm running to my car.

Roaring down the street, I'm trying to figure out what to do. I pull onto a dark deserted road, snaking up a hill, and turn left, trying to backtrack to a familiar road. I have no idea where I am or how to get out of here. I'm reaching over to turn on the GPS, when I see a flash of bright light in my rear view mirror.

I watch, transfixed, as the lights grow bigger, brighter, blinding. Suddenly the driver guns the engine and strikes me from behind at a strange angle that makes me lose control of the steering.

I slam on the brakes, tires screeching, as I ride up on the curb and strike the trunk of a tree. The air bag blows up in my face, a soft white cloud, smelling like burnt rubber and an electrical fire.

I slump back, trying to get my bearings, while pain throbs down my face, head, and neck. My headlights stare ahead, bright columns of light penetrating a cloud of smoke and steam and eerie silence. I hiss and hold my hand to my nose, horrified that in my rush to leave Dan's house, I forgot to buckle up.

My ears are ringing. My vision turns into tilt-a-wheel, and I think I'm going to be sick. I lean over, trying to get into a better position for the coming unfortunate event, but the queasy sensation thankfully fades. I need to get out and exchange details with the idiot in the other car now. That jerk who rear-ended me.

I look up at the hood of my car, buckled and steaming. Shit. I'm scrambling, trying to put this together. I place my hand on my forehead and sit there for a second, trying to gather the strength to get out and talk to that bastard. But I can hardly move.

My nose runs. I sniff, gently touch my nostrils with the tips of my shaking fingers, pull my hand away and look. There's blood. Red dabbles of it. Bright red, not dark red, I tell myself, heart accelerating with fear, trying to figure out which one is deadly, while the taste of metal seeps into my mouth.

With my fingers pressed against my nostrils, I lean over, open up the glove box and fish out an old pack of tissues. Then I gently press a handful against my nose, thinking bright is right, isn't that what doctors say? I don't know, maybe I'm making stuff up.

There's another roar of cylinders, a gunning engine. Instinctively, I cringe and lean away from the sound in a move to self-protect, but I look in spite of myself, and see a red SUV with a blonde driver cruise on by, looking at me, while I look at her.

Erin.

A few seconds later, fuzzy gray stars fill my vision along with a curious neighbor. "Are you all right?" he asks, leaning close. But his voice sounds like radio static beaming in from outer space.

He's asking more questions that I can't quite answer, while talking to someone on the phone. "We need help . . ."

Sometime later, I hear distant ambulance sirens, buzzing in my head like a swarm of bees. Soon, I'm being carried somewhere, floating on a long sturdy cushion surrounded by lots of quick-moving people, asking me if I'm okay. Telling me to hang in there!

A mask covers my mouth, filling my lungs with the crispest, cleanest air I've ever breathed. What is this stuff? I wonder, as someone hovers over the crook of my right arm. Ow! That hurts . . .

My gaze follows a line that leads to a bag of fluid, floating somewhere off planet, where everything is dim and soft and wonderful, where darkness begins to envelop me and finally washes over me completely.

CHAPTER 27

BRYNN

Just one glass, I tell myself as my friend Jaime pours two big ones. As soon as I saw that Peeping Tom dash across my front yard and drive away, I rushed Bear into my car in the garage and drove straight to Jaime's house.

"Thanks for letting me stay over," I say to Jamester. She's a solid friend. She has a tendency to laugh a little too loud, sometimes at inappropriate times, but she doesn't take herself too seriously.

She's also a happy drunk and probably not the best person to be around so soon after almost pickling my liver, but she's my shoulder to lean on. She's also a fellow "wine lover" and that means only one thing.

"You can pay me back in bottles of wine," she says, smirking over her bulbous wineglass and swallowing a good measure, while I nurse mine. "So tell me what happened."

Her dyed red hair is pulled up into a loose bun. She's settled into her overstuffed couch ready for a good story, wearing bejeweled cat eyeglasses instead of contacts, the thick lenses magnifying her round blue eyes. It's called singing for your supper. You get something you need, in my case a place to stay, and the other person gets a good laugh. Except I'm sleeping on Jaime's couch, so I don't feel too much pressure.

"It was horrible," I say, stroking Bear's silky soft ear as he sits next to me, transfixed by Jaime's beige tomcat lurking underneath the dining table. "I was talking to Dan on the phone—okay, we were fighting, and I heard someone knock really softly on the front door. Like creepy soft. Like they'd been standing there, listening, trying to time their intrusion. And that really freaked me out. Plus, I'll be honest, it's not like I was in the mood to talk to anyone. I didn't want to answer the door so I turned off the lights. That means go away. Right?"

"Yeah. Absolutely."

"Then I heard twigs cracking outside my front window. I thought it was a cat or a raccoon at first so I didn't pay much attention. But the leaves kept rustling, and I swear I saw a shadow pass behind the window blind. So I wasn't even thinking that I'd catch anyone red-handed. I mean who stands outside of someone else's window? So I yanked up the blind, expecting to find nothing, and—and someone was standing there!"

"That's crazy."

"Completely nuts. Something like that has never happened to me before. I felt so violated and exposed. And—and what the heck is wrong with that person? What were they looking for? A peep show? I mean, you can find anything you want online. Why stand outside my window?"

"The world is full of crazy cuckoo heads," Jaime says. "Remember that time we woke up wearing Shrek costumes?"

I snort. I can't help it. Then I laugh out loud, and it feels great. That was quite possibly the most ridiculous night we'd ever had, if I could remember what had happened exactly. Dan had been out of town on a training trip. It was meant to be a mellow get-together, but a booze bomb had detonated at a house party in Mission Beach instead, scattering us far and wide. By the time we gained some sort of consciousness the following morning, sun beating down on our throbbing heads, Jaime had somehow donned an ogre costume, and I'd been transformed into a donkey.

"So what do you think the Creepo wanted?" Jaime asks, looking pretty warmed up. "To watch you practicing hair of the dog?"

"A transformative pose I tell you," I say, raising my glass to her. And we both chuckle. "Seriously though, I'm going to tell you something that's even weirder. I don't think it was a guy. I caught a glimpse of the Creepo. Either it was a skinny dude, or it was a girl."

"Skinny dude for sure," Jaime says. "It was a skinny dorky dude who can't get laid through the usual channels, so he has to resort to peeping. I mean who else could it be?"

I think about it for a minute. I could have sworn the figure was female, but that narrows the possible suspects down to about half the population.

I had been so rattled after my call with Dan and shocked to find someone standing outside my window, I hadn't been exactly concentrating on the details. I'd told Dan about the incident report. I wanted him to put on his warm lover voice and tell me it was all a big fat mistake. But he'd put on his angry military man voice instead. *Not on a potentially open phone line!*

"The thing is," I look at Jaime. Her cheeks are bright, her teeth stained red. She's having a great time. She's loving this new dramatic turn in my life. "We kind of partied with Dan's ex-girlfriend at his farewell party."

She nearly falls off her perch. "You what?"

"Yeah . . ."

"I can't believe I missed that!"

"You were out of town. Remember?"

"Oh yeah, the annual Grimes Family Fun Fest. Always worth attending." She rolls her eyes. "So did you wake up wearing a costume?"

I want to laugh, but the pit of my stomach is opening up.

"It shouldn't have happened. It was so stupid. But we ran into her down at Delmonicos, the starting point for the big night, and it seemed innocent enough. Dan wanted her to leave, but she seemed nice and kind of shy. So I called Dan a party pooper and he backed off and then we all drank way too much. You know how it goes . . . everything turns into a big blur, people dip in and out." I leave out the part about how Dan and Erin had *talked*. "And a few days later, she called Dan."

"She called him?"

I nod.

"What a bitch!"

I don't defend her honorable intentions because that would mean mentioning The Photo. So I get on with my hypothesis. "It was just the one call that I know of, and Dan said nothing happened. So . . ." I shrug. "I thought that was the end of it. But then she tracked me down and showed up at my yoga class."

"No. Way."

I think about that nuclear bomb of a photo, but I don't want to talk about it. Not about that. I don't want anyone else to know. My stomach churns, thinking about the image of her bloody nose, her lip split, her swollen eye . . .

"So yeah, I think she's the stalker."

For once in her life, Jaime has nothing to say. Then her phone rings.

"Just a sec," she says to me. And to her phone, "Hello? Oh, hey Tiff . . . uh huh . . . I don't know. Let me check." She covers the phone with her hand, hardly secretive, and says to me, "Do you want to go out tonight? Tiffany's at the grand opening of Ocean Palisades, that new oceanfront bar and restaurant."

"I don't know . . . I'm not sure I'm up for it."

Jaime smiles sympathetically, reaches over, and squeezes my knee. "I think you could use a distraction."

186

I pull in a deep breath. If I stay here, I'll sit on Jaime's couch and drink myself into morose paranoia.

"All right," I say, getting up slowly. "Maybe I could use a change of scenery."

CHAPTER 28

GIA

I'm in an emergency room, I think, with a flimsy curtain pulled half-closed next to my bed alcove. Just beyond, I can see a nurse standing at a wheelie computer station, entering data and struggling with glasses that keep sliding down her nose.

The loudspeaker squawks overhead, "Doctor Chen to room 13." A woman—not Erin—lingers down by the foot of my bed, waiting for the nurse to finish. So much for privacy. I close my eyes, trying to make sense of the last few hours.

I'm still groggy from the sedative they gave me, but solving the mystery of how Erin found me is in the forefront of my muddled mind as well as the memory of screeching tires and metal crunching on metal, both making my stomach roil.

I reach up and gently touch the bandage on my throbbing nose and hiss when pain radiates down my face. My body aches. I feel like I've run a few marathons back to back. I drop my hand and try to relax.

Someone will stop by at some point and tell me exactly where I am, what's shoved up my nostrils, and my medical status. Stable, they'll tell me. Shaken, not stirred, surely. Fractured memories of the accident flash in my mind. The steaming radiator of my car, the deflated airbag, and Erin, driving away.

There's really only two ways she could have tracked me down. Through a GPS tracker physically placed on my car or with my cell phone. If she bugged my car, then she's lost that connection. My car was totaled. It's probably sitting in some tow yard, a certain write-off now.

That leaves my phone. I really don't know anything about tracking people down via cellphones. I've never even googled 'how to be a creepy stalker and use nefarious ways to track someone.' Well, clearly Erin figured it out. Is she tracking me now? Listening to my thoughts? I fumble for my phone, stashed in my back pocket, and power it off. There. That should cut the umbilical cord. I think. But what about Mom? How will she get in touch with me?

Shivering uncontrollably, I reach for a thin blanket and drape it over my body as best as I can, trying to warm up and stop the shaking.

"Over here?" I hear Mom's voice. And the curtain snaps open.

My eyes instantly well up with tears. My throat tightens with emotion. Mom. The only person I want to see right now. The only person who will make this all better.

"Oh, honey," she says. Her dark hair is pulled back, her bangs ruffled, mascara smudged a little. I suspect she's wearing pajamas under her tan trench coat, cinched up tight around her waist, but I don't ask. I'm just happy she's here. "Are you okay? Have the nurses checked you out and everything?" Her pretty almond shaped eyes are wide with alarm. She hovers overhead, looking at my nose. "Ouch."

"Ouch is right," I say, reaching for her hand.

She sits down next to me and takes both of my hands in hers. "As soon as the police called, I rushed here as fast as I could." She frowns. "What are you doing all the way down here anyway?"

I groan and look away, gazing at the gouge marks in the wall, wondering where to begin. It's such a long story, and I don't want Mom to worry. But the bigger problem is that she'll get in my way. She'll stop me, when I'm so close to stopping Erin. But maybe I should stop. Maybe I'm not thinking so clearly, after all.

"What's going on, Gia?"

I look into her honey-colored eyes, bloodshot and tired, and want to tell her everything, but I can't seem to find the words. Instead, I say, "I didn't want to tell you. I didn't want you to worry."

She squeezes my hand. "I wouldn't worry," she says. I look at her and try to laugh but it hurts too much. "Okay, maybe I would worry a little, but you know you can tell me anything. Are you in some kind of trouble?" she asks, all calm and casual, but I know she's desperate for the details. "Is it about Jack? Because I do think it's strange that you brought him over. I mean—"

"Is he okay? You didn't leave him alone, did you?" My skin tingles with goosebumps just thinking about Erin getting her creepy claws on my Jacky-baby again.

"No!" she cries. "Jon came over. I didn't know how long I'd be gone, so he offered to pet sit for me." He's the neighbor, who's quite smitten with my mom. I'm not sure she's noticed yet.

"Oh, that's good. He's such a nice guy . . ."

"Don't change the subject, Gia." She's onto me, snuffling out my problems like a bloodhound. "I want to know what's going on. I want to know why you're here."

Silence.

"Well? What is it?" she demands.

We lock eyes for a moment, and then I look away. "Two weeks ago this girl, Erin, came into my work, trying to drum up business for her nail salon. I could see that she was in trouble. I thought it had to do with money, so I went to her salon to get my nails done, hoping that I'd see something because I think you're right. I think my psychic ability came back for a reason."

"Uh huh."

"Well, the mani-pedi turned out to be . . . not what I expected." Chills race down my back just thinking about it.

"What happened?"

"I saw that someone is going to die."

"What?"

"And I'll tell you what *really* freaked me out."

"Okay . . ."

"Mom." I lower my voice to a whisper. "I found out that she killed her ex-boyfriend and made it look like self-defense."

Mom sits there, stunned. "But why," she asks. "Why would someone do that?"

"I don't know."

Mom looks away, troubled.

"But I believe she's going to do it again," I say, leaving out the part about calling Mandy at the psych ward and poking around outside of Erin's house. Mom would lecture me to high heaven if she found out. "And—and I tried to get the message to her new victim—to the person I think is about to have a bad life, or at least a short one. But Erin found out that I'm onto her, and she stole Jack and left a message on his collar. She said he'll die if I don't stop snooping. And—"

"And that's why you brought him to my house."

I nod. "And that's why I'm down here. Trying to get to her victim before she does. Trying to use this gift for good, trying to make sure I listen this time."

Mom cups my cheek with her hand. "Honey, you can't blame yourself for what happened to Melissa. She was not well."

I grit my teeth and force back the tears. "I did everything I could to help, but I can't keep going. Erin . . . she's scary. She stole Jack. Threatened his life. She left online reviews, practically killing the pet shop. And now the accident . . ."

Mom frowns.

"But don't worry. I'm done. I can't do this anymore. I can't keep putting myself and everyone around me in danger."

"I'm with you. I absolutely think you should stop with this vigilante justice stuff." She leans in and squeezes my hand. "But this—Erin problem? It's big. Real big. We need to get the police involved."

"What are they going to do, Mom? Arrest her based on a psychic's prediction? The whole world would be incarcerated."

"But how are you going to save someone's life based on a premonition?"

I open my mouth to object, but a nurse pulls the curtain open holding a clipboard. She checks my bandage and my oxygen saturation levels. Then she removes the IV drip and gives us the discharge instructions.

I leave it to Mom to ask the follow up questions. Should I go on bed rest? Any foods to avoid? Am I okay to sleep alone or should she keep vigil twenty-four seven?

Finally, the nurse leaves, closing the curtain behind her. Mom turns to me, her mouth turned down, her eyes serious. She leans in close and says in her no-nonsense Mom voice, "You're going to talk to the police. And if you don't, *I will*."

CHAPTER 29

BRYNN

Everybody always flocks to the latest new thing. Ocean Palisades, a trendy bar slash restaurant in a sleek oceanfront property, distracts me from my problems as soon as I walk through the wide front doors.

The restaurant part sits on the mezzanine level, candle-topped tables overlooking the crowded downstairs bar area that faces a wall of windows. In the daytime, the windows look out on the beach and ocean beyond. Tonight, only the outdoor terrace area lined with flaming tiki torches can be seen beyond the darkened windows, where people stand, shivering and smoking.

I had donned Jaime's black sheer-paneled dress, a shade above slutty, but still attractive. I have a boyfriend, after all, even if he does beat up women, allegedly. But you can't show up at these events looking like the help.

"Hey Tiff!" cries Jaime, making her way through the crowd.

"Hey Tiffy," I say, walking behind Jaime.

Tiffy is great fun, but she's a little flaky. She has been a blonde, brunette, and redheaded—at different times. If her eyebrows are anything to go by, I'd call her a dark blonde. She has a penchant for dramatic winged eyeliner and vintage dresses. She also has a tendency to laugh a little too loud, oftentimes at things that I don't find particularly funny. Kind of like Jaime. Maybe that's why they like each other. She's sharp and quick-witted, and her sexual orientation seems a little dubious. Maybe that's also why she likes Jaime. No matter. She invited us to a grand soirée, and I'm grateful for the distraction.

"Brynn has a stalker!" Jaime roars above the music.

"What!" I yelp. "Jaime, you don't need to tell everybody. Tiff—really, it's not—"

"A *stalker*?" Tiffany says, eyes wide, leaning over and giving me an air kiss. Then she straightens. "Do tell!"

More singing for my supper. Except tonight I'll buy my own drinks, thank you very much. "Guys, it's really not that big of a deal."

"Then why are you sleeping on my couch?"

No answer.

"And get this," Jaime says to Tiffany. "We think he is a *she*."

"A she stalker?" Tiffany says, totally enchanted. I consider leaving a sign on my door, notifying the stalker of a more willing subject. "Is that even a thing?" she asks.

"I think they're called shtalkers," Jaime says with her best Sean Connery impression. "As in sh-talkers. Because when they're sh-talking, they're looking—not talking."

Tiffany finds that hilarious.

"I don't know if it's actually a girl," I say above their laughter. "All I know is that . . ." And here I fumble. I most definitely do not want Tiffany to know about my reckless night out with Dan's ex and her photo-documented face. I don't know anything about criminal proceedings (if it gets that far), but I do know that it's definitely a bad idea to go around town and blab. Besides, at this point, it's still an unsubstantiated personal matter. But who else could the stalker be?

Jaime and Tiffany look at me expectantly.

"Okay, I think it's a girl," I say.

Jaime and Tiffany lock hands, eyes bright with—glee? They remind me of couple of Inspector Clouseaus, anxious to make a disaster of things in their haste to solve the mystery.

"We can set a trap," says Tiffany.

Exactly.

"Absolutely," agrees Jaime.

"No," I say. "No traps."

They blink at me, positively ruining their fun. "I'm going to get a drink," I say. "Anybody else want one?"

We three troop over to the bar, where Tiffany stumps for our first round. A tall, frosty glass of white wine arrives in my hand. I feel better, as if life has instantly become more manageable.

"So, how are we going catch the peeper?" Tiffany asks. As if we were all on the same page here, as if this is a big load of fun. Well, it's not fun. It's dangerous and scary.

"We're not," I say.

"First, I think we should come up with a catchy operational name," Jaime says.

"Oh great." I take a big gulp of my wine. I need it. There will be no derailing these Keystone Kops now.

"*Great* idea," says Tiffany, taking a thoughtful sip.

"How about 'Catch the Creeper'," Jaime says, smirking, trying not to laugh.

Tiffany nods her head. "Oh yeah. That's good. Real good."

And down goes more of my drink.

"See?" Jaime says, lifting her glass for a toast. "I'm a genius."

"Definitely an asset to the team," I say, rolling my eyes.

"*Huge* asset," Tiffany agrees, missing my sarcasm entirely and clinking glasses with Jaime. "Okay, so it's all decided?" She nods and looks at Jaime, then me. I'm supposed to nod back in agreement preferably with some enthusiasm. But I just stand there feeling like a stunned mullet.

My phone buzzes. It's a long buzz, which means someone is trying to call me. Dan? I hurry to unearth my phone from my clutch. It keeps buzzing. Good news, that means he's still on the line. But when I pull it out, I see a U.S. based number that I don't recognize with a 213 area code. Los Angeles. So not Dan.

I put my phone back in my bag. Probably a telemarketer, poor guy, sitting in a dreary phone call factory, dialing number after number only to be abused when someone finally picks up, his salary hanging on a thread. Convert or die!

Then I feel a short buzz. A text message. Jaime and Tiffany launch into their Catch The Creeper plan, while I play what the heck with my cell phone.

I punch in my security code and read the message. Then my knees go weak.

Hey, it's me, Erin. I was wondering if I could talk to you really quick? Sorry to bother you.

"Who is it?" Jaime asks, peering at my phone. "Is it *Dan the Man*?"

I so regret telling her Dan's nickname.

"No," I say, holding up my phone. "It's the Creeper."

CHAPTER 30

BRYNN

We hastily relocate to a quieter area, the outside patio of Ocean Palisades, tiki torch flames wavering in the chilly breezes. I'm flanked by Jaime and Tiffany, telling me to: "Call her back! Call her back!"

They can't believe their luck. The Creeper calling me direct? This deserves their one hundred percent focus.

Jaime hiccups. I glare at her.

"Sorry," she says, pulling in her lips.

"I can't call the Creeper back with you two breathing down my neck. You hiccuping and,"—I turn to Tiffany, who's peering down at my phone—"and who knows what the heck you're going to say."

Tiffany tries to look offended, but she knows she's guilty. She has a mouth that knows no bounds, and she never, repeat never, thinks to put a muzzle on it.

"I won't say a thing," Tiff says, pressing her plump hand against her mouth, eyes dancing merrily.

"Yeah right," I mutter, turning my attention back to my phone.

I don't want to mess around with Erin. She has photographic evidence that could completely blow up Dan's life. Even if she had somehow Photoshopped the image and Dan is as innocent as a lamb, a false accusation is as good as a real one in today's climate. Besides this girl is really off her rocker if she faked the appalling attack.

What will she do if I call her back and the Keystone Kops start giggling in the background? She'll probably hang up in a fury and commence Operation Destroy Dan, or me, or both.

I don't know. All I know is that I can't mess around with her. It's one thing to tell Jaime my filtered version of events. It's quite another to unleash Tiffany and Jaime on Erin, without any backstops.

I put my phone away. "No, I can't risk it, guys. If she is the stalker, and I don't know, but if she *is*, then that would mean that she's completely crazy, and the last thing I need is you two clowns giggling in the background. This is serious. She has—" But I stop myself right there. *Don't say another word.*

My phone buzzes again. I look down at the glowing screen.

"It's another text," I say.

"What does it say?" asks Jaime.

I read aloud, "I need to talk to you. Can you call me back?"

My stomach churns. I am well and truly out of my depth here, but fortunately or unfortunately I have two friends standing on either side of me, offering up their version of moral support.

"Well?" Jaime asks. "Talking doesn't hurt anyone."

My thumb hovers over the call button.

"Go on," says Tiffany.

"It's just a phone call," says Jaime.

So I brace myself and push 'call.'

"Hello?" comes Erin's voice, a little breathless.

"Hey . . . Erin, it's me, Brynn." Did I just introduce myself?

"Oh hey, Brynn. Thanks for calling me back."

"Um—how did you get my number?"

"Oh, you gave it to me that night we all went out." *That night.* The gift that keeps on giving. "You don't remember?"

"I guess not . . ."

Her voice sounds weird, a little quivery and nervous. Inexplicably, I feel sorry for her. "Are you okay?" I ask.

There's a long pause. "No," she says. "I'm just—I'm a little rattled."

Rattled because you're a stalker? I want to ask. *And I caught you red-handed?* But common courtesy dictates my next statement: "Did something happen?"

And here she breaks down a little. I can hear snuffles, and my resistance toward her melts.

"Sorry," she says, at last.

Jaime and Tiffany are both leaning toward me, trying to hear. I have her on max volume so they can catch snippets. They're riveted, not moving, like twin stone statues.

"It's just that . . . someone just broke into my house."

Karma.

But wait. If *she* just got burgled that means she's not my shtalker. Right? I'm trying to work this out in my head, matching up the timelines, but everything is a blur. Jaime and Tiffany are staring at me, waiting for an update.

"Someone broke into your house?" I repeat for the benefit of my audience.

Erin starts crying. "Yeah, and I'm just—I'm having a really hard time coping, you know?"

Tiffany tilts my phone toward her face. "Hi, hi—this is Tiffany, Brynn's friend. Do you want to drive over here? We're at—"

I rip the phone away from her, wishing so badly I could set Tiffany's hair on fire with my searing evil eye. I cover the mouthpiece with the palm of my hand. "Don't invite her over here!" I whisper fiercely. "That's the last thing I need!"

"But she's *crying*," whispers Jaime.

"This is Dan's. Freaking. Ex-girlfriend we're talking about here," I say to them both, and then to Erin waiting on the phone, "Sorry just a sec." And I put the call on mute.

"*Everyone* is someone's ex-girlfriend," Tiffany reasons. "Does that mean we're all lepers?"

No, just this one.

"She's really scared," says Jaime. "I mean, put yourself in her shoes."

I really, really do not want to do that.

"I don't want to get involved with her, okay? She needs to go to the police, not me. I can't do anything for her."

"You can be a friend," says Tiffany, her voice cold and accusatory. Ugh. That old bone of contention. We have a little history in the 'being there for each other' department, specifically me not being there for her. Circumstances out of my control. Forgiven. Not forgotten, clearly.

"Fine," I say. "Just fine. Invite her out if you want."

Jaime and Tiffany exchange glances. Had they somehow coordinated this new development by exchanging subliminal signals or something? All I know is that they are mightily pleased about it.

"Think about it," Jaime says, her eyes glimmering with excitement. "We can get her a little tipsy. And we can pump her for information."

"No. Pumping." I look at Jaime, while Tiffany suggests, "Corroborate?"

"No nothing. Okay? I'm serious." They both nod solemnly. "Okay." I switch off the mute button. "Hey Erin, sorry about that. So, do you want to meet us out for a drink?"

CHAPTER 31

GIA

"Knock, knock." The curtain next my bed in the emergency room opens. A policewoman with frazzled auburn hair steps through, wearing a dark blue uniform and a permascowl. I can tell by her unimpressed demeanor that she's seen it all.

"Miss England?"

"Eastland," I say. "Gia Eastland."

The policewoman pulls out a notepad from a tooled pouch on her heavy-duty belt and leafs through the first few pages filled, no doubt, with notes about a gruesome unsolved murder. On the back of one page, I see the word "pizza" written in large block lettering circled a few times. Maybe not.

The police officer looks up, lake blue eyes meeting mine. "My name is Detective Robbins. I'm with the San Diego Police Department, and I'm here to follow up with your recent traffic incident. Let's start at the top, okay? Can you tell me your full name and where you live?"

"Sure. My name is Gia Maria Eastland and I live in Newport Beach."

"And what are you doing all the way down here?"

"I was looking for someone." Robbins jots down some notes. Something incriminating? Oh dear. "And—and let's see, what else? This is my mom." Mom waves.

Robbins nods to her, and addresses me. "Miss Eastland, why were you looking for someone? Did they go missing?"

"No, nothing like that. I was just trying to deliver a message."

"What kind of message?" She catches my gaze and narrows her eyes in concentration. She's trained to read the nuance of the situation, to read between the lines. She's surely also as sharp as an eagle when it comes to spotting lies. Her impassive gaze is fixed on mine, waiting for the wrong answer so she can pounce.

I swallow. Under her laser gaze, I know there's no escape. I must tell her the truth.

"Detective Robbins, I'm a psychic," I begin. The words come out strangely reassuring. "I believe someone is in danger, so I wanted to warn them, but I got rear-ended instead."

Detective Robbins looks dubious. She's not a believer. That's okay. I don't need to show off. I can feel myself opening up, receiving some news. Snippets of her past rise up within me. I want to push them away. Close the opening. Not now. Not anymore . . .

But they're here all right, pushing through. And suddenly I know that she wouldn't be eating pizza alone every night if she hadn't dumped her husband for that hot young stud.

Creaking leather. Gun fire. Correction: her partner. *Listen, Rookie.* So she was his superior. My heartbeat accelerates. I can feel searing pressure on my lips. The affair was hot all right, filled with lots of late night office encounters, lust, and maybe even love. He made her feel young and alive again in her deadened world of investigating death.

You piece of shit! I see a glimmer of a diamond ring, bouncing off a wall. Not Detective Robbins'. Another woman's. So the hot stud was cheating too. Bummer.

A fucking traffic warden? I can hear echoes of Detective Robbin's incredulous voice during her demotion, which is why she's here at an emergency care center, investigating my car accident.

"Miss Eastland? Can you answer the question?"

"Sorry, what was the question?"

"Miss Eastland, we're dealing with a hit and run here. That's illegal in the State of California. The vehicle in question was observed by a neighbor, but he couldn't make out any numbers. Did you see anything? Anything that might help us identify the owner?"

"Yes, I saw a red SUV drive away. A red SUV that belongs to someone named Denise Livingston."

Detective Robbins jots down some notes. "Is there anything you can tell me about this Denise Livingston? Anything that might explain why she drove you into a tree?"

Mom looks at me, her eyes wide, and she's jerking her head ever so slightly in the direction of Detective Robbins. I know exactly what she's saying: *Speak!*

Robbins tilts her head to the side. She's listening. I pull in a big breath, trying to tamp down a rush of adrenaline as I step off the precipice of 'officially involving law enforcement,' and glance over at Mom, who's nodding with encouragement.

"Officer Robbins, I believe something bad is going to happen to someone."

"Okay . . ." Robbins glances over at Mom and back to me. "Are we talking about a bad hair day or what?"

"I'm talking about an untimely end."

"Homicide or suicide?" Detective Robbins asks, sectioning the information into the right bucket. Her blunt dealing with the matter gives me confidence. She's taking me seriously. Maybe she can help, without officially helping. Maybe she can stop Erin.

"I think someone is planning the perfect murder. And I'm trying to stop it from happening again."

"Again?" she asks, raising her eyebrows.

"She got off the first time. Walked free because she made it look like self-defense."

Detective Robbins narrows her eyes and glances away, evaluating. Then she meets my gaze. "How do you know she made the murder look like self-defense?"

I pause, hoping that Detective Robbins doesn't try to arrest me for the crime of reading her mind. "I know . . . kind of like I just know that you were demoted down to a 'traffic warden'." I do the finger brackets around 'traffic warden'—her words, not mine.

I look straight into her eyes, gauging her reaction, waiting to see if she wants me to announce the details. But she blinks a few times, astonished, registering the information, and looks away. *No*, she's saying, *don't say it.*

"Can you look into Denise somehow?" I ask. "Or her pseudonym Erin Lazarus? Or warn her soon-to-be-victim? Dan Evans?"

"Her soon-to-be victim? Miss Eastland, this isn't Minority Report. We deal with facts and facts only. That means the crime has to *have occurred*, before we can get involved."

I look away, deflated. This is exactly what I thought would happen. I give Mom a look. *Told ya so.*

"I'll be in touch regarding the traffic accident investigation." Detective Robbins pulls a business card out from the back flap of her notebook and hands it to me. "And if you happen to come across some verifiable facts about this crime yet to occur, please do contact me."

"Okay, thank you," I say, handing the card to mom. What a waste of time.

Detective Robbins turns to go, sweeping the curtain aside, but then she pauses, hand on the curtain edge. Mom and I exchange glances. Robbins returns to my bedside, fixing her impassive blue eyes on mine.

"I can't promise anything," she says in a low voice, "and my clearance isn't what it used to be . . ." She glances over her shoulder and back to me, leaning in close. "But I'll look into Denise Livingston. And see what I can find."

CHAPTER 32

BRYNN

Erin arrives far sooner than I had hoped. There's the usual flurry of text messages, directing her to the right spot, advising her about where to park, letting me know that she's 'close' and then 'right outside' as my heartbeat rises with sickening dread.

All the while, I'm trying to soften the hard edge of regret that I allowed the Clouseaus dictate my evening. Why did I let them invite Erin over?

Because I'm nice. Well, I'm getting really tired of being *nice*.

I also don't want to hear about her burglary, mostly because I'll have to provide a sympathetic shoulder on which to cry. I'm not feeling very sympathetic. I'm feeling angry because she possibly spied on me and uneasy as if the ground is moving in a slow motion circular pattern under my feet. I can't shake the horrible flashback of that night we all partied and Dan supposedly rearranged her facial features.

But she seemed so rattled on the phone, and clearly she's all alone. Somehow she promoted me to the best friend position in her life. I'm wondering why she called me, when she really should have called someone else. Then I see her walk through the entrance doors, searching for me.

I wave my arm over my head, and she walks over, smiling and looking relieved to see me.

As she makes her way over, I see that she's wearing jeans, a t-shirt, and some white sneakers. Her hair is pulled back in homely looking ponytail. Her cheeks are ruddy, her eyes glassy. I can tell she's been crying.

I feel a twinge of regret for pegging her as a boyfriend-stealing vixen. She doesn't seem to have the confidence needed to carry out such a devious deed, but that doesn't change the fact that she peeped through my windows like a creep, I think, and accused my boyfriend of beating her up.

I elbow Tiffany, who elbows Jaime, and there we stand, ready to receive the new addition.

When I introduce Erin, I carefully avoid adding on the amendment to her name—Dan's ex—and wait on pins and needles for Tiffany to make a foot-in-mouth comment, but she gives Erin a welcoming hug instead.

Dan would kill me if he found out that I went out with his ex again. I look around, trying to spot anyone that I know. Thankfully, I see only strangers.

"Wow," I say. "You got here fast."

Jaime slyly steps on my toes. I keep my smile fastened on tight.

"Yeah, I tend to drive too fast." Erin looks a little rattled. "So, what is everyone drinking? Can I buy us a bottle of wine?"

Well, that's nice of her, even if she was looking in my window. Buying drinks is always regulated. My turn, your turn, my turn, your turn, mostly because everyone is marginally broke, chronically short of discretionary clamshells, yoga teachers especially.

But Erin doesn't seem to have the same monetary restrictions as us regular folk. I had no idea painting nails could be so lucrative. Maybe I'm in the wrong business.

Jaime and Tiffany talk to each other, while Erin orders an expensive bottle.

"Oh hey," Erin says, ordering complete, and reaches into her purse. "I have something for you."

"Me?" I ask, taken aback. She hands me a cream jewelry box topped with a pretty red bow.

"Oh wow. You didn't have to bring me anything!" And suddenly I feel like a shoe heel for not wanting to invite her out. Tiffany catches my eye, looking at the box and then back at me as if to say: see what being a *friend* will get you?

"Oh, it's nothing," Erin says, waving her hand. "I just saw it and thought you'd like it."

212

I open the box and find a rutilated quartz bracelet, each bead faceted and glimmering in the low light. It's delicate and expensive looking, and I really like it. Erin helps me put it on.

"Aw. How thoughtful," says Jaime.

"Thank you," I say to Erin with a warm smile and glance down at my bracelet.

The wine bottle arrives, nestled in a bucket of ice. I busy myself with pouring out four glasses, just a splash for me—I need to stay sober for another night out with Erin—and an extra full glass for her. She needs it. Maybe Tiffany is right. What's the matter with me? Maybe I inherited the gene allele SCRGE, Scrooge not scourge. Though lately, I'm not so sure.

Jaime pipes up. "So Brynn says someone broke into your house?"

"Here you go, hon," I say, handing Erin a very full glass. And dole out the rest of the glasses to Jaime, myself, and Tiffany, who has her eyes locked on Erin, listening oh so intently.

"Yeah, so I got home," Erin says, "and it was really weird because I walked inside and kind of felt like something was wrong, but I didn't even think that someone was actually in my house, you know? I mean, that sort of stuff happens in movies, not real life."

Jaime shares a similar tale of 'stuff that happens in movies,' which she never tires of talking about: a car accident—nothing major, just a newsworthy event worth dissecting.

"No way! The same thing happened to me," cries Erin. They bond over that for a while, but good ole Tiffany, hot on the heels of my would-be shtalker, starts pinning down times. "So what time did you say you got home?"

"It wasn't that late, that's why it was so weird. Probably around eight or eight thirty?"

I look at Jaime, who looks right back at me. That's when I found my stalker, who is clearly not Erin, standing outside my window.

While they all bond over movie matters (Tiffany shares a story that I'd never heard before about catching her boyfriend in bed with another guy). "Oh, I suspected," Tiff says. "I just didn't want to believe it."

I look at Erin, Jaime, and Tiffany talking, sharing their incredible, unbelievable stories and bonding over things that *actually happened*. Is Dan's crazy ex-girlfriend really a part of my friend circle now?

"So tell us about the burglary," Jaime says.

"So I heard someone rummaging around upstairs in the back bedroom," Erin continues. "Little creaks here and there. Footsteps, you know?"

Jaime and Tiffany are riveted. They remind me of an old couple sitting in a movie theater, clutching onto one another, eating popcorn, watching the horrible scene unfold, waiting for the baddie to pop out as the hapless main character creeps around an empty house, calling out: *hello? hello?*

"Then what happened?" Tiffany asks.

Jaime's hand travels up to her mouth in anticipation.

"So I hid in the downstairs closet and waited for him to leave. It was horrifying."

"That's crazy," says Jaime.

"Unbelievable," murmurs Tiffany.

Then Jaime reaches for Erin's hand, her face a picture of compassion, and cries. "Oh, you poor thing!"

"Aw, thank you," Erin says, tilting her head slightly.

I want to hate her so bad. I haven't felt so torn in my life. I don't want anything to do with Erin. But the thing is, I feel sorry for her. And the hell of it is—I honestly don't know if Dan beat her senseless or not.

"Someone was looking in Brynn's window tonight," Jaime volunteers.

Erin gasps, puts her hand over her mouth, and looks at me, eyes huge with alarm. "Do you think someone is targeting us both?"

"That's ridiculous," Jaime barks.

Tiffany agrees. "Totally ridiculous."

While the conversational train chugs on to other topics, I can't shake the buzz of low-level anxiety.

Is someone out to get us both?

CHAPTER 33

BRYNN

Do you think someone is targeting us both? Erin's words from last night echo in my mind. Try as I might, I cannot escape the scary undercurrent that someone is out to get us.

Is someone after me? And why, exactly? There's a modicum of logic in there somewhere. I think. If both her burglary and my Peeping Tom were random crimes, what are the odds that the two events happened at the same time to two people who roughly know each other?

It would take some sort of criminal organization to "target" us both at the same time, wouldn't it? Who are we dealing with here—the mafia? KGB? And why? Why would someone do that?

Suddenly my nervousness about this 'targeting' business comes crashing down like a house of cards. Both crimes were random. It doesn't make any sense that someone would target us both. The only thing I know for certain is that Erin wasn't peeping in my windows. Somehow, this seems to be the only thing that matters.

The sun breaks through Jaime's thin front room curtains, but I'm glad to see the light of day. I sling my arm over my eyes, trying to solve one of the original riddles. Who was looking in my window? And why? Bear shuffles around down by my feet. I roll over and bury my face in the soft cushions of Jaime's couch. I'm not feeling one hundred percent, but at least I'm functioning.

Stress is taking a toll. I roll onto my back and stare up at the ceiling, my feet propped up on Bear's rump, thinking over last night. I remember Erin and Tiffany bonded over something unbearably funny to them; I had no idea what. At some point, I found myself sitting on the outer circle of hilarity, wondering if Erin was stealing my friends from under my nose.

But then she reached out and draped her arm around my shoulders, smiling over at me, making me feel petty and shallow for thinking such thoughts. She's beguiling, that one. And sweet. I feel a pang of sympathy for her.

Snippets from last night float up to the forefront of my mind. I remember Erin telling us she had an abusive ex-boyfriend. Dan? Did she mean Dan? No, his name was Steve or Chris or something. So not Dan.

Finally she managed to leave him, but then he started stalking her, showing up at her work and home. I remember Tiffany's sad face as she reached out and squeezed Erin's hand.

I remember thinking that Erin has had an awful lot of trauma in her life. She must be so brave. She's a picture of survival itself, someone who really does deserve sympathy. I'm happy that we could help her out in her moment of need. Now, I hope she'll go away.

"Hey," Jaime says, wandering into the living room in her cat pajamas. She yawns and sits down by my feet, ruffling the fur on Bear's head. "How are you feeling?"

"I'm okay," I say, rubbing my eyes. "I could use a coffee though."

"I could use a Bloody Mary."

"Ouf. Not me."

Jaime shrugs. "Hair of dog? Best yoga pose ever." And we both chuckle.

"Get showered. Tiffany and Erin are going to meet us at Surfside Cafe."

"Tiffany and Erin?" I ask, a little surprised.

"Yeah. She stayed at Tiffany's house last night. Because Chez Jaime is all full up."

Tiffany doesn't normally do couch-overs.

"What are we—best friends forever? We hardly know her."

"What are we—twelve? C'mon. It's just breakfast."

Surfside is a manky establishment that boasts a convenient beachside location, old upholstered banquet chairs, and chipped tables. The glasses are mostly clean, but the groggy clientele don't seem to notice. Our dearly beloved Surfside has been running on financial fumes for some time now.

I'm a little reluctant to hang out with Erin under the bright, glaring light of day. The last time that happened, she produced a picture of her smashed face.

It's a topic that I don't want to talk about ever again because it tinges the water around us with a faint hue of blood. To stem the flow would mean talking about it, and I want to pretend it never happened.

Erin and Tiffany both sport crumpled clothes and messy buns. They almost look like an old couple, if I didn't know the details. Tiffany spent the night riveted by Erin, oohing and awwing over the poor thing, and isn't she so strong? *You're the strongest person I know.*

Aw.

"Hey," I say to no one in particular as I sit down, avoiding eye contact with Erin. I so want to hate Erin. She's Dan's ex, one. She's stealing my friends, two. And give me a few seconds so I can think of three and four.

I feel a hand on my forearm. "How are you feeling?" comes Erin's warm voice, soft and vulnerable. Suddenly I recall something that she told us last night. *I lived in a shelter for a little while, after my mom died. Some girls in high school found out. They used to call me Shelter Girl.*

Shelter Girl. How awful. Maybe Jaime is right. Maybe I'm not twelve years old. Maybe I'm just a bad person.

"I'm doing good," I say, looking at her and smiling.

We order. I skip the round of Bloody Marys. My pancakes arrive, a great big mountain of them, topped with a patty of butter and no syrup. It's carb overload, and I feel a little sleepy afterwards, so I lean back, listening to Erin, Jaime, and Tiffany talk about the minutiae of last night, helping each other piece together the same picture. I zone out, wondering if Erin is going to drive home afterwards or go back to Tiffany's house and move in forever.

Then I hear Jaime say, "Brynn is staying with me."

"I think I'm going to go back home today," I say, reaching down and massaging my lower back. "I have to buy a few things at Home Depot, replace the outside flood light, stuff like that. I think I'll be okay."

"Why don't I help you out?" Erin says. "It's no trouble at all."

Seems like a decent idea, but a really bad one at the same time. Before I can deliberate and/or think of a reason to say no, Jaime says, "Oh, that's so sweet of you!"

And I find myself in Erin's car after breakfast, driving to Home Depot.

CHAPTER 34

BRYNN

Strange days. Strange days indeed. Dan would explode in a ball of fury if he found out about my new friend. Surprise! It's your ex! Isn't that weird? I'm not entirely feeling like myself these days.

I feel like I'm living in some strange surreal world where my new bestie is Dan's crazy ex, but I'm starting to think that maybe I've been living with the crazy person all along.

Erin and I did my Home Depot run, replaced the outdoor floodlight, and put up better blinds. Erin was helpful and beyond generous. She offered to pay for everything even though her SUV needs some bodywork—that accident she mentioned last night, similar to Jaime's bumper cars episode, except Erin's SUV has significantly more damage. Erin said she's still waiting on the insurance company to pay out, but I couldn't bring myself to let her pay for security enhancements on Dan's house. That just seemed so wrong.

"He hit me," Erin says in a soft voice. Not Dan, thankfully, I remind myself. We're sitting in the front room, talking. She hugs a big velvet throw pillow, recalling her harrowing relationship with her ex-boyfriend, Chris, all the while I'm thinking about Dan.

Her long white-blonde hair is pulled around one shoulder. The slightly bulbous tip of her nose wiggles a little when she talks as sunlight falls into her brown-flecked eyes.

I've never known a victim of domestic abuse before. It all seems so foreign to me, loving someone, but getting beat up by that someone. I have googled it, however, when an acquaintance of mine posted her story of survivorship on Instagram of all places.

Is there a history that predisposes women to fall for abusers? Some sort of hardwiring gone wrong or something? Because after what happened with Dan, this is appearing to be a theme with her. Did I just take her side?

"It all started out so amazing. So perfect. Like soul mates perfect. I felt like we were meant to be." Erin's talking about her abusive ex, but I can't help but draw parallels to my relationship with Dan. "He was so attentive and yeah,"—she shrugs—"he was a little possessive. But you know I thought that was refreshing. I'd dated people before who literally had no clue. I mean, they just didn't care. I had one boyfriend who never even looked up from his computer after I got out of the shower."

"No." I honestly couldn't imagine. Dan has laser beam eyes, pre and post shower.

"So when Chris was very interested in where I was going and with who, I kind of liked it. I felt like he *cared*, you know? But then . . . I remember the first time he hit me." She looks up at the ceiling and blinks a few times as if she's trying to hold back tears. I'm horrified and riveted by her story. Is this my future?

"Then what happened?" I ask.

"So I left. But Chris tracked me down and convinced me to come back. He said he loved me and he was so sorry. He said he'd never do it again. His dad beat him up when he was a kid and he wanted to break the cycle of abuse. I wanted to help him through it so that we could grow stronger and better together. You know?" She looks at me, her eyes swimming in unspent tears. Then she laughs ruefully and wipes her right eye. "I can't believe I was so gullible."

"You can't blame yourself," I say, hoping that's the right thing to say. I really don't know.

"But when these things happen," Erin says, "you can't help but look at yourself and wonder how you got there. My therapist says that it's good to look at yourself, even if it is like looking in a broken mirror."

"I guess that's a good place to start."

Erin falls silent. She plays with the tassels on a throw pillow, her blood red polish glinting in the light drifting in from the bay window.

"Then what happened?" I ask.

"Well, then he—he put me on medication."

My mouth drops open with shock. "He *drugged* you?"

"No, not exactly. Well, I don't know. Maybe. I started off on stuff like Xanax because I was really having a hard time coping with everything, you know?"

"Of course."

"But the pills my ex gave me made me feel strange and disassociated. And when he was at work one day, I upended the house until I found the vial . . ." She meets my gaze. "It was an anti-psychotic medication."

"Holy *shit.*"

"Yeah . . ."

"What does that even do to you?"

"It just makes you feel really loopy. Like you're spaced out and stuck in some strange time warp."

"Sounds unpleasant."

"And then the drug wears off and you feel like road kill."

"Ouch."

"Yeah, it's a really vicious cycle. I wouldn't recommend it. So I pretended to take the pills, but I just spat them out when he left. I guess looking back, going cold turkey probably wasn't the best way to handle everything, but I just wanted to be able to think straight and figure out what to do. And that's when our relationship really fell apart."

"Mmhm."

"I thought he wanted to help me." The venom in her hard eyes makes my stomach turn. "But he only wanted my money."

"Wow." I don't trust myself to speak, afraid that I'll say the wrong thing. Where did she get all her money anyway? I want to ask, but that's off topic. "So how did it end? I mean, is he still around?"

She looks down. "No," she says, almost wistfully. "He's gone . . ." She runs her tongue over her incisor and nods definitively like she's decided on the matter. "He's out of my life forever."

I want to ask about this forever part. Does she mean a permanent restraining order? Did the guy move overseas? Find another victim? I'm trying to formulate my next question without sounding like an investigative journalist, when she looks up at me through her eyelashes.

"Do you remember anything that happened that night we all went out?"

That night. The mere mention of it makes my blood run cold.

"I mean, did you see anything?" she clarifies.

I shake my head. "No. I just know that you and Dan . . . went somewhere and you . . . caught it on tape, so to speak."

I hadn't forgotten. The mere existence of the recording gives me cold sweats and sleepless nights.

"Yeah, I got in the habit of recording everything because of the Chris ordeal. That's what I call it, anyway. Recording became an automatic reaction."

"How do you even do that?" I ask, wondering.

She pulls out her iPhone with its winking bejeweled case. "It's super easy. There's an app pre-installed on every iPhone, called voice memos."

"Really?" I pull out mine.

"It's hidden right there in the extras folder." Lo and behold there it is. I open up the folder, then the app, and push the big red record button. The seconds run along a ticker timeline, squiggles marking the audio. "You can return to your home screen and turn off your phone. The app will continue recording."

I try it, clicking the side button on my phone. The screen goes black. Then I wake up my phone again and go back to the app. There it is. Recording away.

"Very sneaky!"

Erin demurs. "Yeah, there you go. So if you're ever walking into an iffy situation, just start recording. Make sure the microphone is pointing out though. I slide my phone into my bra. I call it my braket, my bra pocket. Plus, you get a nice lift." She laughs a little and slips her phone into her bra, nestled to the side. I can see the very bottom of her phone, microphone perfectly positioned to catch a nice clean stream of audio. "Voilà."

But then my heart sinks. So that's exactly how she recorded her tussle with Dan. The thought of Dan roughing up Erin takes me back to the police incident report. And it occurs to me that Erin has the answers I have desperately sought.

My stomach twists just thinking about bringing up the topic. But I need to know. I readjust my position on the couch and take in a big breath. "Hey . . . Erin?"

"Yeah?"

"It's kind of an awkward subject, and—and if you don't want to talk about it, I completely understand. But I found a police incident report about something that had happened between you and Dan. A domestic abuse problem? It was a two-page narrative. Unfortunately, I can't find the conclusion." Then I wait, holding my breath, but Erin doesn't reply. "So what happened, if you don't mind me asking?"

"What did it say?" she asks, eyes wide. "I mean, you said you only read some of the narrative . . ."

"It said that Dan was agitated and placed in a squad car."

My eyes sting. It's the precursor of tears, but I blink them away. *Buck up, Brynn. Just get the damn facts.*

Erin lets out a big breath, and folds her hands in her lap, recollecting, probably, the terrible event. Then she lifts her chin and meets my gaze, her eyelids dropping into a glower. "Yes, he was placed in the back of a police car. The cops wanted to arrest him." She pauses. "Are you sure you want to hear this?"

I look away and nod, praying I can take it. "He chucked a wine bottle at me and missed, thank God. Then we argued. He roughed me up a little,"—she motions to her forearms. "And he begged me not to press charges."

Wow. I don't even dare speak. Dan, my beautiful tender Dan, is not who I thought he was. And then a surge of relief washes over me as I realize that I dodged a bullet, followed by a stark slap of reality. If what Erin says is true, then I would have been next.

Abusers don't change. Leopards and their stripes or spots or whatever. People don't change. If Erin hadn't reached out to me, it would have been only a matter of time before the cops rocked up to this house and placed Dan in the back of a squad car. Wouldn't it?

Even as I think these words, there's a stirring deep inside of me that makes me hesitate and doubt. I can't reconcile the man that I know with the man that Erin describes. They're like two different people. My Dan and her Dan. Which one is the real guy? And if my Dan is the real Dan, then he's innocent. But why is he so cagey about *that night*?

Erin adjusts the pillow on her lap. "You probably never want to think about that night again—that night we all went out. But I know you want answers . . ."

"Yeah, I do."

Erin smiles sadly. "It's hard. I get it. I've been there. My therapist said to me once that if you hear or see something from the event in question, sometimes memories come back to you. That happened to me when I was trying to piece together some things that had happened with Chris. It's like your brain shuts down around that trauma, but sometimes you can trigger it to open back up, so to speak."

I'd never thought of that. Maybe I did see something, but my mind blotted it out.

"And I totally understand if you never want to think of it again, but you must wonder if Dan actually . . . hurt me, right? Maybe you think I'm lying?"

"No," I say, jumping to her defense. "No I don't think that at all." Yes, I absolutely do.

"It's completely natural." And there she is, making me feel better again.

We sit in a silence for a few seconds. "Okay," I admit, "I do wonder what really happened."

She doesn't seem offended or hurt. She seems pragmatic and confident in the result. "You know I have a recording from that night. And if you ever want to listen . . ."

I hold up my hand. "No. I can't. Not now."

She shrugs. "No big deal. I'll just text you the recording. And if you ever feel like you're ready to listen, then it's there for you."

And by the time she leaves, I've already decided that I want to listen to the audio clip. I want to try and look in the broken mirror.

CHAPTER 35

BRYNN

Later that night, Erin sends through the audio file with the following text message:

Here you go, hon.

The thought of listening to the audio clip that she recorded the night of Dan's farewell party fills me with dread. Will listening to it trigger any memories? I don't know, but I need to find the answer because this uncertainty is pulling on the very last thread that's holding me together.

I have to get to the bottom of this. Did Dan beat up Erin or not? Being in two minds have never been so devastating. Deep down, I cannot actually believe that Dan hurt Erin. I don't believe that the man I love is capable of any violence against a woman. Yes, he has a short temper. Does that make him guilty?

But all the verifiable facts are pointing to his guilt: his cagey behavior, his aggression on the phone, dodging my questions, and stonewalling. Then there's the police incident report stating that Erin had marks on her arms, along with her testimony saying the same, and the fact that they placed him in the back of a squad car. There's the photo, a recording, and Dan's physical advantage.

She must weigh all of one hundred and fifteen pounds. Plus, she's not exactly muscular. I would call her skinny-fat, the type of girl that doesn't need to work out because she looks good anyway. Models are like that, so they claim, until one of them crashes out of the fashion world and writes her lettuce-eating memoir.

I walk to the kitchen, trying to calm the nervous fluttering in my stomach, and pour myself a glass of wine. I should be bigger than my problem, and handle it unaided, but I'm barely hanging on to my sanity right now. I need all the help that I can get.

I sit down on the couch, phone in one hand and glass of wine in the other, wondering if listening to the voice recording will trigger any memories. Has the answer been buried deep inside me all along?

Bear hops up on the couch and lies down next to me. They say dogs and cats are so different, but neither misses the opportunity to get their rump scratched, Bear included. I reach over and pat his back, while he swishes his fluffy tail in my face, his pink tongue lolling out of his mouth. He may not be the brightest spark, but he's friendly and cuddly. And that's all I need right now.

I push his tail out of my face, swallow some wine, and set my glass down on the coffee table. Then I put my phone on the armrest and pull up the audio. It's a black screen with a gray triangle. All I have to do is push "play" ...

I hear a sound of fabric scratching against the microphone and the distant booming bass of the nightclub music. I close my eyes as memories from that terrible night swirl in my mind as fleeting as snowflakes, carrying me back to the night of Dan's D-day party. The night that I want to forget, but can't quite remember. Fragments come rushing back to me, flashes of ragged memories that don't quite fit together.

I remember bright strobe lights and women dancing in cages hung from the ceiling. I think we crashed a Very Important People party. Snippets of a conversation float up like a waterlogged body in a murky pond.

What are you—a human trafficker?

Ha ha ha!

Geez. Who were those people?

I remember the dance floor. And the wraith. I remember the wraith. What happened exactly? He tried to kiss me.

I pause the recording.

Ugh. This is like an out of body experience. My heart is thumping out of my chest. I didn't listen to the audio recording to relive that awful memory. I pull in some deep breaths, trying not to make myself dizzy. And exhale a long breath that I didn't realize I was holding.

Okay, I feel calmer, not quite better, but capable of carrying on. So I push play again.

A door slams shut, blocking out the deep beats of the music.

"What do you want?" I hear Dan say. The sound of his voice makes my heart race. He's slurring a little bit, his mouth sounds like it's full of cotton balls.

I think back to the handful of times I'd seen him drunk. I recall Super Bowl Sunday in particular. He drank the entire day non-stop and still seemed stone cold sober. I remember marveling at how well he could handle his booze. How did he get so drunk the night of his send off?

There's a cut in the audio stream. Then the sound returns, quieter now. For one horrible second, I think I can hear Erin breathing fast. Dear God, not that. I think I'm going to be sick, but it's not that—it's . . .

It's coming back to me in a rush. That night.

I remember pushing an exit door open and looking out across an empty parking lot. There was a black SUV parked out there. A Beemer. The memory stabs through the veil of my subconscious mind like a dagger. And suddenly I remember. I remember it all. I remember seeing the reflection of Erin's blonde hair in the mirror-black hood of the vehicle.

And I remember Dan shaking Erin, his hands gripping her shoulders. And when I hear her cry out—"Stop, Dan! Stop!"—I break down in tears.

CHAPTER 36

BRYNN

Monday morning dawned with depressing overcast skies and drizzle, apropos to how I felt inside. I drove to the local police precinct so that I could give them my statement. Tell them what I remembered. I felt that was the right thing to do. Tell them my truth.

I sat in a soulless room with no windows across the table from an older cop, who looked like he hadn't seen a day of physical activity since Christ walked the dry hills of Jerusalem.

I expected fast-acting police detectives, ready to whisk me into a shiny interrogation room with mirrored windows and listen to my testimony with sharp interest. *Yes? And then what happened*? For some reason, I thought my case would be escalated to the top brass. But it was surprisingly anti-climatic. A bit dull. Filled with lots of paper pushing. I wondered why I had bothered.

The cop asked me impersonal questions, taking notes on a yellow legal pad, while my mind drifted to Erin. She had taken the high road by not pressing charges. Instead, she came to me and told me what had happened because she's a good person and wanted to warn me. She was thinking about *me*.

I had thanked her by treating her with contempt, at first, followed by suspicion and an arm's length friendship. In the middle of the questioning, I glanced down at the delicate bracelet she had given me, feeling a twinge of guilt.

He asked me more questions that raised my hackles. *How do you know it was her? How much did you say you had to drink again . . . ?*

As I sat there regurgitating my memories from That Night, I felt myself slipping into an existential crisis. How could I "know in my bones" that Dan is innocent? *Know thyself.* Well, it's clear that I don't know the first flaming thing about myself! And if I can't trust my own instincts, who or what can I trust?

It's so bewildering to know that I have nobody to lean on, not even myself, that my own intuition about Dan's innocence completely failed me.

Was I so blinded by love that I couldn't see Dan's true character? I don't know. All I know is that I loved him desperately. Now, I hate him desperately. And I hate myself, too, for blithely ignoring his black box of a past. And I'm angry with Dan for dumping this on me right before his deployment.

The old cop with breath smelling of stale coffee and breath mints finished up his case study written in long hand and stapled it to a form. He promised to type up his report and hand it over to the "right department." He said they'd be in touch if they have any follow up questions. So I drove home in a fog, nursing an aching heart and a numb feeling of utter disbelief. I can't believe I believed Dan.

I need to talk to him now and tell him that I know the terrible truth, but all I have is email. It's not ideal, but it will have to do. I sit down on the couch and open my laptop. It's a clunky old Dell that I bought second hand at a local computer shop.

There's the spinning ball, doing its little wiggle dance as the computer slowly boots up. I head to the kitchen for some water, and by the time I've returned, the welcome screen flashes.

I fire up my email program, but my fingers pause over the keyboard. What if he reads my email right before a mission and gets distracted and then hurt? But the United States isn't at war officially, I remind myself. They probably trot the boys off to "missions" to keep them active.

Besides, he's a big guy. He beats up women, small innocent ones at that. He can take a little email.

First stop, the subject line: Liar.

Then I get right to the point.

I know what you did that night. I know you beat up Erin. You're a sad excuse of a man. You're not even a man. You're a walking dick with four appendages. Yeah, I found out. I remembered. How about them apples?

Little drunky-pants Brynn heard the audio that Erin had recorded and it all came rushing back to me like a terrible tsunami. Clarifying remembrances about how you shook Erin in that parking lot.

And you know what I've been thinking? I've been thinking that Erin was kind enough not to tell the police. But I'm not that kind. Do you know why? Because I had a friend in college, who got beat to hell, probably by one of your fraternity brothers. And it ruined her life. You see, women, we blame ourselves.

So I went to the police, you pathetic mealworm. I gave them my statement. You're not going to ruin another woman's life. Not on my watch.

My shaking finger hovers over the send button, while my heart beats high and fast in my throat. Mom's wise words rise to the forefront of my mind. *Write that terrible letter, but don't send it.*

Send or not send. I re-read my missive, and the word *beat* leaps out at me followed by: *not on my watch.*

"Yep," I say to myself, resolved about it. "Not on my watch." And I hit send.

I pull in a long calming breath, even though I feel sick to my stomach, and close my eyes. A hint of peace washes over me as I envision my electronic letter traveling under the great depths of the ocean, scurrying along thick fiber optic cables, and rushing straight up to the military servers, where it will sit for who knows how long before Dan logs in and retrieves it.

I pull in some deep breaths, trying to relax and make me feel better.

Except, I don't feel better. A deep gnawing pit of anxiety opens up in my belly, while I think about my black dove letter, fluttering over to its target.

Maybe I was a tad too harsh. Regret washes over me. Maybe my mom was right. Maybe I shouldn't have sent it. I should have waited until he got home so that I could tell him to his face. In the meantime, I could help Erin by supporting her. What's the big rush anyway?

Now, I'm definitely sick with regret. I shouldn't have sent the email. I grab my laptop and sit down at the dining table. Maybe the email is sitting in my outbox. Maybe I can cancel it.

I open up my email program. First stop: the outbox. Nothing. I look at my sent folder. And there it is. My stomach drops.

It's gone. My black dove is flying off to greet him like a punch to the gut. There's nothing I can do about it now. Is there? I google 'delete sent email' and read the offerings.

There are a lot of technical people, describing the ins and outs of email configuration. There are YouTube videos on how to retract emails, but none of the known methods apply to me. I'm reading an article that looks somewhat helpful, when a little notification bubble pops up on the upper right hand corner of my screen.

I have mail. I double-click on the bubble as tingles of dread race over my skin.

Re: Liar.

What remembrances?? What did you fucking remember? Because it had nothing to do with me! Hey don't you worry about going to the police. Erin beat you to it. They're in the process of pulling me out. I'll be on the first comm flight home so I can face the music. Don't worry about picking me up. I'll find my own way home.

He didn't even bother to sign off.

Slowly, I close my laptop. Comm flight. They're sending him home on a commercial airline. I breathe out. This is bad. Real bad. Face the music? Is he getting discharged from the military?

No, I don't think it happens that quickly. He'll have to go through a military tribunal, maybe spend some quality time in a brig, while they assemble a case against him.

Well, one thing is for certain. We'll need a criminal attorney now, won't we? *We*? I think to myself, pacing the front room.

"Who is *we*," I mutter to myself. This is Dan's problem. He did this all by himself. Except, I'm involved too. I'm a witness to the crime. Or rather, part of the crime.

My mind flashes to the coming courtroom scene, to the bank of jurors, looking at me dubiously as the prosecution tears my testimony to shreds.

"And how many drinks would you say you had that night, Miss Masters?"

Too many. Too many to count...

But Erin went to the police. She must have pressed charges because Dan's on his way home. I'm stunned. And I'm angry. I thought she took the high road by telling me about what had happened. Did I read her wrong all along? Seems like she should have at least told me, since I'm dating the accused. This is like climbing a set of stairs and one rung gives underfoot. Is just a one-off? Or is every stair rotten?

I need to get to the bottom of this. Why did she go to the police, and when was she planning on telling me? It feels like a betrayal, even though I went to the police too. It's just that—what is it?

I feel like she's playing a double game. That's what it is. I don't know what she's doing, but her secret salvo has left me feeling that she working for her own interests—not mine like I was lead to believe.

Because if he did this to me, he'll do it to you...

I believed her. Now, with her motives called into question, I'm not so sure. I have to talk to her. I have to confront her. Prickles of dread race over my skin just thinking about it.

I don't have a steel-lined stomach. I tend to avoid confrontations at all costs, and I hate myself for it. I hate feeling weak. Why can't I just be strong and combative? Because I'm too *nice*. Well, that's about to change.

I'm going to call her up. Invite her over. Because I want to see her expression when I tell her that I know. So I can see for myself—what kind of game is she playing?

And whose side is she on?

CHAPTER 37

GIA

It's been three days since the accident. I'm still sore and stiff, but my power Advils are taking the edge off. My nose is still tender, but I'm on the move.

I ditched my cell phone, cutting off any route for Erin to track me, and bought a new one. Then I called my cell phone company, changed my number, and gave out the new number only to Nikki, my mom, and I sent a text message to Detective Robbins.

I made sure to remove my contact details from the Furry Baby website staff section and my LinkedIn account. I told Mom that it's possible her address may have been compromised, so we upgraded the locks on the doors and windows.

It helps that my mom's place is located on the second floor of the apartment complex, so a break-in would be harder to pull off. But I'm not too worried about a break-in. Erin is much smoother than that. And deadlier. I'm worried about devastating online attacks. I'm worried about a second run-in with a tree trunk or dognapping. I'm worried about my job.

After the accident, I decided to my Palomino back in the paddock and give it a rest. Stop with the vigilante justice stuff like Mom said. Except I'm wracked with guilt knowing that I'm not doing anything to stop her. Doing nothing feels safe. It also feels cowardly.

I know that Erin is moving all the pieces into place. I know she's busy entangling her prey in her web. I know she's waiting to strike. And I'm doing nothing to stop her. Wisps of regret roll in like fog.

But what can I do? I can drive back down to Dan's house. But what will I say? And why would someone believe me and my psychic premonitions?

I have only cold, hard facts that are easily justifiable. Denise killed her ex in self-defense—*he was going to kill me!* Denise is Erin—*I had to change my name!* And "Erin" has no record whatsoever—*See? I'm such a good, upstanding citizen.* Yeah, right.

So my hands are tied, and that's probably a good thing. I try to find solace knowing I tried my very best to stop her, but it's a bittersweet feeling, knowing that she's moving forward and I'm laying on the couch, nursing my bruises.

It's Monday afternoon. It's only been three minutes in bureaucracy land, so I'm not expecting a follow up call from Detective Robbins for another few weeks, if at all. By then, it will be too late.

But my phone does ring. It's Detective Robbins, standing outside somewhere, judging by the breeze blowing across her microphone.

"Listen, I just called to let you know that I looked into the Denise Livingston murder. I can't send you any privileged information because, you know, I'm just a traffic warden now. But I found out the name of the victim. His name was Chris Mabray. I'll email you an article that I found."

"Wow. Thanks so much. And her new victim? Is there anything you can do?"

"Like I said, this isn't Minority Report, so law enforcement won't make any moves to apprehend her or investigate her."

My heart sinks.

Wind blows across her microphone, sounding like hollow static. "But if I were you," she says in a voice so low that I strain to hear, "I'd contact the victim's family . . . and look for parallel motives. Look for patterns."

She texted over a photograph taken of an op-ed, a journalist's opinion, clipped out of the Rocky Tribune. She must have found it in the original case file. The journalist included all the basic facts that Nikki and I had already discovered as well as a few that we hadn't. Denise was emotional on the witness stand and cried when the jury read their verdict.

She'd served time in jail, waiting for the court case to be processed through the legal system, a point that her lawyer had brought up, garnering even more sympathy from the jury. And luckily, finally, the poor downtrodden victim, Denise Livingston, was vindicated. Justice had played its noble role in her exoneration.

Right. Let's hope *that* doesn't happen again. For once, it's easy to find someone's phone number. Nikki got the home phone number of Chris Mabray's parents in the short matter of a few hours, followed by some words of warning.

"Are you still involved in this thing? G, I'll dig up one more phone number for you, but that's it, okay?"

"Absolutely," I tell her. "This is my last shot."

Before I cold-call this number, I want to make sure I have all my facts straight so I look over the notes that I'd jotted down the day that I had called the psych ward and spoken to Mandy, putting them together with what I learned from the article Detective Robbins sent me.

Chris Mabray was Denise's last victim. She stabbed him seven times, and somehow made it look like self-defense.

Find the patterns...

I need to figure out what happened with her ex, how she set him up, and warn Dan or the person living in his house, who hopefully knows him, to look for the same method.

With this phone number in hand, I have one more chance to save someone's life. It's just a phone call, I tell myself. Just a chat. If it turns out to be nothing, then so be it. Maybe the number is no longer in service. Maybe nobody will pick up. But if someone does . . . and if that someone says one thing that can turn this around, then it's worth it.

Kill List's short time horizon is ever present in my mind. MOX. Presently, shortly, soon. So I decide to call this evening instead of waiting. I don't know what to expect, but the chances are pretty good that whomever answers won't want to talk to a stranger about their family tragedy. But I have to try.

The call rings out on the first try. A few minutes later I try again, and someone picks up.

"Hello?"

"Oh hi. Hi, my name is Gia Eastland, and—and please don't hang up on me, but I'm calling about Chris Mabray."

Dead silence, except for my own pulse thumping in my ears.

"Who's calling?" The man's tone of voice is curt and officious. He's about to hang up on me if I don't get this right.

"You don't know me, and—"

"Are you a reporter?"

"No, I'm not. I'm calling—"

"Because you guys came nowhere close to reporting the truth. You just picked over the story like carrion crows, trying to satisfy the *viewers at home*, never once thinking that a real family was suffering and had to watch as that monster—"

"Denise Livingston. I know. Her name is Erin Lazarus now. She's setting someone else up. She's doing it again."

I can hear him breathing hard through the phone line. Is he ratcheting up for another rant? Or is he considering my words?

Finally, he speaks. "Who did you say you were again?"

I need to tell him the truth, but I clear my throat because the truth is still a big pill to swallow. I hope he's up for the task.

"A little while ago, Denise Livingston came to the pet shop where I work. I'm a psychic, and I saw something very strange and disturbing. And so I looked into the matter. I know she set up Chris. I know he was innocent. I know she killed him, but she managed to walk free, claiming self-defense. I don't how she set him up exactly. All I know is that she's doing it again—to someone else."

The line falls silent. I wait, listening to my heart thumping in my chest. Was that too much?

Finally he speaks. "My name is Jacob. Chris was my older brother by three years."

A wave of grief washes over me. "I'm so sorry," I say with feeling. He sounds younger now that he's dropped some of his defensiveness. "Can you tell me what happened?" I ask softly.

Jacob sighs. "It didn't make any sense. Chris was a good guy. My mom, she always used to say that she was doing society a favor by raising men, not boys. We were taught from a very young age to respect girls. To open doors for them. Pay for dinner and what not. And to never *ever* touch them, unless we basically had written consent." He makes a sniffling sound. I think he's chuckling, but his voice comes out strangled. "We were the guys at parties, watching out for the drunk ones, you know? Making sure they got home okay."

"So Chris, he didn't have a history of violence at all?"

"Well, I mean there was this one time Chris got into an argument with some chick from school. She was scary, man.

Like, I wouldn't even classify her as a chick. But she hauled off and whacked him. And—and Chris pushed her back. My mom hit the roof and grounded him for a month. It was a defining moment because you better believe that came up in court. Those subhuman pieces of shit prosecutors brought up ancient history, trying to paint Chris as an abuser with a past. But that happened in the tenth grade. It was crazy. I mean, how do those guys live with themselves? Defending the absolute scum of society."

I make a sound of agreement.

"Anyway, he was out at his favorite bar, partying with his friends, and Denise showed up. And about half way through the night, she managed to get him outside, alone, where she proceeded to . . . well. She pushed herself on him. You know what I mean? She wanted to hook up, but Chris didn't want to. She wouldn't take no for an answer. She kept pushing and insisting. So he shoved her away. Then he left. Not thinking much more about it. And a few weeks later she showed up with a picture of her demolished face."

I grip the phone, afraid I'll drop it.

"That's the set up . . ." I say, thinking of Dan. "Party with the victim. Get him hammered. Get him alone. Push him to the brink, and when he pushes back—collect the evidence."

"Oh yeah. That's the stitch up. But it's not 'get him hammered.' It's get him *drugged*."

"Wow."

He breathes out heavily. "She lorded it over him, said she'd ruin his life, blow it to smithereens, press charges, you name it. She wanted his inheritance. It's payback, she told him, for beating her up. Of course she knew about that—the money. She seemed to know everything about Chris before he ever laid eyes on her. And what was he supposed to do? Call her bluff? She had photographic evidence and her phone was recording the whole time, so . . . yeah. You bet she used that against him."

His words send shivers down my arms.

"Denise was nine miles ahead of everyone else. Chris never saw it coming. He was screwed from the word go. She took his money, of course. She said she'd drop the charges when he paid. So Chris wired it over because he wanted it all to go away."

Money. *Of course* it's about money. So that's how Erin bought her business and luxury town house. How many victims are there? Does she shed her identity each time like a molting snake?

"But that's extortion," I say. "That's illegal."

"You try fighting that in a court of law, her arsenal against your pea-shooter. Maybe he would have won the extortion part, but he'd lose the domestic battery case hands down. So it wasn't worth it. He just wanted the whole nightmare to end."

"But it should have ended. He gave her the money. Why didn't she walk away? She got what she wanted."

"Because a walking person is a talking person. She caught wind that Chris was building an extortion case against her. So she called him over to her house. And I suspect she stuck to her playbook. Like you said: push him to the brink, and when he pushes back—collect the evidence. All I know is that she had everything she needed to frame him for attacking her. Then she went in for the kill. Literally."

"Wow. She makes gold diggers look like saints. I can't believe she targets her ex-boyfriends like that."

"What?"

"Ex-boyfriends. She goes after them for money."

Jacob scoffs. "That chick wasn't his girlfriend. He met her on Tinder and he slept with her on the first date like a dolt. They went out a few times afterwards, but he wasn't interested. So she fabricated a 'relationship.' She targeted him. Stalked him. And showed up at the club . . ."

So Erin must have lied to Mandy about her relationship with Chris. Why? To garner sympathy? And what else has she lied about?

"Jacob, I mentioned this before, but Denise has a new victim. She's going to do it again. Setting someone up. It's not going to end well. I think someone is going to die. I need your help to stop her. To finally put her in jail."

"I wish I could help you somehow," he says, at last. "Save some other family the devastation."

"You can help," I say. "And I know exactly how."

CHAPTER 38

DAN

Numbly, I close out my email program, make my way over to my quarters, and start packing. News is slowly filtering through the ranks, but nobody dares talk about it. I can tell by the quick sideways glances that people are strategically avoiding me as if I have Ebola, and they're afraid of catching the contagion.

Getting sent home early from deployment is the stuff of nightmares. But the reason behind my early departure is even worse than a nightmare. Is there even a word for that? Something worse than a nightmare?

Something worse than a nightmare was standing in my Commanding Officer's makeshift office yesterday, listening to him read out the official accusation that Erin made against me, all the while feeling like hellfire was raining down on my head. The sickening words swirled around in my head, making me feel light-headed with disbelief and despair.

Head bashed against a retainer wall . . . Forced to open a condom packet . . .

"Officer Evans, what the fuck is this?" my CO demanded, his face red, holding up a dossier of paperwork.

I struggled to put two words together, pulse thundering in my temples, stunned out of my mind by her accusation. Brynn told me about the photo and the recording, so I knew I had a fake claim about assault dangling over my head.

But—this? *Bashing* Erin's head against a retainer wall? *Forcing* her to open a condom packet? I feel like I've slipped down a dark dank hole that leads to the land of Utter Hopelessness.

"Sir, that is a false accusation, sir," I managed to say.

"Do you have a fucking hermetically sealed alibi that stood there with their nose shoved up your ass at the exact time and date that is event allegedly occurred? Because if you cannot prove you did not, in fact, force this young lady to kindly open a condom packet for you, then we have a real big fucking problem here!"

Of course, I'm innocent until proven guilty. But that's the problem. All the 'proof' points to my guilt. Plus, Erin has an unfair advantage. She's a female.

"Well?" he barked.

"No sir. I do not, sir."

Stone cold silence ensued, followed by some hurried signing of documents and curt mutterings about a flight that will be arranged to send my "pathetic ass" home so that I can handle this civilian matter without the added headache of burdening the United States government with the disposal of my "carcass" should I suffer a catastrophic loss of concentration and lose my life during an operative mission.

So I pack up my bags, feeling like a dead person walking. Because I am a dead person if I don't find a way to defend myself against Erin's thick fiery wave of absolute lies.

And I am going to find a way.

One that stops her dead in her tracks.

CHAPTER 39

GIA

I shouldn't be driving, but I think I'm okay. The bandage on my nose came off, and the doctor was satisfied that I hadn't suffered any permanent brain damage. But as I drive back down to Dan's house, I begin to wonder if I have. I should give myself more time to rest and relax, and all the recovery stuff that the doctor talked about. But I don't have time for that. MOX. *Soon.*

My car rental is a bland gray sedan that looks like millions of other cars on the road, my second one since the accident, just to keep Erin on her toes if she's still tracking me somehow. I keep checking my rear view mirror for signs of her hungry red SUV, barreling down the road toward me.

In my mind, I'm going over the many logical ways that she can't find me. I've changed my cell phone and ditched my car. I'm still on sick leave from work, so Erin can't scope me out from the comfort of her nail salon. And I've hardly left my mom's apartment.

But I suppose where there's a will; there's a way. I'm hoping this is like dealing with would-be home intruder. You can't eliminate the threat entirely, but if you put up enough barriers of resistance, they'll move on to easier prey. And clearly, she has other prey in mind. She might also be banking on her warnings (two now) registering loud and clear. Fortunately or unfortunately, I'm a little hard of hearing.

Most importantly, I have to make absolutely sure she doesn't know that I'm back in action. An hour or so later, I arrive at Dan's house, walk up to the front door and bang on it, loud and clear. I don't want to leave anything open to speculation. Someone is definitely at the door. Open up.

To my surprise, the door opens. A girl with honey brown hair, sun-lightened locks framing her round face, a small upturned nose, and pretty feline shaped teal eyes stands there. She's tall and lithe, her arms toned, but her shoulders slope as if she's carrying a heavy burden.

"Yes?" she asks.

"Yes, hi. Is this Dan Evans's house?"

"Maybe," she says, eyes shrouded. "Who wants to know?"

I glance behind her shoulder at the front room. It's decorated with seashell bric-a-brac, framed pictures of a couple, and the word "love" carved in large block lettering sits on her mantel.

"Do you know Dan personally?" I ask.

"Yes," she says with a lift of her chin. "I'm his girlfriend, Brynn."

My knees weaken with relief. Finally.

"Oh, I'm so glad I found you. I'm trying to get a message to Dan . . . to you both, actually. Do you mind if I come in?"

She seems edgy and reluctant, but she lets me in. I take a seat on her tidy gray couch, more of a perch really, and clamp my hands between my knees. At the other end of the couch, she sits down and looks at me expectantly, knee bouncing.

"Brynn, this is probably going to sound a little strange, but I want to give you a message—a warning, actually, about Dan's ex-girlfriend, Erin."

Brynn's eyes narrow. "Erin Lazarus?"

"You know her?" I ask, while tingles of dread race over my skin.

She shrugs. "Yeah, I've gotten to know her a little bit. How do you know her?"

I feel like I've stepped into quicksand. Erin got to Brynn first. She's one step ahead of me. Of course, she is. I can only hope that Brynn doesn't know Erin well enough to fill her in about my house call.

"So my name is Gia, and I'm psychic." I pause, gauging her reaction. Brynn seems a little dubious, but interested. "When I met Erin, I saw some things that were very disturbing and unusual, probably because most people aren't out trying to kill other people. And—"

"What?"

"That's the message I'm trying to get to Dan. Erin set up and killed someone named Chris Mabray. I believe she's doing it again. To Dan."

Brynn sits there, stunned. I'm thinking this is a good reaction. My news is a lot to take in. She needs time to swallow it all and figure out what she can do protect herself and Dan. Then she speaks, brow furrowed. "Are you sure we're talking about the same person? Small blonde, right?"

"Yeah," I say, nodding. "Erin Lazarus. Even though that's not her real name."

"I'm sorry, but I think you have this all mixed up." Brynn folds her arms and lifts her chin, her back stiff. "Chris was her ex-boyfriend. He was abusive. He *attacked* her."

"Attacked her? No, that's not what happened at all. She attacked *him*. She killed him and set him up to make it look like self-defense."

Brynn waves her hand and scowls. "I don't mean to be rude, but where did you get your information? Through some psychic *premonition*?" I sit back. That stung. Then she softens. "Sorry," she says, looking away. "This has been really hard for me. And after what happened with Dan, I just—I don't know what or who to believe anymore."

After what happened with Dan . . .

"What do you mean?" I ask, alert as a bird dog now. "What happened with Dan?"

I hear tires on the front driveway. A car door slams shut. I hear footsteps on the walkway and up the porch steps. Dan? I can only hope.

256

There's a knock on the door. Brynn gets up and opens it. And in walks Erin.

Suddenly I'm finding it very hard to breathe. I'm up on my feet, ready to fight or flee, I'm not sure which yet.

"Thanks for inviting me over," Erin says to Brynn, walking into the front room, holding a bag full of groceries, eyeing me. "Hey," she says, cocking her head quizzically. "Mining for more info?"

"What?" Brynn asks, glancing at me and back to Erin.

"It's our *stalker*," Erin says. "In the flesh. I told you someone was targeting us. And now we know who."

Brynn looks at me, eyes huge with alarm.

I am definitely getting hot under the collar. "I'm not a stalker! I mean I did knock on your door, but nobody answered, so I—"

"That was you? You *spied* on me?"

"Not on purpose! Your lights went out so I—"

"And she broke into my house," Erin says.

"Are you joking? *Broke* into your house? Cut the victim shit, Denise, and try telling the truth for once."

"Denise?" Brynn asks.

"Yes, Denise. Her real name is Denise Livingston. Look her up. And while you're at it, look into her *victim*, Chris Mabray."

"Tell the *truth*?" Erin screeches. "I'll *show* you the truth." She dumps the grocery bag on the couch and plunges her hand into her purse, but before she can wrangle her phone out, Brynn wheels on her.

"Gia says you killed him. Your ex. Did you lie to me, Erin? About being in an abusive relationship? You said he's out of the picture. Is that because he's . . ."

Yes! Except Erin doesn't miss a beat. "Wow," she says, yanking her phone out of her bag and punching in the lock code. "She told you all that?" A strange temperature gradient envelops me, making me feel both hot and cold at the same time. "Let me help you understand what kind of crazy person we're dealing with here, Brynn."

She pulls something up on her phone, a black window with a grey circular play button. It's a recording. She pushes play, and my voice comes flying out, "You—you *monster*!"

Brynn rounds on me, her eyes bright with anger. She doesn't know whom to trust, but the scales are tipping in Erin's favor.

"She is a monster! She held my *dog* hostage! Who does that?"

"Who breaks into another person's house?" Erin asks rhetorically, pushing play on a video and showing it to Brynn. I move in for a glimpse, feeling the floor is falling out from under me. It's a CCTV clip, clear as day, of me carefully pulling open her side garage door and looking inside. Oh my god. *"Like* I was saying, Brynn, Gia broke into my house."

Neither one of us speaks.

"And let me show you something else, Brynn. I looked into Gia. This is what I found." Oh no. Erin swipes through her photos, looking for something.

Brynn leans closer, so do I.

"Here," Erin says, shoving her phone in front of Brynn's face, who reaches over and expands the image with two fingers.

What is it!

Erin responds, as if hearing my silent plea. "It's your psych ward papers."

"What!" I cry, looking closely at the image for myself. It's the same document that Nikki and I dug up. Except Erin changed the name. And it looks one thousand percent authentic. "Brynn, those are fake. Erin doctored her *own* psych ward papers and put my name on them!"

"Really?" Erin asks Brynn. "Do you really believe that? Did I doctor the burglary video too?"

Suddenly, I'm angry. Angry that Erin is trying to shoehorn into me into the dubious role of a stalker, when *she's* the one ruining people's lives.

"Have you got any video evidence of me actually inside your house, Erin? Surely you've got some proof." She doesn't reply. I turn to Brynn. "That's how she works, Brynn. Smoke and mirrors. Lies and half-truths . . ."

It's clear from the bewildered look in Brynn's eyes that she's back to not knowing what to believe. More importantly, my window of opportunity is about to close. This is my last chance.

"Brynn, we don't have time for this crap. I came here to help you. To stop Erin. You said something happened to Dan. What did you mean? What happened?"

"Time? What do you mean?"

"She means we don't have much time until I call the police and give them my evidence," Erin says.

Heart pounding, I turn to Brynn. "Tell me what happened to Dan!"

Brynn battles her internal conflict (should she believe me, a psychic who supposedly stayed at a psych ward, or Erin, who supposedly killed someone), while the latter stares at me, eyes hard with venom.

But I focus hard on Brynn, pushing my psychic warp drive nozzle to the maximum. *You can do this*, I tell myself, focusing entirely on Brynn, on pulling in a breath, on finally taking control of my ability. *You can do this . . .*

As I step into Brynn's viewpoint, I feel disoriented. In my ears, I hear the deep bass of club music, so loud you can't talk. But people are talking anyway, drinking and dancing and yelling over the deafening music. I see strobe lights and overlays of dry ice fog, spreading over the crowd. She's stumbling somewhere, stumbling after Dan . . .

"Something happened at a club," I say to Brynn quickly. Her eyes lock with mine. "You were drunk. You saw Dan going somewhere . . ." I pause, focusing on the ghostly impressions.

"What a psycho stalker you are!" Erin cries. "Did you follow her that night too?"

"Tell me what you saw, Brynn. Tell me what happened."

Her eyes narrow into slits, becoming hard and brittle with anger as she recalls her memories. "I saw Dan shaking Erin."

Erin folds her arms, supremely satisfied. "See?"

But Jacob's story is front and center in my mind. *That's the set up.* And I'm thinking about Detective Robbins, too, telling me to: *look for the patterns.*

And suddenly it all comes together. The method. Party with the victim. Get him alone. Push him to the brink, and when he pushes back—collect the evidence. Except in this case, Brynn must have stumbled outside and saw the 'pushing back' part of the program, completely missing the context of the entire incident.

"But that's *all* you saw," I say to Brynn. "You never saw Dan hit her. You never saw him beat her up."

Brynn's eyes flood with tears, her hands bunched into fists. "That's all I wanted to see!"

"You didn't see Dan hit her, did you? But Erin showed up with her *evidence* anyway."

"I think you better leave," Erin says.

I turn to Brynn, heart pounding in my chest. "Let me guess. Did she show you a photo of her face smashed to smithereens? Maybe an audio recording, too, just for good measure?"

"How did you know?" Brynn asks softly, stunned, the anger bled from her voice, but tears remain glimmering on her eyelashes.

"Because Gia is an amazing psychic, I mean stalker," Erin sneers.

I don't even acknowledge her. I look into Brynn's glittering eyes. "Because that's exactly what *Erin* did to her last victim." I pull my business card out of my bag with Jacob's number written on the back and press it into her hand. "Call his brother and find out for yourself."

CHAPTER 40

BRYNN

It's official. I'm falling apart. Gia's gone, but I'm shaking so bad that I need to sit down. Erin is by my side in a flash, rubbing my back, asking if I'm okay. I want to scream. I want to tell her to get out of my house, Dan's house, technically. I want her to stay and save me from myself.

I'm thinking about what Gia said, my mind running over her words like a record player stuck in a bad groove. *You didn't see Dan hit her, did you?*

That line of reasoning takes me back to the old joke about a tree falling in the forest. If nobody heard anything, did the tree make a sound? Did I need to actually witness Dan beating up Erin in order for it to be true?

Common sense says no, of course not. But, there's something about Gia's persistence that gives me pause. Why would she put so much effort into finding me just to make such incredible claims? And that story about Erin killing someone? Geez.

Doubt is back, making inroads into my resolve. I had resolved to stand with Erin, the victim, even if it meant losing Dan, even if it broke me apart.

But ever since I got news that Erin went to the police behind my back, the ground has been quaking under my feet. Hairlines cracks are creeping into my mind, breaking apart my logic.

Is Dan the victim in all this?

I look at the business card that Gia gave me. Her information is printed on the front. She's a manager of some pet boutique. I flip the card over and find a phone number written on the back. *Call and find out for yourself.*

Then I look over at Erin. "Gia said you *killed* someone. Your ex. Is that true?"

I see Erin's face crumple right before she covers it with both of her hands. "It was awful," she says in a muffled broken voice. "He was going to kill me, so I—I just got there first."

Her confession hits me like a punch in the gut. It's true then. She *killed* someone. She took someone's life. And then she starts crying in earnest and looks up at me, face red, tears running down her flushed cheeks.

"It wasn't cold blooded *murder* like Gia would like you to believe. I'd be in jail if that was the case, wouldn't I? I mean that's a jailable offense last time I checked. But I'm not in jail. And I'm just trying to defend myself from Gia's delusional *lies*."

She grabs the business card from my hands.

"Hey!" I cry, but before I stop her, she rips the card into two and then two again.

"Lies like this," she cries, holding up the pieces.

"What are you doing?" I ask, taking the pieces from her and slipping them into my back pocket. "That's mine. Gia gave it to me."

She seems stunned momentarily. Then her face crumples. "I'm so sorry," she says, looking down at her empty hands. "I guess I'm not handling this very well, am I." She sniffles and manages a sad little smile that melts away some of my resistance.

"So . . ."

"So I should have told you, but it was so awful. And it's so hard to relive. I hope you can understand. It's not exactly something I tell people that I've just met. 'Oh, by the way.'" She chuckles a little.

"Yeah, I get that," I say. And I do. That's not exactly something you blurt out to people. Especially if that person is the girlfriend of your ex, who she just officially accused of assault.

"So I changed my name to get away from it. I meant to tell you. I really did. I was just—I guess I was trying to find the right time." She shrugs hopefully and smiles a little. "Maybe that time is now?"

Erin gets up, carries the grocery bag to the kitchen, and starts unloading it. It's awkward having Erin over to Dan's house, but he won't know. The very earliest he could possibly land on American soil is tomorrow morning, taking into consideration flight times from the Middle East to Los Angeles, followed by either a flight or a long drive down to San Diego. My calculations don't take into account flight delays, briefings and debriefings, and the red tape involved with repatriating a soldier sent home early from deployment.

Who knows when Dan will actually show up at the front door, but Erin's presence still makes me nervous. I feel like I'm a teenager hosting a house party while my parents are away. Except I'm not a teenager hosting a house party. I'm Dan's girlfriend, trying to land a solid grip on the slippery truth.

I or

"God, I could so use a drink after that," she says when I join her in the kitchen.

"I'll get the glasses," I mumble, pulling two wineglasses down from the cabinet.

Erin fills up two wineglasses, and hands one to me. "Here you go."

I feel my own strength faltering in the face of this terrible maelstrom. I take a sip, hoping to take the edge off, hoping to deaden some of the noise so I can get the heart of the matter.

"You know what I like about you?" she says, looking over at me. "No scratch that. You know what I love about you?" I cringe inside. Is this the beginning of a girl-mance? I hope Erin isn't getting the wrong idea. "You're so strong and brave."

"Thanks," I say. "But I'm really not. You're the one who could use some support right now, but look at you—bolstering me up instead." If a stranger accused me of *faking* domestic abuse, I'd be utterly beside myself.

"Isn't that what friends do?" she asks, but the soft tone of her voice makes me tense.

I take a sip of wine—not much, I still need my faculties working—feeling a little more relaxed, and exhale a big breath. All these doubts are circling around in my mind like a maelstrom, but one thing is still certain. I saw Dan shaking Erin with my own two eyes. "So I listened to the recording you sent me. But I guess you already knew that."

Erin tucks some hair behind one ear and tilts her head to the side. "I heard, yeah."

"I just—what you said really struck me. What you said about triggering memories?"

"Mmhm."

"And I needed to know. I needed to know if Dan did it or not."

Erin pulls in a breath, her nostrils flare. "That was so brave of you. Wow."

I never considered myself to be the type of person that needs sunshine blown up my nether regions, but all her complimentary words feel good. I smile, despite the fission cracks spreading through my mind.

"What did you see?" Erin asks. "If you don't mind me asking?"

I breathe out. I feel like I've been holding my breath for centuries. My body relaxes a smidgen. I feel like maybe I'm on the right track.

"I saw Dan shaking you. I saw your hair flying. I saw—" But my voice cracks. I can't finish. It's so hard to come to grips with the truth of Dan's character.

She pulls her mouth into a tight smile, pressing her lips together. "Sorry you had to see that."

It's breaking me apart knowing that Dan did this even as Gia's words hammer apart that very truth like a pneumatic drill.

You didn't see Dan hit her, did you?

"Listen, Erin, I asked you to come over because I wanted to tell you that I talked to the police. I gave them my statement for all the good it will do. They seemed more interested in how much I had to drink that night." Big surprise there.

Her eyes are bright and glimmering, her eyebrows raised. "You talked to the police? Oh, you don't know what a relief that is for me! I can't believe you did that."

My pulse is thumping. Confrontation is not my thing, but since we're on the topic of police confessions . . . "And I know you went to the police, too. When were you planning on telling me?"

Erin turns her back toward me, and her shoulders begin trembling.

"Erin?"

"You're right. I should have told you that I went to the police. I guess I'm not handling this whole thing very well, am I?" She sniffs a couple of times, and manages to say, "Sorry," in a soft croaky voice. She turns to me finally, wiping the corner of her eye with her finger. "It's just that it was such a shock to see Gia here. I saw her break into my house. I saw her leaving. She—she walked out of the front door. How brazen is that?" Erin swallows some wine, while I think back to Gia's denial—*that's a lie*! But why would Erin lie about something like that? "I was absolutely terrified because it seemed so random. But now I know why she did it. She was looking for something that would turn you against me. And—and then she comes down here spewing all these *lies*." She flicks her wrist and red wine sloshes dangerously close to the rim. "And—and then she *spied* on you?" She glances around the kitchen and leans close to me, her voice low. "I can't help but think that maybe she's trying to set you up somehow." The idea strikes me like a sucker punch.

"Me?"

Erin's nodding now, gesticulating, wine sloshing, as she details her suspicions. "Isn't it odd that she knows us both? That she spied on us both? You saw with your own two eyes how she snuck into my garage. Did you ever wonder why? And more importantly, how did she track you down? And why? Why would someone do that?"

"Because she wanted to tell me about Dan . . ." I murmur, but now I'm not so sure.

"We need to tell the police. Before she fills their ears with poison. Would you consider doing that, Brynn? Talking to the police again? Telling them what happened with Gia? How you found her standing outside your window?"

"Well . . ."

"I'm going to press charges, but the best way to strengthen our case is for you to testify. If you don't—if you don't tell the police about what you saw, about Gia stalking you, then what are we going to do?"

"We?" My stomach is in knots.

"Yes, *we*. Brynn, Gia is stalking us both. And we were both there the night that Dan beat me senseless." I wince. "And—and we're both witnesses to his crime. You said it yourself, you saw him shaking me, *beating me*."

"Not beating . . ." I say. Erin stares at me, locking her eyes with mine and making me feel so uncomfortable that I look away. "And anyway, is that even admissible in a court of law? I was off my face. Pretty sure the prosecutors will have a heyday."

"Well, I wasn't off *my* face. I know exactly what happened. And maybe,"—the wine is back, slopping over the rim now—"maybe Dan is in cahoots with Gia, trying to scare us into submission."

I feel like I've hopped aboard the crazy train. Toot! Toot! Dan in cahoots with a *psychic*?

But Erin does seem to have a cohesive theory, doesn't she? There must be a grain of truth in there somewhere. I'm concentrating, trying really hard to find that grain . . .

"I mean,"—and suddenly Erin's wine splashes out and douses my blouse and white shorts.

I gasp and jump back.

Erin's there, smothering me with a wet dish towel, offering to stain treat my clothes if I could just go and change, because she knows all about stains, and a red wine stain needs to be treated immediately or else it will set in, and—

"Stop!" I cry. She freezes, kitchen towel in hand. "Just stop." I mumble, feeling wretched for yelling at her, feeling suffocated that she's here. "Maybe you should go."

Erin's eyes well up with tears, making me feel worse than awful.

"Sorry. I'm so sorry," she says. "But think about it, okay? Just a quick chat with the police . . ." And she gathers up her stuff and leaves.

After the front door closes, I dump my wine-stained clothes into the washing machine and start the cycle. Fat chance that will fix up the stains, but honestly, at this point, I really don't give a shit.

CHAPTER 41

BRYNN

After Erin leaves and the house falls silent, I'm more rattled than ever. Erin's words fly around in my mind like a star knife, slicing me apart. *I can't help but think that maybe she's trying to set you up.*

Then I have Gia in my head, the confirmed Peeper, saying: *You didn't see him hit her, did you?*

I wish Dan would just get home already. I'm not sure how much his arrival will improve matters any, but at least I can fall out of this holding pattern: waiting for the other shoe to drop, watching my back, and getting set up, apparently, by Gia or Erin or maybe the Abominable Snowman; I honestly don't know what to believe anymore.

Will Dan even want me here when he arrives? I used some pretty choice words in my email. I wouldn't be surprised if he kicks me out upon arrival. Where will I go? I don't know, but I had better figure it out.

I could move in with my brother (no thanks), but he lives on the East Coast (even worse). I grew up there, suffering hot summers, stifling humidity, and boring bone-chilling winters. I certainly don't want to go back there, but I need to think of somewhere to go. Maybe I'll just dust off Plan B and roll on over to Australia, where I can pick apples and nurse my broken heart.

While I'm considering my next move, Erin's words swoop in and peck at me like carrion crows, cawing and breaking apart my mental stability. *Isn't it odd that she knows us both?*

Followed by Gia's words of wisdom: *You and Dan are in danger.*

But isn't that what Erin said? *I think we're in trouble . . .*

I can hardly get my head around this. Who is lying? And who is telling the truth?

Well, everyone can stop worrying about me because I'm leaving. I just decided. I'll wait until Dan arrives so that I can say goodbye in person. I owe him that much. In the meantime, I need to pack. So I start in the master bedroom closet and begin sifting through my clothes, dividing them in two piles: keep and donate.

I get through the first shelf without a mini breakdown. I'm starting on the second shelf, when emotion overwhelms me.

What do I do with the joke princess t-shirt that Dan gave me? I don't know. I can't decide.

I abandon my project, walk to the front room, and flick on the TV to give my mind a rest. Commercials accost me, so I turn my gaze to the bay window and see clouds in the evening sky turning deep shades of vermillion. I set the remote control down, walk out to the front porch, and sit down on the first step.

As the sun lowers, the clouds fill with hues of vibrant fuchsia and burnt apricot. Across the street, a few doors down, a guy wrestles a box out of his trunk. A woman with bouncy hair jogs past, looking spiffy and carefree in her athletic get-up. There was a point in time when I was that spiffy carefree person.

Now, I'm a shadow of myself, doing my level best just to get through the day. I took the week off from work. I told my manager that I'm sick, and that's not so far from the truth.

I look skyward, watching the clouds grow sharper in contrast to the soft blue sky, trying to calm the chaos in my own mind. Trying to make sense of this.

You didn't see Dan hit her, did you?

The sky turns blue-violet, streaked with spreading golden light, and I find myself wondering how Gia knew that Erin showed up with a photo and a recording? That's the real mystery. How did she know? Is she really a psychic? Or just a crazy faker?

But then I think about what Erin said. *How did she track you down? And why? Did you ever wonder that?* I remember Gia's psych ward papers that Erin showed me. How she creeped around Erin's house, looking in her garage. I recall how she was looking into my windows, and the mystery of her knowledge is revealed. She snooped and spied and made it all up. But why? Now she wants me to call someone and discover something.

Call and find out for yourself.

Is this some sort sick game? It does sound like a set up. Thanks, but no thanks. I don't have time for treasure hunts put together by crazy people. The sky fades into soft pastel hues. Night is coming. Another night without Dan.

I'm thinking about what the following few days will bring and how our love story ended so wrong, when voices from the television drift to my ears.

"And tonight on the evening news . . . a local military man is accused of assault and battery. That and much more. Just after this short break."

My blood runs cold. I get up and rush inside, praying some other military man got caught roughing up a girl. Not my Dan. Please, not *my* Dan.

The commercials are impossibly cheerful, given the topic at hand. How can the TV network be so callous? I watch a nice family buy a new car, the kids tucked into their giant booster seats with big straining smiles. Then there's someone running to catch a bus, only to get drenched by a spray of puddle water. But he takes some cold medicine, so problem solved.

I can't stand up anymore. My knees weaken just thinking about the upcoming news segment. I back up to the couch and sit down. Once there, my knee bounces uncontrollably, but it's okay. I'm releasing anxiety.

And finally, after watching Fido *dig in*, the evening reporters are back. It's a man and woman team, color coordinated. The woman is looking impossibly young, yet exceedingly professional. How is her life so put together when mine is such a wreck?

Quiet. She's about to speak.

"Tonight, we learn about Dan Evans, a local Navy corpsman, who allegedly beat up his ex-girlfriend—a night on the town gone terribly wrong."

I cannot move. They show a picture of the club—"where the incident allegedly occurred"—its double black doors closed, a chain looped around the bars, followed by a picture of Dan looking handsome in his military uniform that sends a jolt down my arms, and a seductive selfie of Erin, heavy on the filters. My knee is working overtime, jangling out of control. Dan Evans. The news network said his name.

This is like an awful surreal movie. I half expect a lighting director to wander into my living room with a light meter in hand, pointing it at my face and reporting his findings. But nobody is wandering into to my living room except Fear.

"Dan Evans, a medical officer in the United States Navy, will face charges of assault and battery in the second degree. A felony charge, if found guilty."

The camera flicks to the newsman, who embarks on the second story of the evening: a cat who saved her elderly owner. And as they rattle off the rest of their program, interspersed with overly loud commercials, I sit as still as a stone.

CHAPTER 42

DAN

This can't be happening to me. This is like a bad dream that I can't wake up from. Getting sent home early from deployment? Facing charges of assault and battery and *rape*? My CO's words ricochet around in my mind like an echo chamber. *We have a real big fucking problem here!*

Yes. We do. The bird finally takes off from Doha. Set in the steep incline of departure, I press my palms into my eye sockets as reality begins to bite. My eyes burn, but the tears won't come. I won't let them come. I won't let Erin win. There has to be a way to get out of this with my career, my integrity, and my reputation intact.

All during the long hours of the flight, my mind clicks meticulously over every last detail, trying to find an angle of attack, trying to find a way to save my ass, but the answer keeps eluding me. About four hours into the flight, I find that I'm just going around in circles, chasing answers like mice that keep slipping away.

By the time we land in San Diego, I feel like a gesticulating corpse. I collect my rucksack from baggage claim and take a taxi to a nearby hotel so I can grab some shut-eye before I'm due onto the base tomorrow afternoon, where my superiors will ease my ass into a sling.

I like to think that I'll be asleep before my head hits the pillow, but who am I kidding? I haven't had a decent nights rest since this whole nightmare broke. Still, I take a hot shower, slide between the crisp sheets, flick on the air conditioning, and hope that sleep will come.

Which it doesn't. An hour later, blue-gray tones of the coming dawn edge around the curtain. I roll over and dig my phone out of my backpack, switch it on, and brace myself for the onslaught. First stop, text messages. Brynn. Mom. Friends, telling me my story hit the evening news. Shit.

I need to take a mental break, so I thumb through my Twitter feed, realizing things are far worse than I could have ever imagined. The online threats are already coming thick and fast. People with way too much time on their hands and a powered up Photoshop program are churning out 'Dan Womanbeater' memes faster than I can comprehend.

What is wrong with these people exactly? And how do they find the time? They're like super-powered robots, spewing their vitriol as fast as lightning strikes. There must be a swilling undercurrent of people that either hates men or feels they have dealt them a wrong hand. I don't know exactly, but they are vindictive, motivated, organized, and they drag around their hashtags like human-sized crosses: #deathtodan, #destroydan, #danthedemon.

I close out my browser and check my voicemails. 'Dan Womanbeater' is a popular guy, likes to shop. There's a message from a clerk at a sex shop confirming my dick enhancement order, followed by a message from Quick Print unfortunately declining my order to print up one hundred t-shirts because the 'nature of the graphic' was against their company policy.

The girl who left the message sounded disgusted and slightly vindicated that she got to personally deliver the news, even if it was through voicemail.

My mom calls. I'm so glad for the interruption. We exchange some pleasantries; I catch her up on the hows, wheres, and whys.

"Are you okay?" she asks.

"Yeah, Mom," I assure her, but I don't think she believes me.

"Brynn told me about the police incident report . . . and the Erin situation."

Of course she did. I want to be angry with Brynn, but in the place of emotions I feel a yawning crevasse opening up, where feelings should be found, but nothing is there.

"Dan, you know you can tell me anything." My mom can take a curve ball. She's about as hardy and objective as my drill sergeant. I admire that about her, but the flat tone of her voice tells me that she's already made up her mind. She doesn't understand how I could have done something like this, beat up a girl, but it doesn't matter right now. Now, she just wants to figure out how best to move forward and what kind of attorney we should hire.

"Don't tell Brynn I'm home," I say and get off the phone, promising to update her after I check into base.

Erin had moved like quicksilver, turning me into a desperate man as I watch my freedom swirl down the drain. And if I lash out in anger or frustration? Well, that's just another arrow in her quiver. Proof positive that I'm a violent man.

Brynn doesn't understand. Why would she? Just thinking about her asking if I hit Erin makes my blood pressure rise. How could she believe for a second that I would do something like that?

Even if I am proven innocent in a court of law, the evening news will cover every 'breaking development.' My story will be old news by the time the rusty wheels of justice deliver my verdict. People will ask, "Weren't the charges dropped or something?" And I'll have to explain boring legal dealings, while their minds glaze over. They will already be convinced that I walked free based on a technicality, not on the verifiable fact that I am an innocent man.

Erin will be free to move on to the next innocent person whose life will be ruined by an unscrupulous pathological liar.

My phone rings again. Good, another distraction.

"Hi, is that Dan Womanbeater?"

"What?"

"Mr. Dan Womanbeater? I got your email, asking to buy a timeshare in Casa Questa Resort? It's one of our best—"

Disgusted, I hang up, climb out of bed, and hit up the shower. After Brynn's email, I feel like maybe I should pass on her phone number to these timeshare people. But that would make me a terrible person, wouldn't it? Just another nail in the coffin of Mr. Guilty As Hell.

I finish up, dry off, and wrap a white towel around my waist. Then I check my phone and see that I have two missed calls. What the fuck? Well, I'm not going to check any more voicemails, that's for sure. I'm whisking my electronic shaver around my face, trying not to cut myself because I am furious with Erin. How dare she. How *dare* she.

My phone buzzes again. Christ. What is going on?

I check my email and see that it's a direct message from my Twitter account.

Hey, bro. I think this the right 'Dan Evans' based on the images I'm seeing on your feed. Contact me. It's about your ex.

Is this some other jerk looking for Dan Womanbeater? Don't these people have any working brain cells? Clearly 'womanbeater' is a joke. Well, the joke's on them. I'll make sure of it. I dial up the number that the guy gave me and when he picks up, I bark, "You looking for Dan *Womanbeater,* too? Huh? It's a fake name, you numb nut!"

"What? No. No—I, I'm just looking for Dan Evans."

"Who's this?" I demand. "And what do you want?"

"Bro, my name is Trevor Whitmore, and this is going to sound a little weird, but I saw that TV segment of you on the evening news. I mean, my girlfriend saw the vid on YouTube and passed it over to me."

"Uh huh," I say, sitting down on the edge of the bed, elbows on my knees, head down, squeezing the bridge of my nose between my eyes. What does this Chatty Cathy want?

"And I called because your ex—the girl that says you beat her up? I know her."

I drop my hand and sit up rod-straight. "You know her?"

"Bro, we used to date. But she wasn't a fuckin' blonde when I knew her. She was a brunette. And her name was Michelle Larkins." My stomach sours because I have inkling of what he's going to say next. "She fleeced me out of a hundred grand, man. Used some fuckin' story that I beat her up, threatened to take it to the cops, so I coughed up the money and ran as fast as I could. I hate to say it, but I prayed she'd forget about me and move on. Latch onto some other dumb fuck. And when I saw that vid . . . I realized that she did move on. And that dumb fuck is you."

I cannot get any words to come out of my mouth.

"And you know what? We're not the only ones, bro. I know of one other. She told some dude that she had cancer and got fifty grand out of him for her *treatment* . . ."

I lurch over to the nightstand, groping for the hotel pen and notepad. "Can you give me any names? Anything concrete?"

"Yeah, bro. I can give you what I have. But I hope you got your seat belt done up tight cuz you're in the middle of a shit storm. And that girl can really bring it."

"I think I have an idea . . ."

"Yep. I'm sure you do. But don't think for a minute that you're innocent until proven guilty. Not after her prosecution gets a hold of you. Sounds like you're already in knee deep, but you better find a way to cut her off at the pass because the minute she gets more evidence on you, dude, you're done."

CHAPTER 43

GIA

I'm spooked. I delivered my message, but I think it fell on Brynn's deaf ears. I promised myself that I would try one last time, and I fulfilled that promise, for all the good it will do. The timing couldn't have been any worse. It was like a bad joke watching Erin walk in the front door, one of those things that you couldn't make up if you tried. And knowing that she has a video of me peering into her garage? That's enough to put chocolate in my drawers.

I'm getting back to my life now, trying to lay low, trying to salvage the shop from Erin's flurry of one-star reviews, trying to save my job, and I'm watching my back, too. She drove me up a tree after I approached Brynn's house last time. What will she do now that I actually talked to her?

It's excruciating to sit on the sidelines, but I need to catch my breath. Fall off of Erin's radar.

I'm living in a state of suspended animation, waiting for Erin to unleash her fury. And I'm in the back office of Furry Baby on the phone with Yelp, trying to get those bombs removed from the shop account, when the other line rings.

I look down at the LED screen and think about letting it ring out, but I don't want to give my boss any more ammunition to fire me. I need this job. I need the paycheck. He said he's "had it up to here," bringing his flattened hand up to his receding hairline, but I think he was referencing shop troubles.

I put Yelp on hold and pick up the other call, thinking that it might be him, checking in on my progress from the comfort of his home. So I rattle off the entire script that my boss wrote, careful not to flub or shorten the cheesy greeting like I usually do. "Thank you for calling Furry Baby, where we love your pet almost as much as you do. Gia speaking. How may I help you?"

"Yeah, hi Gia. This is Foxy Vixen from Babes for Hire."

Foxy Vixen? Babes for Hire? Is this chick for real? I smother a laugh. Crank call for sure. This'll be fun. "Uh huh."

"So, we got your application for our escort services. I was wondering—"

"What?"

"Your escort application?"

She sounds very authentic. She has a raspy smokers voice, and I find myself wondering if she's an old unscrupulous madam, pimping out young ladies and stealing their hard-won cash, no pun intended. Maybe this isn't a crank call. Maybe she just dialed the wrong Gia. Except Gia is kind of an unusual name . . .

"Okay . . ." I venture.

"So I just wanted to talk you briefly about your previous experience and get a feel for your level of comfort with things like threesomes, two guys and one girl type of stuff. And about your name, Gia Fuckmelater? That's another thing I wanted to discuss."

Suddenly I'm not smiling anymore.

"I think we should talk about your stage name, so to speak. 'Fuckmelater' is kind of a mouthful if you know what I mean." She laughs coarsely. "Not that there's anything wrong with mouthfuls . . ."

And I hang up, pulse pounding in my temples. This isn't a joke. This is payback. Gia *Fuckmelater* is screwed.

I fumble through the rest of my day, helping out customers, ringing them up and upselling like my job depends on it, because my job does depend on it. And in my down time, I'm on the computer, typing up the 'nature of the dispute' that Yelp asked for so I can get the reviews removed, trying to push that phone call into the dark depths of my mind.

The day finally, mercifully, draws to a close. Sales were good today. That's happy news. The shop phone is ringing off the hook, but I don't dare pick it up. That's bad news. What on earth is going on?

I don't know exactly, but if Creepy Vixen or whatever is anything to go by, the calls foretell an onslaught of even more bad news, authored by You Know Who.

Just then the shop door jingles. I look up and two cops step through, two men, eyes trained on me, sending my heart rate ever higher. I ring up the last customer of the day, hands shaking, while the cops stand off to the side, watching me.

I'm finding it impossible to hold myself together. My last customer leaves, but I'm desperate for her to stay and save me from the bearers of bad news. But she rushes out of the door, also unnerved by their presence, leaving me alone with two uniformed police officers.

When the shop door closes, they step toward me, faces stern and imposing. I fight the urge to break down in tears and tell them everything, but maybe they don't know about my visit to Erin's house. And is that even illegal? Poking your nose in someone's garage? Maybe they're following up on a lost pet.

The taller cop steps forward, his head as bald and shiny as a billiard ball. His brow deepens into a permanent cop scowl. The same scowl that his shorter counterpart wears.

"Miss Eastland?" he says, folding his arms.

"Yes?"

"I'm Officer Ward, and this is my partner, Officer Ortega." Ortega inclines his head toward me. "We're here following up on a complaint that's been made against you."

I reach out and grab hold of the countertop, steadying myself.

Ortega steps forward. "Miss Eastland, can you tell me if you know someone by the name of Erin Lazarus?"

CHAPTER 44

BRYNN

It's Friday night. Five days have passed since Dan emailed me with news that he's coming home. Will he ever get here? I'm pacing the front room, nibbling on a nail, trying to figure out if I should wait for him to arrive or just leave, when I hear a vehicle pull into the driveway, followed by the solid *clunk* of a door slamming shut.

I rush to the front window and crane my neck to see through the scraggly bush, catching a glimpse of Dan as he grabs his army green rucksack from the bed of his pickup truck and heaves it onto his shoulder. Then he stalks toward the front door. He's here. Yay! He's here. Oh no.

I wish I could play it cool and let him find me in the backyard up to my elbows in potted flowers, happily surprised with his arrival. But I'm not happily surprised. I'm nervous. And I'm scared.

The front door opens. Dan walks inside. He looks skinnier, lankier, and worn out with dark smudges under his eyes, his cheeks sunken and drawn. He looks like he hasn't bathed in recent history. His five o'clock shadow is approaching midnight, and his brow is furrowed into a very deep scowl that instantly sets me on edge.

I've seen that scowl before. It's intimidating. He mostly employs The Look when we're out and about, getting jostled at a lively bar, or when someone cuts him off on the road.

I used to reach over and massage his broad shoulders, making cheesy little jokes, while The Look melted away. I liked that I could tame my lion of a man, who yielded to my touch, growling at everyone else.

But I don't like it anymore.

"How was your flight?" I ask as calmly as possible.

"Shit," he says, dumping his heavy bag on the couch and looking around for Bear, while his bag rolls onto the floor.

Bear, snoozing in the back room, finally senses his master has returned and shuffles into the front room, sheepishly wagging his entire body, a blur of blonde fur, white teeth, and pink slapping tongue.

"Hey, Buddy Bear," Dan mumbles, allowing Bear to lick his face and neck. After Bear settles down, Dan walks into the kitchen still ignoring me. I follow, heart thumping in my chest, feeling a little breathless. "Well, it's good to see you too."

He doesn't reply. He opens the fridge and grabs a beer that I had kindly stocked for him. We can still be civil, can't we? He cracks open the can and pounds the contents in three long swallows. Then he crunches up the can, stomps on the trash can pedal so hard that I jump, and chucks the beer can inside.

"I'm surprised you're still here, social justice warrior," he says. "Don't you have a rally to attend?"

I fold my arms and sigh. "So that's it? We're going to start calling each other names?"

"I think,"—he scratches his chin and gazes thoughtfully up at the ceiling—"dick with four appendages was a good start, don't you?" He cocks his head a little to the left. "Or pathetic mealworm? That was a good one. On military comms no less."

My stomach drops. "I didn't—"

Dan steps toward me, his lips twisting into a snarl. "You didn't *what*, Brynn? You didn't know? Of course you knew. But maybe that was all part of your plan to publicly lynch an innocent man."

"Publicly *lynch*? You're the one who rearranged Erin's face!"

Dan turns and punches the wall; plaster explodes around his fist. My breath catches. It was stupid to provoke him. If I'm not careful, I might find his fist up my nasal cavity.

We both stand there in tense silence.

Finally, Dan looks over at me, eyes bloodshot and weary. "Brynn, I'm on the verge of losing my career," he says in a quiet voice that unnerves me. "I could lose everything over a false accusation." He paces the kitchen like a caged animal. "They're talking about a dishonorable discharge if I'm found guilty. Everything I've worked for—poof! Gone in a puff of smoke."

"Maybe you should have thought about that before you attacked Erin," I say, but my voice sounds small and frightened. He shoots me a murderous look. I inch closer to the block of knives.

He heaves out a big breath, walks to the sink and leans over, his hands on the edge of the counter. For a long while, he stands as still as a gravestone, staring out of the kitchen window.

"Dan . . ." I move close to him, but he moves away from me.

"I'm going to lose it all, Brynn. Everything. For something I didn't even do."

Gia's words echo in my mind. *You didn't see him hit her, did you?* And Erin's are in there too, showing me Gia's psych ward papers. The words. The accusations. The lies. The video. The recording. And one simple truth. They're all swirling around in my mind like a snowstorm.

All I have is my own truth. All I have is what I saw with my own two eyes. His anguished voice takes me back to the audio recording that Erin had sent me, and the flashes of my memory that it triggered. I remember the mirror black SUV and Dan with his hands wrapped around Erin's narrow shoulders, shaking her.

I step away from him, squeezing my eyes shut, my throat aching with tightness. I don't want to speak, but I have to.

"I saw you that night," I hear myself saying. "I saw you with Erin." He stills. "I saw what you did." He doesn't speak, of course not. What would he say? My throat closes down with pain and regret and anger. How could he have done this to her? And to us? "I can't defend you, Dan. I can't stand by your side."

"Brynn, I don't know what you saw that night, but you *never* saw me hit her."

Gia's words rush to me again, her eyes hot with vindication. *You didn't see Dan hit her, did you!*

Then I'm back to thinking about that tree falling in the forest. Did it make a sound? But I'm tired of going in circles. If a tree fell in a forest, then it made a damn sound.

"I saw enough," I say, but somehow the words feel hollow.

He looks over his shoulder at me, his eyes narrowing. "You saw *enough* with your own two eyes that were swimming in booze?"

"Dan, don't go there ..."

"Call Erin."

"What? What for?"

"Call her. Now."

His hard tone of voice tells me I don't have a choice in the matter. So I take out my cellphone and call her. She picks up, but before I can speak, Dan snatches the phone out of my hand.

"Erin, you liar! Yeah. Yeah. You go ahead and get an innocent man hung out to dry. *No.* You listen to me. Brynn is right here. Yeah, she said she saw it all. But I want you to tell her. I want you to tell her what *really* happened that night." He jerks the phone away from his ear and jams his finger onto the speakerphone button. "Go on!" he roars.

I listen, heart skittering in my chest, but all I hear is light snuffling.

"Don't do this to me, Dan," Erin pleads. "Haven't you done enough?"

"Me? Haven't *I* done enough?" he yells.

I've never seen him so apoplectic. A vein bulges on his forehead. His eyes are enormous.

"You tell Brynn what happened that night!" he yells again.

"Stop!" I cry, trying to take the phone away from him. "Leave her alone!"

And suddenly Erin's voice turns eerily clear and quiet. "Meet me at my place. Come over and we'll talk this through."

My heart sinks. Meet at her house?

Dan scoffs. "There's no way in *hell* I'm going to meet you at your house. Ever. Meet me at Trestles. Down at the end of the trail, next to the train tracks, and we'll sort this shit right out." He jams his finger onto the red hang up button, tosses my phone onto the kitchen counter, and moves to leave. Then he pauses, his back to me. "Brynn, you asked about the police incident report when I was on deployment. And I didn't want to talk about it; I couldn't. I guess that does make me an asshole."

"Dan . . ."

He walks into the bedroom. A little while later, he returns with a pink paper in hand, heavily folded and creased.

"Here's the rest of the police report," he says, tossing the square onto the counter. "Read it and weep."

CHAPTER 45

BRYNN

A surreal feeling descends on me as I unfold the paper, my gaze skipping straight down to the narrative.

Con't. After placing Evans in the backseat of the squad car, I then proceeded inside the premises to make contact with Lazarus. Upon entering the kitchen, I found Lazarus with sand paper in hand, roughly rubbing her arms, causing self-inflicted wounds.

I placed Lazarus in handcuffs for making a false statement to police and escorted her outside. Victim Daniel Evans declined to press charges. Suspect was issued with a warning instead.

The final conclusion hits me like a body blow. *Victim Daniel Evans.* I'm having a hard time putting those words together. I put my hands on my forehead and pace the kitchen. Erin hurt herself! Who does that? Crazy people do that. Insane people do that. Maybe that's why Dan was so adamant about avoiding 'drama' when I met him. He'd had his fill of it.

"Dan the victim" carries my thoughts back to Gia, who also said he was a victim. What else did she say? *Call and find out for yourself.*

I rush to my bedroom, trying to remember what I was wearing the day of her visit. There's a laundry basket over by the closet. I quickly ransack the clothes, digging my hands into all the pockets and finding nothing.

I step back from the hamper and look around the room. Where would I have put that business card? What was I wearing that day?

White shorts.

Wine.

The laundry.

I rush to our washer dryer combo set in a small alcove just off the kitchen, yank open the lid of the top loader, and peer inside.

My heart sinks. My wine stained shorts lay crumpled at the bottom of the stainless steel drum. There, plastered against the wall, are chunks of paper that hold the secret to Gia's message.

I reach inside and carefully peel away the shredded pieces from the side of the drum. They're dry so at least I have that, but they've been pulpified. I'm not holding out much hope that the number is still intact.

My mind flashes back to when Erin had "accidentally" sloshed her wine on my clothes and the fuss she'd made to treat the stain. As I collect all the pieces of paper, I realize, with a pit opening up in my stomach, that she planned to ruin my clothes all along so she could get her hands on that business card. And stop me from calling the number.

As careful as a surgeon, I lay the pieces down on the tile countertop and start piecing them together like a fossil, but hardly anything fits. I peel apart two layers that are stuck together. The permanent marks of Gia's ballpoint pen survived, but the ink was mostly erased.

I can still make out the bare outlines of the number and trace depression lines from the tip of her pen. I put together the pieces in what looks like the correct combination, area code first, followed by three numbers and a dash. The last piece holds the final four digits, except the last number is hopelessly mangled.

I'll start at the top, nine to zero, and hope that I reach the right person. I'm a little breathless at the prospect of dialing a stranger. What am I supposed to say?

First things first. I need some liquid courage. I need some wine. I open the fridge door, and search around for the familiar red foil finish of my favorite bottle. There it is, tucked behind the carton of soy milk. I yank it out and shut the fridge door. The bottle is half empty; the perfect amount to get me over the hump of self-consciousness.

I start unscrewing the cap, but slow to a stop. No. I put the frosty bottle down on the counter. No, I'm tired of needing a crutch to function. I'm tired of looking to a bottle of wine for courage.

I look again at the series of faded numbers. I need to do this sober. I *want* to do this sober. My mouth goes dry. My stomach is roiling. With shaking fingers, I pick up my phone and start dialing. Hopefully, the right person picks up. Which they don't. Next try. And someone picks up on the third ring.

"Hello?"

"Hi, my name is Brynn. I'm sorry to bother you, but someone named Gia gave me your phone number. She told me to call you and find out something that has to do with Erin Lazarus? She's harassing my boyfriend. Erin, I mean. I think she's framing him for assault and battery, but I don't know why . . ."

Silence. Maybe this was a bad idea. Maybe the last thing this guy needs is a stranger calling him up, rambling on about set ups and harassment.

"I'm really sorry," I begin. "Sorry I—"

"No," he says. "No, I think we should talk. I think you should know what happened to my brother. To Erin's supposed *ex-boyfriend*."

CHAPTER 46

ERIN

Dan's got me on the back foot, but I can recover. I always have. Chris also had me on the back foot. That's why he died. If Chris had been a good little Trevor and handed over the cash without any kick-up, he could have lived to tell his sad little tale of woe to his next girlfriend in search of a man improvement project.

But he didn't. Chris decided to try and catch me at my own game. That was his undoing. It was messy business getting rid of him, and not at all an experience that I would like to repeat. That's why I'm hoping Dan doesn't try to throw any punches.

I was scrupulous with laying down the clues in Chris's case, but I'm not going to lie. I was stressed to the maximum during my time in jail, after they decided to deny me bail and leave me there to rot during the long legal battle.

Eventually, my exorbitantly paid bulldog attorneys did their job and convinced the jury to find me not guilty, but I had to endure a brutal and agonizing stay in jail, even faking a suicide attempt so I could hide out in the psych ward and escape the lesbians looking for fun and favors.

All in all, I think I paid for that crime, even if the victim's family found the verdict "unfair." Well, life is unfair. Don't they know that? This wasn't supposed to happen to them, a good family happily ensconced in suburbia with their comfy beds, Sunday roasts, and a big trampoline in the backyard with yapping dogs and barbecues and laughing friends.

Well, my question to them is this: why *not* you? What makes you so special? So immune to heartbreak and turmoil?

I've had my share of it. And I'm busting my buns so that I'll never have to taste the hollowness of starvation again. Why do they think they get to sit on their fat fannies and eat popcorn and watch movies, while I have to work so hard just to get food in my fridge, a roof over my head, and clothes on my back?

Never again. That's what I swore to myself.

When I was twelve, a walking bag of bones with lice crawling in my hair, I swore that I would do *anything* to make sure I never starved again. *Never again.* Never again will my stomach crater with hunger. Never again will I beg for a morsel of food. Never again will I be ridiculed for wearing dirty clothes and having unwashed hair, getting unmercifully bullied because of circumstances that were out of my control.

That's the plight of the child who nobody cares about. That was my plight. Getting shunted from foster family to foster family. Many of those "families" were poor and down on their luck, looking for an easy paycheck. Growing up, I was just a meal ticket, a way for some "mothers" to pay for a fix.

I worked hard to get to where I am today. Now, I can shower when I please, however long I want to. I have a beautiful house and a closet filled with beautiful clothes. And I have a business and a great life, as long as nobody comes along and tries to screw it up.

All this doesn't come easy, I can guarantee that. I almost missed Gia, stumbling away from Dan's house and running to her car. I'd been sitting outside of Dan's house for hours, starving and in need of a restroom break. So I made a quick dash to a taco restaurant. By the time I drove around the corner, Gia was peeling away from Dan's house.

That was a scary near miss. What would have happened if I hadn't driven around the corner just then? I would have missed the golden opportunity to paint her as a stalker. Then where would I be? Nowhere. That's were I'd be. I deserve that bit of luck. Luck favors those who are prepared. And I'm always prepared.

Yes, I've come so far, and I'm proud of myself because there's nobody else around to be proud of me. If Daddy was still with me, he'd be proud . . . I know he'd be proud.

Now, I have to deal with Dan. I had hopes that our relationship might survive. But I guess I couldn't contain my volatile temper. And I went too far one too many times. Well, all learning lessons for next time.

I park in the dusty parking lot close to the trailhead that leads to the spot where Dan and I spent some Saturdays. It's the place where we will meet again under much different circumstances.

I reach under my car seat, pull out a switchblade, and slip it up the sleeve of my coat, the tip of its handle resting in my palm. Let's hope Dan's a lapdog like Trevor, and doesn't give me any problems.

I've got him right where I want him. Brynn went to police, gave them her statement. I wanted to toast to her gullibility that day that at Dan's house, and her exasperating dithering, but I had to get that business card out of her hands. Well, I failed to get it, but at least I ripped it up and rattled her cage. But you know what? I don't think it matters.

She went to the police. She stated on record that she saw him shaking me. Now, I'm about to meet Dan in a dark isolated place. It will be easy enough to get some more evidence on him. Making my final plan just that much easier.

I get out of my car, lock it up tight, and head out into the night. Soon enough, and if I step very carefully, it will be yet another "job done."

CHAPTER 47

DAN

Driving up to meet Erin brings this whole nightmare into surreal focus. This is like a bad dream that I can't wake up from. My own girlfriend thinks that I beat up my ex, and she doesn't believe a word I say. Brynn's calling now, but I let it ring out because I don't want to pick up and listen to more of her *remembrances*.

I strike the steering wheel with the palm of my hand instead. The sharp jolt of pain feels good somehow, a nice contrast to the aching, spreading, intangible miasma that is growing inside my chest, robbing me of air. I wake up in a living nightmare every single day now. Well, at least I'm not alone.

There are others. She told some dude that she had cancer and got fifty grand out of him for her treatment . . .

Erin thinks she's so smart. Well, we'll see about that. Ever since my call with Trevor, Erin's ex-victim, I've been busy laying out a plan that's going to put her nose out of joint.

"You gotta play with the same deck of cards," an ex-operative pal of mine, Ken Walker, had advised me after I called looking for advice. He's a retired CIA agent that lives out at Joshua Tree. We meet up occasionally to rock climb some of the less technical routes and sit around a campfire at night, the cold desert to our backs, whiskey warming our insides, talking about close shaves and his days of old. "You gotta play the same game as her," he said, his voice gravelly. "But play it better."

Her game is extorting money. Am I surprised? Not exactly, but I am taken aback because I realize that she's far more unscrupulous than I could have ever imagined.

I always wondered why she never had cash liquidity crises that seemed to plague every other girl I knew. At one point, I thought maybe she was a stripper on the side, so I investigated the matter. I toured the main 'topless dancing' establishments in San Diego with two of my friends, who were only too happy to help with reconnaissance. My friends got souvenir lap dances for their efforts, while I just pocketed a complementary bottle opener with two big boobs as a handle because I didn't have one at home.

I found the atmosphere at the strip clubs to be depressing, the ladies desperate and hollow-eyed. Some were clearly on drugs. And after a quick look into how many strip clubs I'd have to visit in order to chance upon Erin, I decided to give up my mission.

Attending grimy strip joints was certainly not how I intended to spend my down time. So I let the mystery of Erin's finances fade.

After Brynn apprised me of this looming shit storm, I'd hoped to handle Erin's false accusation through the criminal justice system, even if it meant facing her bulldog lawyers in court. I consulted with a lawyer that my mom had found, and he wasted no time laying out the legal mountain that lay before me which appeared as formidable as K2, patiently waiting to dispatch me in the death zone five hundred feet from the summit. In essence, victory is a treacherous journey and far from certain.

Even if Erin's Photoshopped *pièce de résistance* along with her carefully curated voice recordings are debunked and thrown out of court, I'll be on the hook for hundreds of thousands of dollars in legal fees, not to mention the many months, if not years, I'll spend legal limbo land until the jury delivers their opinion. Do you think the military would welcome me back in the interim, while my case works its way through the legal system? Not a chance in hell.

Trevor's sage words of advice come back to me. *You better find a way to cut her off at the pass because the minute she gets more evidence on you . . . you're done.*

Not if I can help it. I exit the freeway and park next to a red SUV. I told Erin to meet me on a mostly deserted stretch of beach where we spent a few Saturday afternoons, back when we first started dating and she'd given me every reason to think she was completely normal. Erin with her picnic spread and word salads, me with my surfboard.

Brynn calls again. I let the call go to voicemail.

I pull on my puffer jacket, lock up the truck, start off down the sandy trail at a brisk pace, and break into an easy jog.

The wind blows sharp and frigid. The night is moonless and inky dark, the kind of darkness that steals away your depth perception and makes you feel like you've fallen through a trap door.

I reach the end of the trail and sweep my gaze up and down the vast empty beach. A storm had blown in overnight. I can hear the ocean pumping waves onto the sandy shoreline and the hissing sound of retreating water. It would be magical if it wasn't so eerie, if the temperature wasn't so bone-chilling.

A little way up the beach, I see a glowing cell phone illuminating the face of a blonde sitting among the small rolling sand berms, hugging her knees. Erin. Behind her I can just make out the train tracks that follow this stretch of coastline.

She looks small and vulnerable. If it were any other person, I might go to her and see if she needs help. But not this one. She looks my way, switches off her phone, and rises to standing. I can just make out the edges of her dark silhouette.

I feel a twinge of nervous anticipation. I pull in a breath and memorize the feeling of being alive and vital as cold ocean air fills my lungs. Then I exhale and make my way over to her, finding strength in the knowledge that I have a plan.

A trap, waiting for her nasty right foot.

CHAPTER 48

BRYNN

I'm racing up the freeway toward Trestles, praying for no traffic, for a fast commute, that my car won't run out gas or blow a tire. And I'm praying for Dan. I'm praying that he'll blow a tire instead, or maybe get abducted by aliens—anything that will stop him from meeting up with Erin.

I put my ear buds in my ears and dial him up. "Please call me back," I mutter to myself. *Please please please.* But my call goes to voicemail.

My hands are shaking. My heart is thumping so hard that I'm having a hard time catching my breath. I take a few deliberate big ones and focus on calming down.

The traffic slows, making me grind my teeth with frustration.

Hopefully, Dan got caught in the same knot of traffic.

Trestles is a long stretch of rugged coastline, home to a beautiful unspoiled beach with lots of great waves. I'm not exactly sure which exit to take, but I know that there's a dirt parking lot just off the freeway, close to the trailhead for a coastal path that weaves through dry shrubbery and under a train overpass to the beach.

I program the directions into my phone as I speed up the freeway, while my thoughts turn to Jacob. Or rather, the eerily similar story that he shared with me, followed by the chilling final end.

Erin operates by collecting her evidence, by hook or crook. If she gets any more evidence against Dan, or if he's put into a position where she can concoct some, then it's one more chain around his neck.

I listen to the peppy roar of my car as I press my foot on the gas pedal. The central panel glows blue as I watch the speed dial climb. And finally, I reach my exit. I hope it's the right one.

I follow the signs and flick on my brights. There's a dirt parking lot where people leave their cars close to the trailhead. It's empty—except for two vehicles: Dan's and Erin's.

Thank God. I park next to the 'no kooks' sign, and before I climb out, Erin's words of warning come to mind: *if you're ever walking into an iffy situation . . .*

"Thanks for the advice," I mutter, punching in the passcode of my phone and starting up the voice memos app. Then I slip my phone into my 'bra pocket,' and I'm down the trail in a dead run.

CHAPTER 49

DAN

Erin stands there, watching me approach. The shadows cloak her face, but her eyes are gleaming, and a hint of wickedness curls her mouth into a smile. I would be lying if I said I wasn't nervous. It's surreal coming face to face with my ex-girlfriend turned enemy. It's excruciating to think about what happened the night of my farewell party.

We're a few feet away from each other now. She smirks; her eyes narrow. I see the familiar features that I used to like—the smattering of freckles across her nose, the deep Cupid's bow on her top lip—and find them repulsive now.

I want to mention Trevor and all her past victims, just to

wipe that nasty smirk off her face, but she can't know that I know. She has to think that I'm just another innocent little lamb, trotting off to the slaughter.

"You need to stop this, Erin. Drop the charges. Get your goons off my back. This is my *life* you're screwing with here. You can't make these false allegations against me. You can't—"

"Yes, I can. I can because it's all true."

"You know it's not true though," I say evenly. "You know I didn't hit you." *See if you can squeeze out a few pathetic tears*, I tell myself.

She steps forward, her index finger jabbing my chest. "Yes you did. And Brynn saw! She saw you *shaking* me."

My hands curl into fists, thinking about how Erin turned my own girlfriend against me. I'd like to shake Erin now, but that will just give her the ammunition she needs. "Yeah maybe I did shake you. I tried to shake some fucking sense into you."

Erin folds her arms; one corner of her mouth turns up. "Thanks for admitting that."

My stomach sinks. That's one for her, zero for me. *That's okay*, I tell myself. The game isn't over yet.

"How do you even know what happened that night anyway?" she asks. "You were so shit-faced, you hardly knew your own name. I made sure of it."

Flames of anger shoot through me. "You . . . made sure of it?"

She shrugs as if to say, *Yeah? What's the big deal?* "Just a little GHB. Nothing deadly."

There's a timer counting down somewhere inside of me as inevitable as a nuclear core meltdown. *Of course* she drugged me.

I felt like death warmed over the morning after my farewell party. It took a Herculean effort to drag myself out of bed. It was by far the worst hangover I'd ever experienced. I hadn't suspected *drugs* though. I know for a solid fact that I did not touch the white powdery substance on offer that night because I could have lost my job!

Keep a lid on it, man, I'm thinking to myself. *Calm down. Don't let her win.* But my pulse is racing.

"All part of your big bad plan right, Erin? Framing me for assault and battery wasn't enough for you, was it!"

She makes a mock pouty face, her fat fish lips forming words that I wish I could obliterate. "Oh, poor you," she says. "Losing your jobbie-wobbie." Then the pout disappears, and her eyes turn hard. "Well, you deserve it after everything you did to me."

Two. One. A shutter raps down on my vision. I see a fuzzy terrain of whiteness. Erin is in there somewhere, a great gob of a shape, yammering about her clever little plan, how I never had a chance, how she set me up, how Brynn is going to testify against me, how she has a recording—and then she's screaming, "Hit me, Dan. Hit me! I dare you! You pussy!"

In my mind, I imagine the ropy cords of her neck pressing against my palms. It's a vividly satisfying image. The helpless choking sound that she might emit is like a salve to my torn and ravaged soul.

No.

I dial back my rage so that it's manageable, barely, and say, "No. I won't hit you. Not now. Not ever."

Erin doesn't reply. But her eyes bulge with fury. Suddenly

she screams and hurtles her own fist at her cheek, hitting herself instead. She strikes her own cheek twice in quick succession, making a muffled *thwak-thwak* sound, and a small lump rises up on her cheekbone. Then she scratches at her own face and neck with a screaming vengeance that leaves me breathless.

Finally, she wraps her hands around her own neck and tightens, making a gurgling choking sound, crying out the same line she'd used the night of my farewell party, "Stop, Dan! Stop!"

After she's done, she moves a few feet away, snuffling or snickering, I honestly can't tell, saying, "Dan just choked me. He tried to kill me."

Is she serious? Who the fuck is she talking to? Every bone in my body is dead tired of her. She's still got a hand around her neck, but her eyes are dancing with what I can only describe as glee.

My heart sinks all the way down my feet as Trevor's words come back to me: *the minute she gets more evidence on you . . .*

I never worried about Erin getting evidence because I knew I'd never touch her. But after the police incident, I should have known that she'd hurt herself again, and blame me for it. I just should have known.

The malice emanating from her feels white-hot. She reaches up to the lapel on her coat and plucks something off. It's small and black, attached to a thin cord that is plugged into her phone, which she produces with great satisfaction.

"Thanks for that," she says, without a tremor of emotion. "That's all I needed." She shows the face of her phone to me. "A nice recording of you *assaulting* me again." She tucks her phone safely away in her pocket and looks up at the night sky, rubbing her neck and tilting her head left to right. "I hope you left a mark." Under the bright smattering of stars, light years away, stand thousands of silent witnesses that I wish could talk. Her cold voice startles me from my reverie. "Do you want this to end?"

"Yeah. I really do," I say, my anger bleeding out.

"All you have to do is pay me off," she says.

I tamp down a little thrill as she steps into my carefully laid trap. Checkmate.

"How much?" I ask, looking down in feigned defeat.

"Half a mil. Then I'm gone. I'll drop the charges. You'll never hear from me again."

One half of one million dollars. That's far beyond the measly fifty or one hundred thousand she tricked out of her ex-victims. But she knows I have it, sadly, so I start mentally earmarking the money. I have some equity, the benefits of buying young (except I still owe my mom the down payment), plus I've been lucky with my investments, and I have about a hundred thou in savings. It would have been a heavy toll to pay, but she's not going to get a single dime of it.

"Yeah, I'll give you the money," I say in my best approximation of a beaten man.

Actually, my retired CIA operative pal, Ken Walker, wired up with a concealed body cam, is going to give her the money. As soon as she takes possession, he's going to rain hellfire down on her head, while I watch the comedy unfold from the comfort of a car. He said he couldn't wait. "Retirement's a little dull," he told me when I asked. "I could use some excitement."

"All cash. No bank transfers," she says.

I'm glad she agrees. "Exactly."

She lays out her terms like a mobster, while I smother a smile. Small unmarked bills, stuffed into a duffle, or something equally as ridiculous, when I hear my name.

"Dan!"

The clear voice startles me. I turn, trying to identify its owner. Who in the world could be out here on this deathly cold night, calling my name?

Brynn!

She's running toward us in a tired lope. She's giving it all she has, sprays of sand airborne behind her feet. My heart lurches in my chest. Brynn. She's here. She's yelling something, waving her arms. I hold my breath, listening.

Before I can understand her words, Erin says in a cold hard voice, while she fiddles with her coat sleeve. "When Brynn gets here, tell her to go back."

CHAPTER 50

BRYNN

My lungs are burning, but somehow my legs are still moving. I see two figures standing among the ice plants in the distance. Behind them, the train tracks curve into the darkness. One figure is the same height and build as Dan. The other one, with long blonde hair streaming behind her head, is a dead giveaway. It's them. I pick up the pace.

"Dan!"

"Go back!" he yells, waving his arms over his head. "Brynn, go back!"

But I can't. I won't. I jog up to them, breathing so hard from exhaustion that I'm having a hard time catching my breath. Erin's mouth is drawn down with anger, her brow furrowed into a deep scowl. She looks none-too-happy about this late addition to her party. Good. I glance over at Dan, my sweet Dan. Even better.

I throw my arms around his neck and try to stem the rising tide of guilt and shame surging through me. "I'm sorry," I say against his neck, my eyes pricking with tears. "I'm so sorry I didn't believe you."

He pulls away, his eyes sharp with alarm. He's squeezing my hands so hard they hurt. He's trying to communicate something vital, probably an apology, but it doesn't matter now. It's all over. I know the truth. And soon, so will Erin.

Dan catches my gaze. "Go home, Brynn. Please."

"No, I won't. Not without you." I turn toward *Shelter Girl*, her eyes gleaming in the moonless night as dark and fathomless as pits.

I hardly recognize her real persona. I had become so accustomed to poor little Erin, always on the verge of tears, always ready with a sad tale of woe, always pawing at people and gazing into their eyes with adoration. I've never seen Erin, the stone cold killer.

"I know what you did," I say to her, my heart beating fast and high in my throat. "I know that you killed Chris Mabray. And it wasn't self-defense like you claim. It was *murder*."

"You *killed* someone?" Dan asks Erin, his voice soft with

disbelief. He's stumbling to keep up. He's falling out of the clouds. But I'll catch him. I'll break his fall.

"You don't know what you're talking about," she scoffs, glancing at Dan, with a hint of defensiveness.

"I know exactly what I'm talking about." I move toward her. She steps back. "It's so uncanny how you partied with both Chris and Dan, and they both *beat you up* the night of the party."

"That was just a coincidence," she says.

"Amazing coincidence right? Wow. You should buy a lottery ticket."

She shrugs, trying to look like she's not sweating the small stuff. I push on. "And you then you partied with Chris and everybody got really drunk, except you." Her eyes narrow. "You pulled Chris aside for a little private chat. And so off he went, a little worse for the wear, not thinking very clearly. That's because you drugged him."

Dan tenses, but I keep talking, the words flying out of my mouth. I'm so close. I've got her. I just need to deliver the final blow.

"So he stepped outside with you, and you pushed yourself on him. You wanted to go the whole way, right? But he turned you down. And you wouldn't take no for an answer. You pushed and pushed until he pushed you back. Just to get his point across because you were being so pig-headed about it. And you made sure you got that part recorded. Right? So diligent. And then what? What did you do? Go ahead and say it. I think Dan deserves to know. Since you did the exact same thing to him."

Erin's eyes glitter with malice. Her mouth is curved into a smile, but it holds no goodwill. I can tell that she wants to brag about her foresight, her cleverness, and her wonderful perfect plan.

"He never saw it coming," she says coolly. "It was my story against his." One corner of her mouth curls up. "Except I had a photoshopped image and a recording. And he had nothing."

"And with your *evidence*, you set up Chris and extorted money from him. Lots of it. But you didn't stop there, because you knew he was working to have you arrested. So you lured him over to your house to deliver your final blow."

As Erin speaks, I watch the dead gleam in her eyes. "Chris thought he was so smart. He thought he could out-step me. That was his undoing. He tried to beat me at my own game."

"Oh my God," Dan says, grasping the parallels between Chris's story and his.

"It wasn't so hard to do," Erin continues. "Chris came over enraged, angry that I'd ruined his life. I prodded him further, making sure he was nice and furious. As soon as I got some marks on my body, I had everything I needed to get away with it."

"The perfect alibi . . ."

"Self-defense," she says in a flat tone. "Works every time."

"With victim after victim, including Dan. Right?"

"Why change a winning formula?" she says with a self-congratulatory grin.

"Except you didn't think this one through, did you?" I say to Erin. "You must be getting soft." I wrinkle my nose. "Maybe a little lazy."

"Oh, really?" Goaded, she pulls up a voice recording on her phone. It's the sound of a voice, followed by some gurgles. It's a choking sound. Dan's weight shifts as if his knees are buckling. And then I hear her voice, shaking and soft. "Dan just choked me. He tried to kill me."

"I never fucking touched you!" he yells. "Put that on your voice recording!"

All part of her game. I tighten my arm around him. I'm here for you, Dan, I'm saying to him. I'll get you through this. *I believe you.*

Erin speaks. "You have—"

I hold up a finger. "Quick question. Did you try to extort any money from Dan yet? Or did I show up too early?"

Dan looks at me aghast.

"You can jump in front of a train for all I care," Erin says, "Dan just *choked* me. I have evidence. It may not be permissible in court," she says, waving her hand like she could care less. "But it will change the course of the investigation." She shrugs. "Like, in my favor."

"Wow," I say. "Wow wow wow. You really know your stuff. You're really a forward thinker. So thorough." The corner of her mouth perks up. She's loving all this praise. Well, she's not going to love it much longer. "You should write a book," I continue, while her smile fades. "Maybe an instruction manual. Have you thought about YouTube videos? You really have a winning personality." Her smile is long gone now, but I continue. "Do you think I could ask your advice about something? I'm just a stupid newbie, after all." I pull out my phone and navigate to the clearly recording app. "But do you think this will change the course of Dan's investigation?" I shrug. "Like, in his favor?"

The corner of her right eye twitches, while I press the home button, leaving the app recording in the background, and push the side lock button. Her lips draw tight. Then she shakes her head. "No way. There's no way you caught that on audio. For one, your jacket is covering the microphone. Two, there's a ton of wind."

I smirk and pull out my ear buds, the wire looped around my neck, the microphone tucked tidily along my collarbone, just under my chin, shielded from the wind by the collar of my coat, unzipped just enough to catch Erin's confession. "Bet you didn't think of that."

"It's all over, Erin." Dan says. "I know about Trevor and everyone else you screwed over. You've really made a career of destroying people. You ought to be ashamed of yourself, but of course you're not."

Trevor? I look at Erin, expecting a smart rebuttal, but instead I see the imperceptible twitch of her mouth as her mask slips. Her eyes widen. She's struggling to hang onto her composure, but she can't quite get that mask fastened back in place.

Finally, she gives up. She looks like a different person now with veins roping across her forehead, a big one pulsing between her eyebrows. Her eyes are wild, her lips pulled back against her clenched teeth.

My amusement turns to alarm when she withdraws her arm from behind her back. And in her fist, glints a long sharp blade.

CHAPTER 51

BRYNN

"Brynn," Dan roars, throwing his arms around me and pushing me out of the way of the blade's slicing arc. I feel his body move in a quick flinch. He doubles over, arm clamped around his abdomen.

"Shit," he mutters, peeling back his arm slightly and looking down at the damage. I see dark, inky fluid seeping into the white fluffy interior of his jacket. Blood.

"Dan!" I try to hold him up, but he sinks onto his knees with a soft grunt.

"Give me your phone," Erin says in a flat even tone, one hand extended. Hot fear surges through me. I need to help Dan somehow, but I've got a big fat problem on my hands called Erin. "Give it to me now!" she screams.

"Okay, okay," I say, backing up, trying to lure her away from Dan, trying to buy some time so I can figure what I'm going to do about this rattlesnake.

A gust of wind bellows, cutting me to the bone. My teeth chatter. But I clench my jaw, stopping the noise, because I hear something: the sharp, shrill blow of a train whistle. The ground rumbles under my feet. Erin and I both look at the rails curving into dark hills like black ribbons. It's coming. A train.

"I'm not going to ask again," she says, jerking the knife toward me. "*Gimme your phone!*"

"You don't know my passcode," I yell against the wind. "You'll never get access to the recording."

"I don't need the passcode," she says, glancing over her shoulder at the oncoming train. She's going to throw my phone at the train and destroy it. That's her plan. What's mine?

I have no idea. But I'm going to fight to keep that recording intact. I need her confession. I keep moving backwards, away from Erin and the approaching train, watching Dan, hoping he can come back online sooner rather than later.

If I distract her long enough, maybe Dan can summon enough strength to get that knife out of her hand. She's inching toward me, away from Dan. My plan seems to be working.

But then my heel catches on something substantial, a piece of driftwood maybe, and I'm stumbling, falling backwards, watching Erin hurry toward me. A spray of sand blows into my eyes and blinds me.

Erin rams her shoulder into my diaphragm on the way down, jolting the breath out of my body. I land and roll onto my side, trying to clear the biting sand from my eyes and gulp some air. Meanwhile, she rifles through my coat, trying to grab my phone. I curl into a fetal position, protecting it from her grasping hand.

Then I feel a cold, sharp sensation against my cheek that instantly stills me. I freeze, eyes locked on the blade that fills my vision with terror. I'm thinking about the tough ridge of a scar that I'm going to wear on my face for the rest of my life if I move. I'm thinking about permanent disfigurement, when I feel her fingers clasp around my phone, tearing it from my grip, and wince when I feel a thin line of pressure around my neck as my earphones snap out of the jack. I want to get up and fight, but fear keeps me rooted to the ground.

Erin straightens, my phone in her hand. "Thanks," she spits.

Tears of loss sting my eyes. She won. The recording is stored on my phone. After she destroys it, I'll lose her full confession, and we'll be back to he said/she said backed by her mountain of evidence. Oh, and my police statement that I kindly provided. Can I redact that?

In any event, Dan will be left to battle it out in court. If he loses, his career will go up in smoke, and I'll be relegated to weekend visits, sitting across a plexiglass barrier, pressing my hand against his.

A shadow moves behind Erin. Dan. He's lumbering, but the deep crease on his forehead tells me he's wearing The Look. Bad news for Erin. I keep my eyes glued on her, afraid that the quick flick of my gaze will betray him. She's turning. She'll see him.

"Hey!" I yell above the wind.

She turns back to me, an automatic reaction, just as Dan hurries up to her and snakes his muscled arm around her neck. Her eyes fly wide, one hand tearing at his forearm. With the other she takes a backward stab at him, but the tip of the knife catches his jacket and shreds the pocket instead. I scramble up to standing and inch closer to her.

Erin suddenly twists to the side, but before she can strike again, I land a grip on her slashing hand and dig the knife handle out of her closed fist.

The blade feels substantial and powerful. A surge of relief rushes through me, now that the outcome is tipped in my favor.

Hands shaking, I point the blade at Erin, careful not to touch her. Adrenaline is flaming through my body. I hardly feel the cold anymore. What does it feel like to stab someone? Will the sensation even register against my palm?

"Careful with that," she says, nodding to the knife. "Don't want to *kill* anybody." And she laughs, which is really more of a high shrieking sound that speeds my pulse.

She can laugh all she wants. The tables have turned now. I'm the one making demands. "Give me the phone," I'm saying, but the dead gleam in her eyes and her distinct lack of fear sends chills down my body. I can't *stab* her. I can't take her life. And she seems to understand my moral and legal dilemma. All I can do is bluff and hope. "Give me the phone!" I yell, carefully placing the blade against the cords in her neck. *Be careful*, I tell myself.

Erin speaks up, eyes narrowed into slits. Her dark eyes meet mine. "Go ahead and *slit my throat*. I'd like to see you explain that to the police."

I pull my lips tight against my teeth and press the blade closer, praying she won't move or that my hand won't slip. I'm watching the hairline edge of the blade press into a crease of her skin. And I'm panting, trying to fight back hot tears of defeat. I can't do it. I can't hurt her. Not with a knife.

Finally, I drop my hand.

Erin smiles, watching me, her mouth curling into a sneer.

"Drop the phone!" Dan yells, shaking her. And when he's done jerking her left and right, she laughs again, her high voice carrying on the wind. She's laughing at my incompetence and my inability to shunt aside my conscience so I can slit her neck.

The horn blares. The train headlight bears down on us, a monocle of blinding light. In the bright light, I imagine seeing the knife handle sticking out of her back, between both shoulder blades. I imagine her reaching behind, grasping for the handle, trying to pull it out, but it's just out of reach. She's twisting and fighting, and she's losing her balance . . .

But I blink away that version of my future because it will never happen. She's right. If I try to bury that blade into her back, even if I merely cut her, I'll be tried for attempted murder or something equally as horrific.

Dan weakens; his grip slips. Erin breaks away.

Frustrated, I turn away and scream, heaving that useless knife into the edge of darkness, watching the metal blade spin and disappear into the shadows where it can neither hurt nor help anyone.

I turn to her, panting, eyes alive to her next move. The horn blares again, warning us away. We both look at the oncoming train. Erin moves forward, my phone in her hand, silhouetted by the train's headlight as blinding as stadium lights.

Erin turns back to me, raising her voice above the clamor. "Sorry your big plan didn't work out, Brynn!"

Then she turns and walks toward the train. The train thunders closer, growing in size, towering over us with its deadly unstoppable speed. Erin steps closer still, with my phone in her hand, the small rectangle of hope that can save Dan.

"Stop, Erin!" I call out, but the train's horn blasts, loud and deafening, swallowing up my voice. I should heed the warning and move back, out of the way, but there's still a chance.

As she watches the train approach, timing her moment to dispatch my phone, her arm cocked back, I rush up and grab hold of her hand. But the sucking wind of the passing train almost knocks me off my feet.

"For God's sake! Let go of it!" Erin cries.

"No, I won't!"

I'm fighting for balance, to save the recording—her confession, for justice, for Dan, and I'm bracing my feet against the sand, trying to gain some purchase, while the deafening roar of the wheels clattering over the rails and the squealing of hydraulic brakes rattle me to the bone. But I hold fast to that phone.

Erin screams and tears at my hair, pulling me toward the thundering train, while hot pain sears down my head and neck. She punches me, trying to get me to let go. Then I gouge my thumbs into her palm, trying to break her grip. But she's a madwoman, screaming, pulling me toward the train, and gaining the upper hand.

The train thunders, sucking us closer with its blinding velocity. It's a freight train, not the light rail commuter type that's here and gone in a flash. This is a heavy-duty worker with lots of cars, an unending amount seemingly, rushing past and pulling us closer.

I have to get my phone. I have to save that recording.

"Brynn!" I hear Dan's small voice from what sounds like another dimension.

Erin jerks me closer to the rails. The whirling axles loom enormous in my eyes, the wind whipping around me in a blurry vortex.

"Stop, Erin! You're going to kill someone!"

"Whatever it takes," I hear her say.

She's pulling me, heaving me toward the clattering axles, toward death, because she has nothing left to lose.

If she can't destroy her own confession, she'll be looking at life behind bars. If I happen to be collateral damage, well, she'll just dig up that knife and use her old line of self-defense. My prints on are the handle. She'll have the troublesome detail of Dan's testimony, but I'm sure she'll think of something.

Like Polaroid snapshots, my life flashes before my eyes. But instead of happy memories, I see Dan and my family ravaged with grief because I was too nice, too eager to put everyone else above myself. I see Dan convicted, carrying a felony charge for a crime he didn't commit. And I see Erin walking away, free to destroy someone else's life.

"Not on my watch," I say, gritting my teeth. "*No more Mrs. Nice Gal.*"

I crook my elbow and slam it into her ribcage. Her grip suddenly breaks. I grab hold of my phone, and scramble backwards, a wave of relief rushing through me.

But she's falling now. She's teetering on the heels of her feet, pin-wheeling her arms, trying to win back her balance, while the train shudders behind her, a blur of flashing metal and blaring horn. I only wanted justice. Not a death.

"Grab my hand!" I cry, reaching for her.

Her eyes are huge and scared, her mouth making a perfect O as she leans just out of reach, her fingertips brushing mine. Like the tail of a scorpion, the last few cars whip by and strike, pulling her inexorably forward, sucking her into the vortex.

The train thunders past, leaving us with stunned silence.

And Erin's mangled body.

CHAPTER 52

DAN

We're in Brynn's car, driving to the nearest emergency room. I can see from the wide blank look in her wide eyes that she's in shock so I put my hand on her knee and squeeze. I have never loved her more.

I pull out my phone and check for messages. I'd already called the police and told them about the accident. Where to find the body. And I left my contact details with them for the inevitable exhaustive follow up. No messages yet. That's good news. I'm not exactly ready for an interrogation.

Pain flames through my body. I hiss and set the phone down on my lap.

She looks over, worried, and reaches for my shoulder. "Are you okay?"

"Yep," I say, trying to downplay the seriousness of the matter. Depending on the cleanliness of blade, I could be looking at blood poisoning, sepsis, or a nice Staph infection. I have to go with the lowest common denominator. We're dealing with Erin, after all.

Brynn doesn't know, but this isn't the first time Erin has pulled a knife on me, though it is the first time she used it. In fact, the knife episode precipitated our breakup, but the police incident was the final straw. Erin couldn't understand that I was unwilling to 'forgive' her for waggling a carving knife at me.

I should have known that I was dealing with somebody dangerous, somebody unstable who should be dumped with a little more finesse, but I wanted her out of my life. Stat.

I grit my teeth. Flames of regret spread through me. There's so much that Brynn doesn't know, stuff I never wanted her to know, stuff that I never wanted to resurrect. I just figured that if I left the bones undisturbed, then they would sink down the deep depths of my internal ocean, never to be thought of again. So I fought for secrecy, and the bones did sink down, but instead of disappearing, they began to fester.

There's something else too. I was ashamed to tell Brynn, this brave magical creature, who had journeyed across the country alone in her car, that I'd been in an abusive relationship. It's one of those weird things where you have to google it to find out if it applies to you.

No man ever thinks of himself as the type to get abused. And what is abuse anyway exactly? Is it getting insulted? Nagged? Does brandishing a knife really qualify if the other party doesn't draw blood? Or if the other party is a woman?

Of course Brynn wanted to know about my past relationships, but I wanted to her to think of me as brave and dashing, not loathe me for being weak and abused.

"We're almost there," she says, her hand on mine. I wriggle my thumb out from her grip and hold her hand back. I never want her to let me go.

"All good over here," I say. She shoots me a worried glance. "I don't think she got my gut. The cut is too low." I desperately hope so anyway.

"Mmhm," she says, taking her hand back and placing it back on the steering wheel. She needs to focus on driving, and she has a tricky exit coming up. She glances over at me. I can tell she is waiting for more information.

"Okay, you're debriefed," I say with a smile, but wince as we drive over a bump.

She pulls into a brightly lit hospital parking lot and parks. It seems so surreal that moments ago, I was down on my knees on that dark isolated beach, staring down the barrel of a felony assault charge, figuring out how to get Erin to step into my trap. And now . . . it's all over.

Thanks to Brynn.

Of course, I had my own plan catch and kill plan in play. But that happy ending was dependent on the legal system, which may or may not find in my favor. And how many years and hundreds of thousands of dollars would I have thrown away trying to catch a lucky break? Too many. Too many to count.

She helps me out of the car, and I hobble inside, Brynn under my arm, propping me up. As soon as I get this wound stitched up, I vow to tell her everything that happened the night of my farewell party and never keep her in the dark again.

CHAPTER 53

DAN

I wake up in a hospital room, the vertical blinds to my right are pulled shut, the curtain to my left drawn closed. I feel like I'm in a suffocating cocoon, tied down with IV lines and hand restraints.

Groggily, I struggle to lift my arm and maneuver my hand into my fuzzy field of vision. No hand restraints. I drop my arm down, exhausted, and a fiery rim of pain blazes up my body so I reach for the big red help button and push it.

Then I close my eyes, pulling in shallow breaths, trying to manage the pain.

In—calm and relaxation.

Out—jagged pain.

The door opens. I hear footsteps belonging to a number of

people. The curtain swishes aside and Brynn rushes to my bedside, eyes wide with concern, followed by two nurses. The older woman checks my IV drip bag and asks about pain levels, while the younger one hangs back.

I over-estimate my pain levels and watch them leave, hoping that they'll hurry up with the goods. I'm post-surgery. From experience, I know that the intravenous good stuff will wear off, leaving me in limbo land until I can get ahead of the pain again.

But I feel stronger somehow with Brynn sitting next to me, both of her hands clamped onto mine.

"Hey," I say, trying to squeeze her hand back, but I don't have much strength.

"Ssh," she says, stroking my forehead, brushing aside my hair. From the soft look in her eyes, I can tell she doesn't hate me, but this whole thing isn't over yet. Committed to the vow I made pre-surgery, I want to tell her everything, even if it means dousing that pretty expression on her face.

"How are you feeling?" she asks.

"Could be better . . ."

She smiles, weakly. In her eyes, I see that she's filled with sadness and regret. Well, that makes two of us. "The doctor said that your surgery went well. Your intestines are okay, but the cut went straight through your abdominal muscles." Her eyes sparkle a little with wry humor. "Looks like you'll have a nice caesarean scar."

"No more bikinis?" I ask, falling into her eyes.

"Not for a while anyway." The corner of her mouth curls up. "But you always did look good in a one piece."

I smile and look away when I catch a smirk on her lips, already thinking about my next question that fills me with dread. "And the police? Are they here?"

"They were. They're still investigating obviously, but my phone was recording the whole time. They heard everything . . . including Erin's confession. They understand that she set you up. And they're treating her death as accidental."

My whole body feels lighter somehow, more buoyant.

The nurses are back with a wheelie computer station and two blue pills in a tiny plastic cup. The veteran nurse shows the younger one how to scan the barcode on my ID bracelet and enter the medicine information into the system. Then she hands me the cup, and I swallow the pills dry.

They leave the room after some fussing over the machinery. Then the door clicks shut, and it's just Brynn and I.

The pills are already nibbling on the edges of pain, making me feel vague and grateful. Now, for the hard part.

"There's so many things I didn't tell you, Brynn. And I'm sorry about that. You asked so many times about my relationship with Erin. And I—I didn't want you to know anything about it because it was really hard for me to admit that—that I was in an abusive relationship. It was so hard for me to think of myself as a victim of domestic abuse. But I was." I gesture down to my taped up belly. "This isn't the first time she pulled a knife on me."

"Oh babe," Brynn says, scooting her chair closer to my bedside. "I had no idea."

"I know you didn't," I say with wan smile. "I made sure of it."

"What else did she do? I mean beside the police incident thing."

I fight a knee-jerk reaction to deflect. But I'm not that guy anymore. My silence is what got us into this big mess to begin with. Brynn had every reason to doubt me. Where there is silence, suspicion grows, but not anymore. Not with me.

I decide to start at the very top, and work my way down through the relationship, detailing the first signs of control, of isolating me from my friends, pulling me away from my mom, and the police incident.

Erin worked fast. Erin always had a fresh batch of tears to dispatch. She accused me of not taking her side, not protecting her. Then came the knife incident. The wine bottle incident. And the much contested punch-not-a-punch. The breakup was nasty. And then she started stalking me. Showing up at random places.

"To be completely honest, when we ran into her that night, I wasn't surprised. I should have told her to beat it, but you guys were fast friends by then, and it made me wonder if I was just being paranoid. Nobody wants to be a Debbie Downer . . . or a Dan Downer." I smile a little at my bad joke, wanting nothing else but to see Brynn smile at me.

"Dan, you couldn't have known. I mean, look at how she played me. I was just a pawn in her game. She glommed onto me so that you wouldn't tell her to leave. It was all a part of her sick game. You can't blame yourself."

"But I do," I say. "I blame myself entirely. I just hope you can forgive me someday."

"That's what I was going to say. . ."

I look into her gold-flecked eyes. The softness is still there, even though I've told her absolutely everything. "What do you mean?"

"Dan, I saw you shaking Erin that night. I saw that part, but now I see it was completely out of context. But I . . . well, I gave my statement to the police. I told them what I saw. And now it's my turn to apologize for not believing you. For not taking your side. "She looks down and bites her lower lip. "I hope you can forgive me."

The shadows have fled the room, banished forever. "Why don't we start over?" I ask. "Try again? I would really love that . . ."

Then she smiles that smile that I'm so desperate to see, leans over, kisses me softly on the lips, and says, "I would too."

CHAPTER 54

GIA

Two Months Later

You know the wedding singer? Well, I have a similarly entertaining job now. I'm the 'happy event' tarot card reader. It's a strange gig. Getting booked out like a face painter for a kid's party. *Okay, great! So I'll see you on Saturday at 4pm.* But I had to think of something since I got fired from the pet boutique.

I'm on my way back down to San Diego to meet with Detective Robbins, the one that investigated my car accident. I've been working with her to resolve the 'slight' (read: astronomical) increase in my car insurance premium.

While I had her on the phone, I went ahead and shared the conclusion of the Erin's story. Erin tried to take Brynn's life, but she fell, instead, in front of a train.

And Robbins suddenly found herself back in her element, handling the meaty case file of Erin's murderous misdeeds.

Driving down the freeway, my thoughts travel back to the last time I had driven down this long stretch of road. Racing, more like. Trying to outrun Storm Erin and move people to safety, myself included, wishing for a bit of normalcy, which returned alongside news that the burglary charges against me were dropped.

Nikki and James are still together, better than ever actually. "So can you read my mind?" James had asked me at a beach party celebrating the opening of Psychical Wonders, the business that Mom and I set up. Nikki, James, and I sat on a mandala beach blanket, while I gave them a tarot card reading. "If you're blocked, we can always try to catch another lightning storm," he added, with a wry smile.

James had finally opened up to Nikki about the loss of his baby, and they managed to move forward together. Nikki is mad in love, a bit crazy in fact, and slightly annoying about it. And all signs point to the feeling being mutual. And yes . . . there in the center of my mind, I saw it. A gleaming diamond stone, already bought but not set yet, floating in a soft hue of green—the color of the heart chakra.

"Yes," I said to James, his blue eyes sparkling with mischief.

"Yes, you can read my mind?" he asked, his smile bright. "Or yes you'd like to go hunting for bad weather?"

I swallowed hard, emotion forming a little knot in my throat. Nikki is going to be beyond thrilled. I looked up at him, catching his gaze. "She's going to say yes."

James's eyes grew huge. He was shocked out of his knickers, trying to wipe the wide grin off his face and keep his future proposal secret.

"What?" Nikki asked. "Who's going to say yes?"

"Never mind, babe," James said to Nikki, taking her by the hand, and pulling her up to standing. "Do you want to go for a swim?"

"Sure," she mumbled, glancing at me.

"See?" I said. "I told you she'd say yes!"

And Nikki laughed, crisis averted.

Soon thereafter, I met with Brynn and Dan for lunch a few weeks after he was discharged from the hospital. We met "halfway in the middle" at a cliffside restaurant in Laguna Beach, overlooking the smooth sparkling ocean.

"Should I call you my guardian angel?" Dan had asked, smiling, extending his hand when Brynn made the introductions.

"Crazy psychic will do," I said, smiling and trying not to wince. He had a really firm grip. I hope I didn't come across as a wet noodle. Brynn and I hugged. "It's nice to finally meet under normal circumstances."

"You mean one that doesn't involve wrestling with our overgrown front bush?"

"Exactly what I was thinking."

We made our way over to the table draped with a white linen tablecloth blowing softly in the breeze and sat down. "So it's all over? Erin is ah . . . vanquished?"

By the resounding silence, it was that clear nobody wanted to talk about her horrible ending.

"So . . . crazy psychic, huh?" Dan asked instead.

"Well, Brynn knows the whole story. But I guess I'm not very good because I always thought I was seeing your death. Definitely not Erin's."

Brynn's voice went soft and quivery as she reached over the table and squeezed my hand. "I can't thank you enough for what you did. I know you risked your life. I feel like—I feel like we can never repay you." She paused. "And I'm sorry, I'm so sorry I called you a liar, when you were telling me the truth."

"It's okay," I said, trying to diffuse the ticking emotional bomb. I've been called worse." Then I heard a voice—*Is that Dan Womanbeater?*—and the corner of my mouth lifted into a smile. "And I think you have too, Dan."

I ate a beautiful dish of linguine alle vongole and left that day feeling like maybe Nonna knew what she was talking about after all. That I finally was becoming the soul reader she had predicted so long ago.

Finally, I arrive at the police precinct where Detective Robbins said to meet. Inside her small office space, sitting across from her desk, I listen with sharp curiosity. What does she have to show me?

"So I had a better look into Erin slash Denise. The defense attorney from her murder trial passed over some of the case file. It was . . ." Robbins pulls in a breath, trying to find the right word. "Surprising."

I have to agree with that. "I'm sure it was very surprising. What a way to make a living, huh? Setting people up and extorting money from them? I can't believe she literally got away with murder. But I did think something was off when she called her dad 'Daddy'."

Robbins narrows her blue eyes that remind me of glacial waters and shakes her head a little. "Erin never knew her father . . ."

"That's weird." I think back to that day at Nail Palace, when Erin painted my nails and told me about her father's philosophy on finances. *A penny saved is a penny earned. That's what Daddy always said.* "She definitely did. She said he passed away."

Detective Robbins looks down, straightens a few pens on her desk, and then meets my gaze. "Denise had a very . . . turbulent upbringing. She was shunted around the foster care system from a very young age. Her birth mom was a drug addict. Denise's biological father, from what we can tell, was nothing more than a John. Her birth mother needed the money, you see . . . And when she was one year old, she became a ward of the State. She grew quite close to her foster 'father,'"—she brackets the word with two fingers—"but he stepped in front of train when she eight. Unfortunately, she witnessed the event, which I believe had a significant impact on her mental state."

I'm floored. So that's what I saw that day in her nail salon. Snippets of past, reaching forward to the future. "So her Dad . . ."

"I think that was the one thing she really wanted. A real father. She developed . . . well, we speculate that she formed a very loose grip on reality. And that's why I called you in today. Denise was motivated by money, that part is quite obvious. But it appears she was also motivated by something else."

Suddenly, I'm not feeling very well.

"We found a journal in her house. In it, we found a list of names. People she decided to target. I think this is something that you should see."

A shiver traipses over my skin.

Robbins slides over a purple journal with faded unicorns and clouds of glitter on the cover. I open it up and find pages of journal entries, written in childish handwriting, but as the years passed, her handwriting became smoother and more controlled, all written in block lettering.

There a list of names, two names scratched out violently: Arthur Williams and Chris Mabray. So did she kill before? What happened to Arthur? Dan Evans is the third name on the list, thankfully untouched. Followed by someone named Trevor Whitmore and another name I don't recognize, also not scratched out.

I stare at the last name on the list, but my vision seems a little blurry, my mouth dry. The letters don't quite register. As I try to pull together the meaning, my mind races back to the night of my car accident. The night Erin tried to drive me up a tree. I wanted to quit and leave Erin to her nefarious devices. I wanted to walk away.

I'm struck thinking about what could have been if I hadn't tried one last time, if Mom hadn't insisted that I talk to Detective Robbins, if had hadn't decided to saddle up my Palomino and get back on.

The letters fall into place. And written in bubble block lettering, I find the next person on her list:

GIA, THE PET SHOP BITCH.

AUTHOR'S NOTE

Thank you for reading *Keep Me In Sight*. This book was a long time coming, but it's always a thrill to see a project finally come to fruition. The original premise was an ex-girlfriend with a penchant for killing her exes, but as the book progressed, I realized this was really Dan's story, hands tied in the face of a false accusation.

I want to first and foremost thank all the readers who take the time to read my books. A book is a just a seed. Readers are the soil and water that gives a book life so it can grow and mature and find its place in the world. I do appreciate you all.

Many thanks to Patricia Sainte, a very gifted and scarily accurate psychic, who helped advise me about the psychic process, sensations, and methods used to intuit.

And a huge thank you to my editors Daphne James and Lisa Wong, who attention to detail is always superhuman, and to my wonderful beta readers, whose early comments helped shape this manuscript into what it is today.

ABOUT THE AUTHOR

An American expat since 2008, Rachel has sailed over 11,000 nautical miles, rounding the Cape of Good Hope and crossing the Indian Ocean three times. After living in Sydney, Australia for a number of years, she moved up to Singapore with her husband, son, and rescue pup named Jessica Shadow Shady Lady, which unfortunately doesn't fit on a dog tag. But no matter, Shadow hates going outside anyway.

Do consider joining Rachel's Exclusive Reader's Club, where giveaways and free Advance Reader Copies of her latest releases are just the beginning.

For more information, please visit: www.rachelsquared.com

Made in the USA
Columbia, SC
17 May 2021

38081905R00196